Joseph

www.peterceren.com
www.orionsbride.com

ISBN 978-0615604329

Joseph

EVERYONE KNOWS WHO HE IS

BUT NOBODY KNOWS WHO HE WAS

PJ Ceren

Published by Orion's Bride
Memphis
2012

To Gabrielle, who appeared as a messenger in the form of a baby on Saint Joseph's feast day to teach me about Joseph's love.

Is this not the carpenter's son? Is not his mother called Mary?
And are not his brothers James and Joseph and Simon and Judas?
And are not all his sisters with us?
Where did this man get all this?

The words of the people of Nazareth in Matthew 14:55

Instruments

Joseph caressed her scar, remainder of some forgotten injury healed over with time. Barely visible to others, it was clear to his trained eye. He would watch for this flaw when he made use of her since this imperfection could make something exquisite instead of ordinary. It was always what he looked for as he worked, because scars from some old struggle left a beautiful memory he called character. He closed his eyes to know her more as he filled his fingertips with her. He wrapped his arms around her and breathed in her subtle scent of life and listened for her whisper as the wind increased.

Now that he knew her fully, he was ready to begin. She was what he needed for what he had to do. He saw a vision of what she would become; just like the ancient Joseph he was named for, who changed his world with dreams. He felt aptly named since he lived in dreams himself and knew they could become reality if he used them well. What he saw she would become was real already. His touch knew from experience. "I hate to hurt her, James. It's hard to be gentle with an axe, but it has to be done."

"You're an idiot, Joseph." James shook his head and snorted. "You hear trees talking and see angels in your dreams. A carpenter ought to be a practical man. I really wish you wouldn't say these things to other people. I'm afraid they might think my friend is mad. Sometimes *I* wonder. Joseph, it's a *tree*."

"But she's *alive*, James. I can feel her." Joseph pointed to his heart with his calloused hand. "Sometimes I can hear them talking to me. I hear God speaking through them all the time. Quiet … please … just listen."

James closed his eyes. "I hear the wind rustling the leaves. I hear a dove in the distance. I hear the gravel crunching under my feet." He shuffled his sandals and the noise barked. "I suppose you think these stones are crying out to us, too." He cupped his hand to his ear, bent down low to the ground, and looked puzzled. "Oh yeah! I hear it now! They are squeaking up at me. *Hey, you big ox! Get off of us, you're crushing us to dust!"*

Their laughter bonded them as it always had since they were curious children eavesdropping on Roman soldiers gathered around their fire at night. The sentry caught them and only James' outrageous story saved their lives. He told them they were hunting invisible hares at night because that was the only time it was quiet enough to hear them. He told the centurion they were waiting for them to poop so they could find them by the sound and smell. And *of course* hare poop is *not* invisible; *everyone* knows that! The soldiers laughed so hard they let them go. James bragged he could talk himself out of anything. They made an odd pair, the singing carpenter overflowing with dreams, and the merchant with a skill for making money in the worst of circumstances. Best friends are often unlikely pairs.

James rolled his eyes and said, "If you are going to cut that stupid tree, *start* already. Otherwise let me get back to my work at home. What are you going to do, contemplate that tree to the ground? Or convince it to gently use the axe on itself? But, you know, Joseph ... now that I think about it, you *are* right about the material I work with. Money does talk – loudly. But out here I think your ears might be a wee bit too sensitive. But ... wait a minute ..."

James cupped his hand to his ear again and closed his eyes. "Wait...shhh...I hear something... I hear that pretty tree talking now. I can hear it! Listen Joseph, there it is! *I want to be a table. Please make me a table, I'm tired of being a tree, these birds in my branches are driving me crazy, and messing all over me, and I can't do anything about it. Make me a table and save me from them, pleeeeeease.*"

Joseph growled and raised the axe over his head, circling it like a sling ready to loose toward the offending head. "All right, that's about enough. Would you like to rest your tongue for a while now, or do you need some help deciding?"

"You're awfully good with that axe, so now that you mention it, I am a little tired. Maybe I'll lie down in the shade on the other side of this tree before it is gone. Uh, it *is* going to be gone soon, isn't it?" The whoosh of the axe-head an inch in front of his face assured James that it would be.

The deep thump and crack of axe on wood echoed from the surrounding hills. The double beat with the softer accent was a heartbeat for this valley. It was constant as a pulse as he worked. Joseph could always find peace in the music of his tools. The rhythm of work cleared his mind from troubling visions. He had seen moving shadows out of the corners of his eyes again this afternoon. Shadows that usually dissolved when he looked at them. Sometimes they didn't. The heartbeat of his axe brought him peace as the strokes fell with the regularity of waves on the shore.

James relaxed on his back with his fingers interlaced to pillow his head. He closed his eyes and spoke in the intervals between axe falls. It set the pace he followed between resounding hollow sounds of axe biting deeply into wood, with the close echo that followed. "What will this tree become? ... Who is it for?"

Joseph replied between the resonating strokes, "You heard the tree correctly ... it *is* going to be a table ... for Abraham and Esther ... now they have grandchildren ... they need more room."

"Grandchildren. ... Do you think either of us ... will ever see grandchildren?"

"Not at this rate ... since neither of us has found a wife yet ... or even started looking."

"Speak for yourself ... I've been looking plenty and enjoying the view." James laughed. "I just haven't had any great views ... look back yet."

A woman's scream broke the silence between two blows of the axe. Joseph jerked around, his grip on the axe tightened involuntarily as he searched for the source of the scream.

"She's close James, but which way? Nothing's moving in this valley."

Joseph listened, but his ears roared so loudly from his excited pulse that he could hardly hear anything else. His legs were hot, filled with blood for running and wanting to know where. "The scream came from over one of these hills, but which one?"

James was on his feet, a broken branch in his hand as a club. "I can't tell, either."

At the sound of the second, shriller scream, Joseph sprinted with his axe in his hand.

"I'm right behind you, but I can't run as..."

"Her voice is coming from this direction."

"Joseph, this scream sounds younger. I think it's a child – a little girl!"

Joseph slipped and fell as he scrambled up the hill. *Can't my feet take me any faster? God, please don't let me be too late, help me run faster!*

Joseph's mind outran his feet. A third scream quavered, weak and wet as a sick infant's cry. *I was sure it was a woman before, then a child; and now it is getting weaker by the second. Has a wolf carried away a baby? Is it a mother and a baby both in trouble?*

Cresting the top of the hill, they saw a naked man hunched over his victim, tearing wildly with his hands and teeth. His hands were bright red to his elbows.

"Get off of her! Leave her alone!" Joseph screamed as he ran.

The nude man turned his face, revealing his meal that was now mercifully still. He wiped the blood from his mouth and cheeks with the back of his hand, then he turned to continue eating.

Joseph stopped to hold back the sickness that wanted to rush out of him. He staggered and steadied himself with his axe like a cane. He closed his eyes but the picture wouldn't go away.

"I'd forgotten how much a screaming hare sounds like a woman's voice, James. Thank God, that's all it was."

"He lives like an animal in the wilderness, eating like a wolf." James spit and threw his club on the ground in the direction of the mess. It clattered across the rocks past the right side of the man who growled without bothering to look. He was focused on his meal.

Joseph turned his face away before opening his eyes to avoid seeing that scene again. His heartbeat slowed. Dizzy, he had to sit. Against his will, he was drawn to turn back. Madness demands attention. The savage wiped his bloody hands on his thighs, then scraped the furry skin clean with a sharp stone and gnawed the bones.

James and Joseph leaned against each other, catching their breath. Disgusting sounds from the meal were punctuated by disconnected words of a song. Broken melodies started, then ended abruptly - smothered by wet sounds like a rooting pig.

Done with his meal, he performed some unholy ritual, singing freely now as he stretched the hare's entrails above his head between the branches of two trees. He danced beneath them and painted the blood across his chest and face. He ignored the flies that covered him, sharing his meal. He shook the remains that were connected by their joints and pretended the hare jumped in the air. He sang of bringing life back to it as he hooked the skeleton by its teeth to swing from the glistening gray intestines. It swung slowly in the air. He circled it and sang louder as he spun. He sang of resurrection from the dead. He waved the pelt like a flag in the wind as he turned like a whirlwind orbiting what looked like a miniature flayed human dangling in space.

James and Joseph climbed the hill to return to the tree he had been cutting. "I bet those trees don't enjoy this horror in their branches any more than his singing. What are they telling you now, Joseph? Are they having a good time?"

"I don't imagine they appreciate it any more than we do, James. And they can't walk away. I'm glad I can still hear him singing, so I know he isn't following us. But I want to get far enough away so I can't hear his madness. I'm afraid it might be contagious."

During the short walk over the ridge, Joseph struggled with the more difficult task of clearing the picture from his mind. He hated the way that kind of image stuck and then returned uninvited.

"James, next time it could be a small child – some child we know and love. Nothing is too horrible for this one touched by madness. Like this one who embraced that touch and let it own him."

"Touched? Who touched him, Joseph - God or Satan? If by God for what reason? What possible reason could God have for that?"

"Madness doesn't come from God, but we don't need Satan. We craft madness well enough ourselves. And feed it. Ah, don't we love to feed madness? But it is never full, always looking for another meal. Sometimes I fear it is looking for me. I get too close in my dreams that overlap the daylight." Joseph sighed and looked down at his foot as he drew a curve in the dust, then another intersecting curve. It was the start of a word unspoken. He looked at James and then wiped the letter away with his foot. "Sometimes my dreams won't let me go and that frightens me." Joseph saw a familiar dark figure move just at the edge of his vision; he knew James could not see it, or anyone else. It was something only he could see. He knew better than to mention it anymore. It looked like a shadow, but a deeper black that moved like a person. Sometimes it just sat and watched him. It was so dark it was like looking into a hole in the world shaped like a man.

James placed a hand on Joseph's shoulder to reassure his friend. "You're not like that bloody mess. You're just a little innocently crazy, but he's completely mad.

Naked, screaming, bloody-faced, out of his mind mad. What did he think he was doing by stretching the hare's guts out like that? First the blood and then his performance almost wasted my good lunch. There is gentle madness, and then there is *that*. There is violence and evil in what he did."

Joseph looked at the hill and seemed to see through it to the madman on the other side. "I think I understand him. I think that was his twisted attempt at prayer. "

"Prayer? Are you crazy? How could that be prayer, Joseph? That man is an animal – the donkey waiting for us is much more human than this thing. Prayer?"

"I think he believes it is some sort of sacrifice. Somewhere down deep he still hears the voice of God distorted by the noise that must live inside his head. You heard his songs. There were bits of the Psalms and Prophets, all mixed up and repeated in a way that made no sense to us. He must have heard them often before. He sang something about the Messiah. He must have been like us until something happened. Something horrible that shook his world loose from him and left him stranded in that other world. But James, there is still hope for everyone. He was singing about hope, but he doesn't understand love - that's his problem. No love, just hope with no reason. If he could know love then his hope would have meaning."

"Hope, huh? Well I hope we get that tree cut and loaded and get ourselves out of here before dark. I don't like the idea of him surprising us - hope or no hope. And I don't feel like joining him in his messy style of prayer. Besides, even including the donkey, we don't make a minyan – the quorum for prayer."

Songs

The saw set the rhythm. The pitch rose and fell with the resistance of the wood. Just before the blade broke through, the wood sang high like a cantor at the end of a phrase. Joseph joined the song, as he always did, in duet alone with the wood.

He sang with the spirit inside the wood and inside himself. He crafted practical things with care, the way his father, Jacob, and his grandfather, Matthan, had taught him. Joseph grew up swaddled in the sweet smell of sawdust, the sugary sharp smell of oak, the incense of cedar, and the aroma like his mother's cooking that came from olive wood.

Since he was a baby, Joseph was lullabied by the song of saw and plane. He fell asleep and woke to the comfort of the music of work merging with his father's voice. Over time, he adopted his father's songs and made them his own. The Psalms, their ancestor David's songs, flowed from his father's lips, reformed into his personal music of carpentry. Somewhere David must have smiled to know his songs lived on in his children after a millennium.

Joseph's fingers cherished the feel of wood with rough texture he could smooth. He loved the testing touch, as each proved the work one step closer to complete. He always closed his eyes and smiled as he rubbed the final smoothness. His work was always better than it needed to be. The hidden side was always finished, though no one's eyes but his would ever see. It was a waste of time, he knew, but gave a holy sense of completeness to his work. It showed respect for the wood, the work, himself.

He loved his tools and tended them constantly to keep them sharp. It was a patient business, sharpening an edge; it was easy to go too far. Joseph had a feel for how much the metal would take before the edge became so fragile it would fold or break with the work. An edge that is too sharp is too weak; there is a balance in the compromise.

Each scrap of wood was precious. Joseph carved them into spinning toys, whistles and flutes that charmed children's expectant eyes. He knew how to free the spirit from the wood. It once had been alive - and still was to him.

Joseph had a carpenter's physique, with broad shoulders and strong arms. His voice was deep, with the lungs of a man who could work hard for hours without needing rest. He could fell a tree and cut it into lengths without getting short of breath. His songs gave him more wind while he worked.

His voice had merely a touch of a rasp smoothing rough wood, but mostly the smoothness of a finishing polish. His brown hair and beard were always full of sawdust. His eyes were dark as the heart of the darkest wood polished to a bright shine. His young skin was burned from long hours in the sun, and premature wrinkles surrounded his laughing eyes. His stride was long and sure as a warrior, but his touch was gentle as a mother to her newborn's face.

Joseph's powerful voice was made for chanting the Torah in the synagogue. He filled the room and the hearts that heard the words. The stories moved him until sometimes tears flowed down his cheeks as he sang. Time disappeared when he talked for hours with the other men about the Prophets and their mysterious words about the future. He wondered at the hopeful poetry that promised a free future for Israel after so many centuries passed from conqueror to conqueror. Empire after empire rose and fell, but still Abraham's children were not free.

Jacob spent most of the day in the workshop with his son, but he tired more quickly every year, so Joseph took more of the harder work. Jacob was over sixty but his only child, Joseph, was seventeen and strong. Joseph loved to twist words in his songs and jokes to keep his father laughing.

Joseph brought the experience of two generations but added more than his youth and strength to the craft. He felt the wood inside and knew how to be a partner with it, using the strengths of the individual pieces, not struggling against them. He brought his passion for the beauty of the wood into his work. Beauty that was the natural outgrowth of using wood in a loving way. A deeper beauty came from the strength and the personality of both the wood and the craftsman in a fine duet.

One wall of the workshop was covered with their tools, organized where they could be easily reached. The saws were lined up in order of size: the two-man saws, the ripping saws and crosscuts, and all the smaller special saws for intricate close cuts. The blades were burnished by years of use and care, the wooden handles oiled and tight. Tools that had been made with great craftsmanship by Joseph's grandfather and lovingly maintained in memory of the man who started this family's love affair with wood.

Three generations had polished the handles of these tools to butter smoothness. It comforted Joseph to hold wood in his hands as he worked with wood, and let the metal be just the point of contact in between.

Below the saws hung the files and awls and augers and clamps and chisels and nails. On one shelf by themselves lay the complicated drills with the rawhide and bows that gave the twisting power. And safely alone were the measuring tools for length, and the all-important squares and angles and plumb. These were the measure of the work to keep it true.

Next to the door the axes were lined from the big ones to the small. These were the tools of first work of felling a tree. The axe was a tool unlike any of the others, for rough work without finesse. For brute work there was no substitute for an axe. The sheer power of this tool sometimes satisfied Joseph in a way no other work could. When his rhythm took him over it was a primal music that woke a sleeping part of him. They never used the axes inside the workshop, so they remained gathered in a row by the door.

The other wall of the workshop was piled high with curing wood, stacked and turned like slowly cooking food until it was ready. This aging process prepared the wood so it wouldn't crack and check to spoil the finished piece. Joseph tended his wood from living tree through years of careful curing until it became a finished piece ready for delivery. He sang to the wood as he worked, and sang with the children who often filled his shop. He thought the wood enjoyed music while it rested. He made up songs for the cedar, the oak, and the olive. His father thought this a little odd, but smiled at the inner connection with the wood that showed in every step of his craftsmanship. It made Jacob proud of his son, who used what he had taught him so well.

More than the wood, Joseph sang of the children who played in his workshop. Each child inspired a verse in at least one song. Sometimes he made up songs with the children for their mothers, who often came to enjoy these songs about their children. And Joseph helped the children create songs for their parents. These loving gifts from their children were more precious than any other gift they could have made. Love songs are a direct route to the heart.

Jacob had taught his son to sing as he worked, but Joseph made up songs of his own, as well as the Psalms his father had taught him. The old words were holy, but so were the new, just holy in a different way. Joseph laughed as he worked the wood and sang to the rhythm of his saw. The children joined in, enthusiastically singing songs about themselves. The streets of Nazareth echoed with children's voices repeating his tunes as they played.

The melody always began with a steady beat, then slowed like a saw approaching the end of a piece of wood.

Moshe was a clever one,
He remembered all he heard,
His mind would jump from thing to thing,
As quickly as a bird.
He often would be deep in trouble,
But escape with a crafty word.

Suzanna is as beautiful as the flower that is her name,
Her eyes are bright, her spirit sweet
As the fragrance from the field.
She will find a broken heart
That with her love is healed.

Joseph knew that if he saw the best in a child and encouraged it, they would grow in that belief. Like a seed in rain and sunlight.

A new child peeked shyly in the door today, drawn by the laughter and singing. He had always felt an outsider. While others played, he watched quietly from a safe distance. His back was slightly bent and twisted, and this made him walk hunched over. He had a hard time running like the other children.

Joseph gestured to welcome him in. "What is your name, son?"

"Daniel, sir."

"Welcome Daniel, to the house of work and play. Everyone please introduce yourselves by your song, so he will know just who you are."

A girl with a round face and bright smile started the songs.

Joanna is the happy one
Who laughs and smiles all day
Whenever she is at her work
Or while she is at play
Her giggle and her joyful words
Makes any dark day fun.

Each child shared his own song in turn. Then there was awkward silence as Daniel looked down at the floor. Joseph pretended a surprised scowl, "What? You don't have a song? We'll have to do something about that, won't we?"

The children responded in unison. "Yes! Let's make Daniel's song!"

Jacob looked up from his work and smiled at his son.

Joseph sat on the floor facing the boy, putting his hand on his shoulder. "Tell me about yourself, Daniel."

Daniel looked at his toes in the sawdust. "I don't know, there is nothing special about me."

"Nothing special? There's something special about everyone. You just don't know how to see it yet." Joseph leaned forward at his eye level. "What is your favorite animal?"

"Well … hawks and eagles, I guess. I love watching them soaring in the air. It looks so easy for them, spinning slowly higher and higher into the clouds. It makes me feel happy inside to watch them"

"And what do you like to do, Daniel?"

"I like to climb trees and swim and watch dragonflies dart around the water."

"Do you know how to play a flute?"

"No, sir." Daniel shook his head. "I can't play any music or even sing." He hung his head and seemed to be shrinking into a very small child, even smaller than he was in reality.

"Sure you can! Take this drum." Joseph handed him the drum he had ready waiting within his reach. "Everyone can play a drum. Now, let's all help make Daniel a song. What does his love of eagles and dragonflies and climbing and swimming tell us about him? What do all those things have in common?"

Suzanna shouted, " I know! He doesn't like to be stuck on the ground!"

Thomas added, "He is good at noticing things in the air. He looks up into the sky, not down at the earth."

Joseph asked the group, "What do you think it feels like to be an eagle?"

Daniel jumped in. "Free and exciting! And they can move quickly out of sight, a lot faster than a horse can run."

Joseph smiled and closed his eyes for a moment and then began to sing.

> *Daniel's spirit can't be caught*
> *By the heaviness of earth*
> *His mind soars like the eagles*
> *As he peers from his high perch*
> *Where he can see beyond today*
> *To surprises that he sought.*

All the children joined in with Daniel's new song. Laughter filled the workshop. Daniel pounded a drum and beamed as he sang the words about himself his new friends had made just for him.

Joseph led the music with his saw.

…

Joseph loved to search for the trees that would become his craft. But he was torn. He loved trees and he loved making things from them, but he hated killing them to use their wood. By the time a tree died on its own, the wood was usually useless for his craft. He had to take the life he loved to love it more. Whenever he was lucky enough to find a dead tree that still had suitable wood, he was overjoyed. He planted three seeds for every tree he harvested, to make sure there would be a supply for his children and grandchildren.

He apologized to the trees, silently if there was anyone else around, and told them what they would become. He respected their life, and knew it would continue in another form. Their beauty would be revealed by his craftsmanship.

When he needed to make something tall and straight, he would find a peaceful tree that had lived a peaceful life. But when he needed extra strength to stand twisting forces, he would search for a tree that had lived a tortured life and survived with interwoven grain. These alone were suited to take great force and bear up safely. When lives depended on what he made, he sought out trees that had endured great trials already.

He listened to the diverse accents of God's voice in nature, in dreams and visions as much as in the Temple. He often saw puzzling pictures of the future in his mind. He often told the children, "God speaks to all of us in subtle ways. God is always speaking, even in the silence; we simply need to listen."

Last night a confusing dream had visited him, one he still struggled to understand. It told him this day would be an important day that would change his life. After the dream pushed him from sleep, Joseph was wide-awake. He felt sometimes he let the dreams speak to him too much; sometimes he saw things in the daylight, too. He worried he was not in control of his mind. But he saw things and knew it, even if no one else could see them. *Didn't the great men of Israel's past see angels and even eat with them? Why should that stop now? Does God care less about his children than he used to? Or am I just seeing things? How can I know?* His visions were maddeningly unclear, but real. Real like anything too great to hold in your hand.

Sleep would not come again for him this night, so he walked under the silent stars to think and talk to God. He didn't want to wake his parents, but he had to talk out loud. It wasn't that he didn't think God could hear his thoughts, but somehow, speaking them made them more real. And real was what he needed now.

Dark and silence wrapped him more deeply into the memory of his dreams. A walk alone in darkness is in the style of dreams. Even the owls held their voices this night. Maybe they were listening. He whispered so only God could hear this private conversation.

"So, God of David, what are you trying to tell me? As usual, you just give me hints. *What?* What is this? What do you want me to do? This dream has left me with no clear memories, just feelings. Vague, disturbing feelings. You are telling me something important is going to happen. *What?* Good? Bad? All you gave me was a feeling. A feeling without any facts. I need more."

Joseph dropped his head and shrugged. "It will be wonderful and terrible. I know that somehow. I don't know how I know that; I just do. I feel it. I know it. If you have something for me to do, you better give me the strength and wisdom to do it. And the grace to be able to do it properly, whatever it is."

Joseph looked up at the sky, desperately looking for some sign for clarity. "Is this what it was like for the Joseph I was named after, another Jacob's son? You spoke to him in dreams. Dreams that brought terrible betrayal and great destiny. He kept his faith and kindness and saved our people in the process. But he suffered through awful pain. What is it in this dream? What are you trying to tell me? I'm a little bit afraid. No, more than a little bit."

There was a constellation in the night sky where Joseph imagined God lived. It comforted him. It felt like home to his heart. He knew God was everywhere, and in the Temple in Jerusalem, but this spot felt like heaven to him. God's primary residence. God's home. This group of stars brought his eyes and heart peace every time it reappeared in the seasons. This night was the dark of the moon and so the stars owned the night without competition.

Joseph sat in silence, waiting for an answer. The only answer came as he rested against a tree and watched the almost imperceptible movement of the stars. He closed one eye to watch a brilliant star slowly disappear behind a twig to reappear again in a few seconds. Joseph loved the night sky, this shadow of the earth that revealed the uncountable stars that were hidden by the day. Without this shadow they would never be visible, he knew. It was obvious to him that there was a journey that moved his view of the stars through the cycle of the year. It was predictable and comforting. Slow movement that marked time in circles like the rings of a tree.

God wasn't talking. Not loudly, at least. His whisper was inaudible this time. Just the movement of the stars, the beating of his heart, the steady flow of breaths. Nothing changed. And everything. He couldn't sleep more this night, so he went to his workshop to start his day.

Oil lamps lit his work until dawn. The dark night easing to morning was full of wondering in silence without vocal song. The comforting touch of wood and the song of his tools left his mind free to look for answers, but none came. What did come was silent peace and the feeling that if he relaxed it all would be revealed. Something would start this day, but only if he worked and played with children as he normally did.

He worked on a simple table through the night. He imagined the family that would gather around this table as he chose the wood. He chose grain that would remain interesting as it filled their eyes through the years. The beautiful pattern of the grain would always be in the background of their home. It would be noticed occasionally as a reminder of beauty like a sunset when the mind was at rest. Or sometimes the beauty of the grain was a place the mind could go to find solace in a difficult time. It was a place to hide for a private moment touching a map of time and growth written by God in a tree. A promise of survival through a struggle, like a rainbow.

Joseph imagined how the family would come to know this grain as a comfort and a bit of nature in their home. Something that was always there. Something unique and personal where each one would find a favorite place. A place where the heart could rest peacefully like the eye.

The sun rose golden, streaming across the wood and throwing the grain in relief. The paper-thin curls of wood rolling off the plane were lit from behind, bright as glowing embers fanned by a breeze.

Jacob joined him later, asking what troubled him from sleep. He shared glimpses from his dream as they worked and talked the way they always did. No answers came but waiting.

Gradually his workshop filled with children and song. New songs were forming and loudly as the children brought him back to the love of life and work and the confidence of every day as usual. He had forgotten this day would be special as he was lost in the love of life.

The new boy, Daniel, sang the loudest this afternoon. In the few hours since he was welcomed, this place had become a home to his heart. All the children joined in a song they made today about Joseph and his songs and wood. It wasn't very good, but he loved it, and Jacob pretended he had sawdust in his eyes.

Near the end of the day, a lovely young woman stood outside his open door. She had come to fetch her little sister who had lost track of time in the songs. She watched through the door in secret, without his knowing. She had seen him over the years, seen the toys he made, heard his songs spread from the children's lips throughout the village. She knew him even though they had never spoken.

In these secret moments she fell in love with him. She imagined him as a loving husband and a wonderful father to their children. He was just a few years older than she was, but an experienced craftsman already. She smiled a woman's powerful smile, knowing. And secretly practicing her smile, so it would be perfect when she first used it on him. She watched his strong hands, powerful with the tools and gentle with the children. She imagined how those hands would feel on her as they touched with both kinds of touch. She blushed across her entire body. And smiled.

Her little sister saw her in the doorway and called her name. "Mary, look what Joseph made for me." He turned, distracted by her smile as the saw blade slipped across his left hand. Blood covered his hand and dripped into the sawdust. He heard the soft plops as the heavy drops landed; he held his hand up and felt the warmth of the blood as it ran down his arm in bright streams that shocked with the purity of the color red. He smelled the wet smell again his tools had demanded so often as a payment for his work with wood. A smell like earth and flesh; the smell of Adam made from clay. He was surprised at the lack of pain. It seemed the red that shocked his eyes just decided to flow like a spring from desert rocks without a cause. It would become a scar he would carry the rest of his life as a fond reminder of the day their love began. But he concentrated on the memory of her smile that had changed into concern. Still, some of that smile lingered behind the concern, comforting him and disturbing him. He didn't move to stop the bleeding; he had more important things to think about. The children were confused. How could he ignore this blood?

Mary did what Mary always would do. She held his hand and washed it with warm water from the pitcher in the window. He had no idea what she was saying to him; he just stared at her as she took charge. She wrapped his hand in the clean blue cloth that had held back her hair. Her long dark hair fell free and bounced as she cared for him. He felt it brushing his arms, his cheek. He saw it pick up sawdust from his beard. She smelled like flowers and spice and something else he had never smelled before, the smell of Mary herself. *Like ...* he struggled and closed his eyes and realized she smelled like nothing he had known before. The smell of this woman that drew him into her soul. She sang a comforting song that was almost a whisper as she worked. A lullaby.

Her eyes matched the touch of her gentle hands. He knew he was in love forever.

Duet

The moon had grown from new to full in the two weeks since they met. So had their love.

"It's almost healed, Joseph," Mary said, kissing the rough ridge on the back of his hand. Her lips lingered, and then formed a kiss as she reluctantly released the warmth of his skin. Joseph felt the puff of air as gentle as a butterfly's breeze. She rested her cheek on his hand. She loved his hands. She even loved the touch from the back of his hand with the scar. It was him.

"Ah, I'd run the saw across it again for another of your kisses."

"Please don't, you idiot! Let me put another kiss on the hand without the wound. You'll be able to feel it better. In the future, how 'bout I just reward you for not being clumsy instead? Can you manage that?" Mary explored his other hand with its complicated map of carpentry scars then turned it over to kiss the sensitive skin on his wrist beyond his calluses. She felt Joseph shiver and squirm, pleasantly uncomfortable. He looked forward to more. He was a man.

"Umm, you're right, I do feel it better on this one. Now let me kiss that charming sick head of yours, Mary. This one so full of strange thoughts inside." He wrapped his arms around her and kissed her forehead, and closed his eyes to enjoy her scent. He had grown to love that part of her that was remembered in his nose. It brought back that first day when her scent first entered his soul. Two weeks had been a lifetime in lovers' time.

"Strange thoughts, you say? But all my thoughts are about you now, dear. So I guess that does make them pretty strange now, doesn't it?"

"You're lovely in this moonlight, Mary."

"So you're saying I don't look so good in daylight?" She pulled away from him and put her hands on her hips and twisted up her face.

"You look fine in any light to my eyes, and you feel even better." Joseph pulled her back with force and hugged her tightly. He nuzzled her neck. His lips rested as he let her warmth flow into him.

"You feel good, too, my dear one. I love holding you, it makes me feel … *home.*"

"Watch out, I smell a love song coming on."

> *The moonlight makes you glow like and angel,*
> *Your soft voice sings like the stars,*
> *You move like the wind through rattling willows,*
> *And you smell like spring's fragrant flowers.*
> *Your words and your touch make me dizzy.*
> *I just wish they made a little more sense.*

"Oh really, Joseph? Well, I have a few words to sing about you, too."

> *You're tall and strong as a cedar tree,*
> *And just about as smart….*

They laughed and then sang in duet:

> *You're so beautiful my dear, but weird.*

Their song and laughter disturbed the sheep and amused the shepherd resting in the pasture below.

The hills wrapped the moment after their songs in silence. All lovers think they are the first to discover this overpowering world. The stars of eternity and the clock of the moon watched these two exploring the hills as they explored each other's heart. It is the furthest journey one can take, until lost in another's world without a map.

The evening dew released the scent of flowers in the night air. Joseph thought it blended well with the warm smell he had come to know as Mary. The sound of her breath next to his ear harmonized with the soft wind in the weeds. Her heart beat against his chest, echoing his own. His cheek muscles ached from his long held smile.

Moonlight revealed the exquisite sculpture of Mary's perfect skin of youth. *Greek and Roman marble sculptures seem rough and mottled by comparison*, Joseph thought. He kissed warm alabaster that responded. Time waited, holding its breath. A turtledove sang in the distance as his mate answered more softly, her song woven inside of his. They recreated the simple chords pairs of doves have shared since the dawn of life.

"I baked a gift for you, Joseph. Honey cakes with almonds and cinnamon. Let me feed you so you won't make such a mess on your beard for once." The smell of fresh baked sweet bread with cinnamon reminded him of his mother's favorite treat. Mary had secretly learned from her what pleased her son. They conspired to win him. Joseph's mother understood Mary, and wanted her for a daughter-in-law already. She reminded her a little of herself when she was young. She thought her boy needed a woman with that kind of spirit and strength. All mothers want their sons to have a good woman just like herself. Or better. Joseph's mother was a bit wild as a child, and never entirely gave it up. She loved to laugh and play games and see the men in her family happy and full. And she was a trickster who loved to laugh. She said it was God's greatest unnamed gift.

Mary fed him like a new mother feeds her baby, placing each morsel into his mouth. He closed his eyes and cooed like a contented baby. She brushed the crumbs off his beard and laughed at him. He kissed the side of her neck, and then moved to the soft skin of her throat. Mary shivered and leaned her head back to feel more. Then he reached behind his back and pulled something out of the bag he carried over his shoulder.

"I have a gift for you, too." He handed her a package wrapped in fine blue cloth. Mary unwrapped this loving mystery slowly like she unwrapped his soul.

"I carved it for you from olive wood, and polished it with beeswax. See how it shines in the moonlight."

She opened the cover and understood. It was almost empty now, but full of the promise of a lifetime. She smiled the smile he would always remember; it would return to her face every time she opened it for the rest of her life.

You're acting like an idiot again, Joseph." James brushed the sawdust off a bench to sit down. The workshop was more cluttered than usual, and sawdust was overtaking it.

"I'm just happy, James. I've found her!" Joseph ran the plane across the tabletop then blew the curls of wood out of the way.

"I didn't know she was lost. She looks like she knows precisely where she is and where she is going, which is a lot more than I can say about you!"

"James, isn't she the most beautiful thing in the world? Her voice sounds like the stream at the bottom of our favorite valley – the one that bubbles over the rocks. It sounds just like her laughter."

"Leave it to you to fall in love with a stream, Joseph. At least she isn't a tree. But you are so lovesick I'm afraid to leave you near sharp tools. Look at your hand; you've already proved me right."

"Well, you've got me on that one. I did run a saw across my hand the first time I saw her. Ever since then, I have seen her eyes wherever I am all day and all night. And I hear her voice. Soft with beautiful words, and I know she loves me, too."

"You're doomed, Joseph."

"How can I be doomed when I am in heaven, James?"

"What day is this, Joseph?"

"Tuesday? Why?"

"It's *Thursday*, Joseph, do you see what I mean? You don't even know what day it is you are so crazy in love."

"So I forgot a day."

"That's two days. You can't even count in the state you are in!"

"Yeah. And I like it."

James grabbed his friend around the shoulder with one arm and bumped his head with his fist repeatedly. "Where did my friend go? What happened to your head?" The only answer was a hollow thump. "Is he still in there?"

"I'm all here for the first time in my life, James." Joseph twisted his head free to face his friend. "She walks like a hawk flies overhead between the clouds, James. She moves like the waves on the sea. Her hips sway like willow branches in the wind, and ..." Joseph's voice trailed off as he smiled with his eyes closed. "I want to be with her, like in those branches by the bubbling water that is her voice. She is springtime and all the fragrant flowers. I want to feel those branches wrap me ..."

"You are a madman, my friend, and gone. So far gone ... I'm taking all your sharp tools away so you can't hurt yourself again. What is so special about *her*? There are many other attractive women in Nazareth."

"It is more than just the way she looks and the way she sounds. It is more than just the way she feels when she leans her head on my shoulder. She is smart and ... she's ... deep." Joseph's mood darkened when he noticed the shadow figure hiding in the corner that he knew James could never see.

"Ah, Joseph, *deep*, huh?" James chuckled and shook his head. "Having *deep* meaningful conversations with a *deep* woman, are you? You're too far gone for hope now. *Deep*. What am I going to do with you? *Deep*." James buried his head in his hands.

"Mostly, James I feel it because I can tell she loves me - really loves me. She understands me and she understands my dreams. And we can talk about anything. She knows what I mean when I talk with her about the great mysteries. She helps me understand them better than I ever could before. I love it when she cuddles into me when we walk and look at the stars, but I think I love it more that she is not superficial. She's deep."

"Joseph, what is it that she says that is so deep? I'm not doubting you, but I want to understand."

"I don't know. It is everything and nothing. It is just the way she feels. I feel like she looks deeply into my soul and understands it all and accepts me for all I am and will be." Joseph finally set his plane down and felt the surface of the wood, testing for smoothness unconsciously. "She sets me on fire and calms me at the same time. She tells me with a few words that she loves me. She tells me with no words. She tells me with so many words that I get confused. And she understands our history and feels our future at the same time. Maybe she sees more than I can and in a different way. Women have a way of knowing that we can't know. She's deep, James, she understands the important things."

James threw two handfuls of sawdust into the air like confetti. "Well then, I celebrate with you and I am happy for you, idiot though you be, at least you are a happy idiot. My dear love-idiot friend. *Deep* in love. And probably deeper in trouble than you can imagine."

Psalm

I t's a perfect dawn, Joseph. The red glow of morning is painting the clouds, and look, the morning stars are still bright above the horizon." Mary kissed his cheek as she pointed to the star.

"And if you look the other way, Mary, the shrinking moon that was full a few days ago is low in the west. I'll always remember the way your smile looked in the light of the full moon the first night we walked together last month. The full moon is ours. Every time it returns we'll remember. It is a quieter light than the sun. It doesn't shout, it whispers."

"Let's go to our hills, dear. But *you* get to carry this heavy basket I prepared to satisfy your giant appetite." Mary pushed the basket hard into his belly and lowered her face to look up at him like a playful child. Mary closed the door of her parents' home after they waved to her mother.

The western hills welcomed the first light of that day. Blueness chased into the deepest shadowed valleys by the gold that crept down from the tops of the highest hills. The lovers watched the transformation and embraced in the shadows as the new light of this day eased toward them.

Joseph kissed her cheek and then again, slowly. "You are much more beautiful than those golden hills. Your eyes are brighter than the moon and morning star."

Mary yanked his beard. "Enough! Stop before you start composing another love song. Enjoy this sunrise with me … silently." Mary dropped her chin, looked up at him mischievously and said, "Let's race to the sunlight on the top of that hill!" Then she suddenly turned and ran, laughing at him as he tried to catch her and the light.

She bloomed into glorious light as her white robe turned a brilliant gold in the dawn flowing down the hill. Her dark hair blazed like fire and her face glowed like a joyous angel, as she laughed over her shoulder. Joseph stopped to watch her run. He thanked God for the gift of this day. He thanked God for this woman he wanted to be his wife, and the mother of his children. He knew she would be the most wonderful mother in the world. He could tell by the way she cared for her little brothers and sisters, and every baby she held.

Mary turned and looked at him, into him. She realized what he was thinking - she could read it in his eyes. She smiled the smile that women have always smiled at that moment. She tilted her head to an extreme angle to watch him approach where she stood inside the growing morning light. The top of the hill was still far above her. Joseph smiled as he reached her and told her to close her eyes so he could kiss her. He smiled at her closed eyes as he took his opportunity - and ran off. He called over his shoulder, "The race is still on!"

Mary opened her eyes and yelled, "You cheater!" Then she ran as fast as she could to catch up with him.

Joseph held back his pace, so they reached the top together. She pounded his back with her fists, and then he turned to feel her beat resonating in his chest until he held her wrists to stop her. Their laughter silenced as they looked into each other's eyes. She loved to feel his strength that could so easily overpower her. Birdsong rose from the valley that was still shrouded in blue mist. It was the only sound except for their breathing coming hard and fast from their run, their play, their love. Young lovers at the top of a hill in dawn's first light of this perfect day.

Mary pointed to the sun now completely above the horizon. "It's golden and full like a ripe apricot." They rested against an acacia tree as she cuddled up against his left side peacefully. Sheep spread in the valley below, seeking new pasture for this day. A lone shepherd led them. Mary said, "I wonder what his life is like, how lonely he must be out here all day and night."

Joseph squeezed her hand with a pressure that was neither hard nor soft, it was a pressure that was somehow a caress the way he shifted his fingers. "He isn't alone; he's close to God under the stars and sunsets. Like David, our great common ancestor."

Mary said, "I wonder how much of David still lives in our blood after all these centuries."

They had grown up in a terrible time, yet with a pride of heritage. They were *David's* line. The line had split for them with David's sons. Joseph came from Solomon, while Mary came from Nathan. Nathan and Solomon were full brothers, two of the four children of David and Bathsheba's love. Mary and Joseph shared the blood of David the tragic hero, flawed but faithful. Repentant after the prophet Nathan told him a story about a single beloved lamb. He touched the shepherd-boy's heart that still lived inside the jaded king. Touched his heart enough they named their son Nathan so they would never forget. And they shared the blood of magnificent Bathsheba. They shared the blood of forbidden love. But strong love. And a chastened, wiser love.

David knew the prophet Nathan had saved his country. And David knew he had saved him from himself. He had forgotten who he was and was lost inside his power as a king. It took a lamb to remind him. Yet the prophet Nathan also spoke of a curse because of what David had done to Uriah, a curse that the sword would not depart from his family forever. Every time Joseph thought of that he shivered. Forever is a very long time. But with that curse there was the blessing that the throne of the family of David would never end, either.

"I'd say David was a complicated man, Mary. Wouldn't you, my love? He started as a simple shepherd boy who loved to make music."

"And he had great faith," added Mary, cuddling closer. "I bet most of the people who knew him as a child were sure he had no sense. Challenging a giant to a duel when all he knew how to use was his little slingshot." Mary circled her hand over her head, then twirled her finger to gently touch his forehead. She made a thudding noise with her mouth and they both laughed.

"Why did he choose *five* smooth stones, Joseph? That has always puzzled me. I doubt if the giant would have waited for him to use them all before he ran him through with his spear. But Goliath was hit in mid-laugh at the boy and died before his last laugh had time to echo back."

"That's easy. We read later of the Philistine's four giant brothers. That crazy little boy figured he might have to take them on, too. *OK who's next? Line up!* But they ran. Four more giants ran from a little half-naked boy with a handful of pebbles. Of course, they were the giant's *smaller* brothers. Giants still, but a couple inches shorter. I guess they only had about six or seven feet on him, and there were only four of them left to stand against him now."

Mary snuggled closer, "Cowards. Running from a little boy. I think I see his bravery in you, my dear. You are strong and I have never seen you afraid of anything."

Joseph squeezed her hand the way she loved as he said, "You embarrass me. I'm just a carpenter, and I have plenty of fears of my own. But David was not just a brave warrior; he was a poet and musician, too. He was chosen to be the musician for the troubled King Saul, to ease the madness in his mind. When he played his harp, the disturbed king could rest at peace and sane for a time. That is something much more powerful than killing a giant, healing madness in a king."

"Yeah, Joseph, and if there were any giants hiding in the palace, he could take care of them too, I guess. I know I'd sleep better with him watching over me."

Joseph gestured with his hand in a rising spiral. "And he was a dancer, dancing in front of the Ark of God when it was returned, dancing so outrageously that he was mocked by the sophisticated princess in the palace."

"Our greatest warrior, our greatest King, master poet and musician who wrote most of the Psalms. I like having him as our ancestor."

Joseph drew Mary closer to him; she snuggled into his warmth and rested her head on his chest. She loved to feel him this way. She imagined entering dreams and waking each day comforted by his warmth and the smell of sawdust in his hair. She loved the way he smelled of cedar, pine and oak.

"I wonder if that is where you get your music, Joseph?"

"Maybe, but I've never been able to hit anything with a slingshot, so it's just as well we have no Philistine giants here." They laughed, then Joseph darkened and looked off into the distance. "There were other times when he played crazy to escape danger and maybe times he wasn't playing. There are some strange stories about him, that's for sure, when he sounded deranged. Maybe his dreams had that effect on him. And he was capable of terrible things in his moments of pride. Like calculated betrayal and murder of an innocent man to steal his beautiful wife. But able to repent and start over again humbled and ashamed."

Joseph sat up and looked to the sky as he continued. "He was real; a real person full of life and passion. Full of every kind of emotion - maybe that is why God loved him so much. He wasn't boring."

Mary stroked his arm and said, "And once a simple shepherd like that boy in the valley below us."

They watched the flock gradually spread from a tight clump of white to fill the field below. Dawn's light made them look like grounded clouds that were not slaves to the movement of the wind. They watched these earth clouds mirror the ones overhead. Natural arrangements like birdsong to the eye. The other morning birdsong filled their ears. Their own song of love filled their hearts. Harmony. A solo can be moving, but harmony brings a whole new dimension to music. And harmony is love.

Mary broke the silence. "Remember, there was another shepherd boy besides David. Joseph, the one you were named for. The dreamer who was betrayed by his brothers and sold as a slave in Egypt. Later, he was falsely accused by an angry amorous woman and thrown into prison. It is not a good idea to make a woman angry with you."

Joseph raised his hands in a gesture of surrender. "I'll try to always remember that!" Then he continued musing about the first dreamer-Joseph. "His faith sustained him through those dark days, far from home. In the darkness, he dreamed again, and listened to others' dreams. Dreams eventually brought him to power in the palace. He interpreted Pharoah's dream and saved Egypt from famine. And God used him to save his family as well. If it hadn't been for him we wouldn't be alive today. Pharoah put him in charge of all of Egypt and named him *Zaphnath-paanead* which means *the man to whom mysteries are revealed.* Dreams are powerful things."

Mary touched his forehead and said, "And dreamers. Dreamers like you, my dear."

Joseph used this as another excuse to hug her, then continued. "And he could see the future long after his death. He made his family promise to bring his bones back from Egypt to rest here in the Promised Land. Forty years his bones were carried in the desert as a token of his faith. His coffin followed the Ark of God back and forth across the desert for forty years in the longest trip to a cemetery ever. It was two hundred years after he died before his bones could finally rest not far from here. He saw in his dreams his people here today and wanted to be part of us here in this land."

Mary nuzzled him and kissed his neck. He closed his eyes and smelled the comforting smell that told him she was near, then interlaced his fingers behind his head as he leaned back and said, "God works in dream-like ways we can't foresee in the wasted intricate workings of our minds. That doesn't work. Only when we let go with a child's trust can we see the miracle that is our lives. I know, Mary. I never imagined someone like you would love me. But I dreamed it."

Mary looked at his face and smiled, although his closed eyes could not see it. This smile was for her instead of him. "I love you, Joseph," she whispered. "I love the way you understand me. I love the way you make exquisite things. And I love the way you are with children, the way you bring out the best in each of them. You will be a wonderful father someday."

"I love you, Mary. I love your soft eyes, your cute nose, the way your hair dances when you move. I love your compassion. I even love your strange sense of humor. But mostly, I love it that I don't feel so crazy when I am with you."

The moment was shattered by the metallic sounds of soldiers marching on the road below from the Decapolis to Sepphoris. They were dressed in so much metal that they sounded like a synchronized battle when they walked. Their swords made the loudest clank as they bounced off their armor with each step. Mary shivered and pulled Joseph close again. The Romans brought unexpected pain that never let the Jews relax. Someone could die with no warning or reason, and many had. No family had escaped the pain.

Mary and Joseph watched them disappear, frozen in the watching. The frightening iron and bronze song faded before the lovers' attention could return to each other. The direct light from the climbing sun now lit the scarlet fields of wildflowers that rejoiced in this time of year. After winter's drabness they sang like one of Joseph's songs. Yet, the color of blood wrapped the hills in a hint of something terrifying. But soon the beauty of this day of love pushed all fear away.

From the top of this hill they could see all the way to the Mediterrean to the east and to the Sea of Galilee to the west. From here, all the mountain ranges arced through the landscape with Har Megiddo rising from the plain to the southwest. Nazareth was nestled in a bowl between the mountains that surrounded it and provided only a limited view. From Nazareth all one could see was Nazareth and the walls of mountains that fenced it in. But from up here in the hills, the world opened to their view, and they loved the way that made them feel. Most of the time they turned their backs to Nazareth to see the larger world that spread as a mystery in every direction.

Before the day was done, Mary found a dove with a broken wing struggling on the ground and calmed it. She cupped it in her hands as she sang her soothing song. She put a splint on the wing and carried the bird next to her chest to keep it warm. They talked about all the doves that were killed each year as sacrifices in the Temple as the offering of the poor for sin. They were symbols of humble innocence. Song and flight sacrificed for human weakness. Weakness that was songless and earthbound. This dove would not die, and if she could do anything about it, would fly again some day.

The journey of the sun warmed the day. They rested and ate beneath an ancient oak in a valley between two hills. The wind kissed them with a cool breeze in the shade. Mary stood and swayed before him as she sang so only she could hear at first. She undulated as the wind blew the loose cloth around her like smoke from incense. Mary closed her eyes and let her body weave to the music she heard inside her soul. She rotated in serpentine cycles that varied with each turn. Patterns of movement repeated with new variations. The music inside her escaped from her lips silently at first; then more audibly. Her arms and hands traced intricate patterns through the air, as if she were swimming through fields of grain or a bird negotiating a complicated path through a dense forest. It was a search for something larger coming from within. It was pleasure in movement for itself. And it was more.

Joseph swayed with the rhythm of her song. Moving his shoulders and head mirroring her movement. He could feel her body moving inside him. He wanted to share this movement with her, to feel her body next to his. She opened her eyes and continued singing into his soul. She was a virgin, as was he. But she liked the way he looked at her. She imagined love with this good man. She imagined it vividly. It made her blush. It made her smile.

It filled him like a lot of wine. He stood to walk to her. He held her face in his hands and kissed her, then stepped back, holding her at arm's length. "I love you, Mary. I know you are the one I have been hoping for. Will you be my wife?"

Shock, joy, fear, and hope all crowded for control of her mind. Love won. She realized she was caressing his hand and the scar from the day she first realized she loved him. The day they fell in love. Now this, already. She knew it was too soon, they had to think, spend time to know. But they knew. Already they both knew.

She didn't answer him; she simply told him that she loved him and, "I need to think."

He would wait. He wouldn't ask again until she was ready.

They sat listening to the water that wound down the hills toward Nazareth. The blue shadows climbed back up the hills. They rested and held each other as sunset sang across the sky in a symphony of change. The gold light rose to the tops of the hills, then flew off into the clouds. They waited until the sky cooled to blue and the first stars appeared. Mary held the dove close to her breast to keep it warm. Joseph joined his heat to hers.

"I hate to leave, it was a perfect day," she told Joseph. "I love you. I want to stay here in this peaceful place next to you forever." But, it was time to go. Nazareth waited.

Song of Home

Joseph had already completed most of their furniture in two months of hard work. Today he and James began building a house although Mary still hadn't given him an answer. She brought him lunch while he worked and ate with him.

"You know I am making this for you, my love. For us to raise our family."

Mary tilted her head and said, "We'll see."

"I've already seen us together in my dreams, and all my life I have learned to listen to my dreams. My name is Joseph, remember?"

Mary stood with her arms crossed then gestured with a low arc and back. "All I see so far is a man with a lot of pieces of wood on the ground right now. Maybe that is a house in your dreams, but so far your dream won't keep anybody warm and dry."

James smiled at their play. He thought her pretence was thin, considering the way she looked at Joseph. "Strong as you are, I don't think you can build a house alone, my friend. Unless your love can raise the beams into place. I am no carpenter, but I will do what I can to help. And for goodness' sake we need to hurry and finish this house so we can hide you two behind some walls so we all don't have to watch all the incessant kissing anymore. You'll become a scandal to the neighborhood."

Mary stuck her tongue out at him as she twisted herself into that gesture all children seem to know as instinct. The universal gesture that goes with the tongue. The gesture that says *nyaaaaahhh*. James returned the same. Joseph shook his head.

James continued, "I'm not particularly good with my hands, but I can lift the lighter half. I'm a merchant, so I can count nails real well, if that will help. I'll pretend they are shekels."

James carried numbers in his mind like Joseph carried songs. And he could turn a catastrophe into a profit.

No loving woman lit up James' life; he was too busy finding ways to make a good living despite the Roman restrictions and arbitrary taxes. Like everyone else, he tried to find a way around the Roman stranglehold on life. There was no freedom here, even to make a sale. *Unless they didn't know.* But he had seen Roman punishment upon those who didn't obey their laws. The Empire was merciless when it made an example. It had invented horrible ways to die, and intentionally made them very public. The discipline imposed on Roman citizen-soldiers was strict and cruel, so these Judeans and Galileans would not be allowed to weaken the Empire. Rome was a dangerously overextended empire, and now needed to bleed the provinces to survive. Rome was far away and the armies were spread too thin for comfort. Just below the surface of their power hid fear. Fear uses desperate cruelty to bluff an image of strength.

Still, James took chances. "Calculated risks," he would say with a grin. He loved the *art* of making money. He hated seeing all his profit stolen, so that sometimes what should have been a profit ended up as a loss. He often said, "Where is the sense in that?"

When they worked on the house together, James bragged about all the clever ways he had outsmarted the Romans. Joseph was afraid for his friend, and warned him to be careful. But he also laughed with him, since he struggled against the same restrictions. He hated paying tribute to them, especially with the sacrilegious coins they had to use. Images of emperors who claimed to be gods were an unavoidable abomination in direct contradiction to two of the Ten Commandments.

James composed awkward rhymes about them, mocking Joseph's songs. But under his teasing, he was overjoyed that Joseph had found such a good woman. She had maturity and grace, but with the spirit of a happy child with a great sense of humor. But most important of all she was very much in love with his friend. James had never seen Joseph so blissful. He looked forward to seeing the children these two would make inside the cheerful home that would sing between these walls.

Canon

The strenuous work of raising the roof beams required all the men in Joseph's extended family. Joseph's uncle poked James as he yelled, "Where will bedroom be, where the great craftsman will do his best work?"

Jacob added, " Yes, it's time to make grandchildren for me and your mother. You're our only son, so the whole job is on your shoulders -- and lower."

Mary had not given him an answer yet, but everyone knew what it would be. She was stubborn and would fill his life with as much as he could handle, everyone was sure of that. She would fill him with love and surprises. It could never be a boring life with this woman.

But Joseph was sure enough to build a house. He knew Mary's father would give his blessing, but she had asked him to wait until she made up her mind. She was a woman who would control her own destiny in this world of patriarchs and empires. She came from a long line of strong women who had changed history throughout the centuries. Not only was she of David's line, but Bathsheba's. She understood the subtle power of a woman in a man's world. It was often a hidden power men never spoke of as it changed their world.

The blue sky was finally divided over the sweating men. The beams were all in place, now it was time to rest and eat lunch before the afternoon work began. As the tools were being stacked against the wall, Mary entered with the meal. James called out, "Here comes the Queen of Nazareth, to feed her loyal subjects building her palace!" He bowed deeply from the waist.

Mary crossed her arms in front of her and sniffed. "Let's not be making any assumptions, James. We don't know who will be living under those beams with Joseph yet now, do we?" Everyone snickered, but Mary barely cracked a smile.

"The Queen of Nazareth" served them warm bread with cheese and fruit to fill them. And wine to relax their sore muscles. It also loosened Joseph's tongue. He started singing love songs to her, as all the men groaned. Mary blushed as he neared a line she knew well that she would rather they all not hear, so she stuffed a large hunk of bread into his mouth. "You must be hungry, Joseph - have some more to eat!" She pushed more on top of the other he was struggling to chew. "You have a lot more work to do, so you better save your wind."

James was rolling on the ground, choking with glee. Mary crossed her arms and scowled at him. "Are you having some kind of fit, James?" Joseph's muffled laughs escaped through his full mouth and nose. This made James laugh even harder, as did all the men in Joseph's family. Mary gestured across the room. "You all think I should sign up for a life of this? Look at you men!" Joseph's father, Jacob, shook his head at his son. "You two might as well admit it - you are made for each other. Heaven help all of us."

Mary looked up at the beams dividing the sky above them. It would be a solid house, made of laughter and love. And she *would* be the queen of it.

Song of the Dove

Sweet dove, your song is always so sad.

Sweet dove, don't feel so bad.

Sweet dove, you calm me in the morning to ease me out of my bed.

Mary fed the dove as she sang. She called her Jonah, the Hebrew word for dove. This morning Jonah's voice was answered with a second harmonious voice outside the window. *They always sound so lonely, even when they are a loving pair, these turtledoves.* Mary wondered if her mate was waiting for her and lonely. As Mary stroked the bird's soft back she felt the feathers' softness stiffen as she reached the tail. *Soft feathers for warmth, and stiff feathers for flight.* Mary marveled at the miracle that is a bird, and wondered if such pure song could exist except within the freedom of flight.

Joseph had made a cage to protect her while she healed, and Mary taught her younger sister to care for the fragile bird. Mary saw gratitude and hope in Jonah's eyes.

"What is more hopeful than flight and song, my little friend? Soon you will be well, free to fly over these hills again," Mary shared one of Joseph's love songs with the dove. It started with her ancestor Solomon's song comparing his beloved to a dove. Joseph had built upon the ancient words to praise Mary at length. The dove cooed along with her.

Mary's mother, Anne, listened behind her, glad for her daughter who was in love with this good man. God had blessed them and answered her prayers. Every mother wants a secure and tranquil home for her daughter. Every mother dreads what an evil man can do, and fears the helplessness of an abusive relationship. She had watched Joseph since he was a child, seen the kind child he had been and the fine man he had become. Mary had been a difficult but loving child. Independent to a fault, she questioned everything. She was kind and sensitive with a strength of will that fueled her curiosity. She always explored her world a little farther than her mother thought was safe. Since Joseph had come into her life, she worried about her less.

Anne hummed along as third voice with her daughter and the dove in Joseph's song.

Staccato

I have to admit you were right, Joseph. She is all you could dream for. And for you with your dreams, that is saying something."

"I truly am a fortunate man, James. God has smiled on me."

"Wh-wh-who are y-you t-t-talking about? Wh-who's all y-you could d-dream about?"

Joseph grimaced, then closed his eyes and sighed.

Agabus stood in the open doorway into James' home and workplace. He was also a merchant and a Jew, although he tried to hide it as much as possible. Agabus was short and almost round, but dressed impeccably in Roman robes. He trimmed his beard as much as he could get away with and still appear to be an observant Jew. He never used his Jewish name in business, but a Roman name. James did the same thing, of course. Seeming less Jewish and more sophisticated in the world of commerce made dealing with the Romans easier. But Agabus went farther than he needed to, and almost seemed to be embarrassed to be a Jew. In a lot of ways he seemed to be embarrassed by who he was - a short lonely merchant.

He was obsessed with his fingernails. He carried a pouch with four sandstones and a limestone he used, in order of roughness, to file down his fingernails. Just like he trimmed his beard as much as he dared without offending his people, he filed his nails so far that his fingers were raw with the quick exposed. There was always a little bit of blood showing in the red soft flesh beneath his nails. As soon as a bit of nail began to grow, he would start his ritual again until he bled. And he was always itching and needing to scratch, but because he had no nails to scratch with, he carried a curved stick shaped like a scoop that he used constantly to scratch his back, his head, his ankles. Worse, he stuttered, and stuttered more the more nervous he became.

He was difficult to be around in every way. But James and Joseph liked him more than they pitied him. He had a dry sense of humor and was so much a character that they simply had to like him, despite how annoying he could be. He had no real friends, and so he came to them more often than they would have wished. He had just returned from a journey lasting months and wanted to hear the local news. Having overheard their conversation, he rushed in talking, as was his way.

James gave him the news. "Joseph is in love, Agabus, with Mary, Heli and Anne's daughter."

"Y-you're lucky, J-Joseph, sh-she's b-beautiful. And sh-she's one of the f-few women who w-will e-even b-bother to sp-sp-speak to m-me. I think sh-she likes me a little. Sh-she takes t-time to ta-taa-talk to me."

"Yes, she is beautiful and she is sweet to everyone." Joseph struggled a smile. There was no telling what Agabus would say next.

"Sh-she has some body on her, as w-well as a b-beautiful face. I s-s-sure w-wish I could g-get to know her b-better, if y-you know w-what I mean."

"I'd back off I were you, shorty! Joseph is an awfully strong carpenter." James laughed.

"I d-don't care, if I had a ch-chance w-with her it w-would be w-worth a b-b-beating or two."

Joseph shook his head.

"I m-mean … sh-she's s-so s-sexy!" He pulled out his roughest stone and started filing his nails so hard the blood started to flow.

Joseph put his hands to his forehead and dropped his head on James' shoulder with a thud.

Mary's announcement to her father was sudden and brief. "It's time." Then she immediately told Joseph that he was allowed to ask for her hand now. Neither man was surprised at the way she finally decided to follow tradition, but on very much on her own terms. She was like her mother, Anne, only more so. Heli, Mary's father had warned Joseph what he had in store. This world where men were in control of everything was just an illusion for fools.

When Joseph delivered a dowry that night, he was welcomed with hugs and wine. Heli and Anne were relieved the betrothal could finally begin. There were no grandchildren on either side of their family yet, so there was much pressure to bring a child into this world soon.

After the celebration, Joseph needed to tell his friend. James responded at his door with mock seriousness, "Really, are you sure, Joseph, that you really want to do this? Are you ready, this is all so very sudden and unexpected."

James threw his arms around him. "Hang on, Joseph, you are in for a wild ride, this is no ordinary love. We can all be sure of that. Let's celebrate, my friend - or mourn - either way, the wine's the same." James poured the wine. Their tongues were set loose and looser as the night grew later.

"Joseph, remember Esther? Remember when we were fourteen, and she matured overnight? She looked like a walking mountain range bouncing down the street. We used to stare and make excuses to talk with her. I remember how much we both wished we could catch a glimpse of her to see what she looked like under her clothes. She was our age, and we had grown up playing with her - it was not like looking at nursing mothers. She was different. Now her husband certainly smiles a lot. She was my first love, even though she never knew it."

Joseph mussed James' perfect hair and said, "My friend, what are we going to do with you? We must find you a loving wife. What about Leah?"

"The one with the tongue that can rip a man's soul out? She will say *anything* when she is angry. I've never heard such hurtful things from anyone else. But most of the time she is very gentle and kind, and she is a real beauty. But I would be afraid of living in a house with that tongue." James winced in a gesture of pain and put both hands over his ears.

"What about Miriam, Simon's daughter? She is Mary's closest friend. She is a bit young, but not as young as she looks. She is petite and a little mysterious. Unlike some women, she doesn't have to say everything that is in her mind. And I have seen the way she looks at you when you aren't watching. She seems to like the way you look." Joseph said with his twisted smile.

James took another drink from the wineskin. "She *is* pleasant to look at, and gentle. She never raises her voice. I like that. I like that a lot. But she is so shy; she never looks me in the eye. She always looks down at the ground. I think she is afraid of her own body; I'm sure she is afraid of mine!"

They both laughed at that, and Joseph said, "Sometimes women learn to love the things they fear a little. If they can conquer their fear and learn to trust, it makes a finer love. Women want to love something they think is stronger than themselves - even very strong women. Maybe the strongest most of all. She might surprise you, James, sometimes great strength lies just below the timid surface, waiting to be freed by love."

More wine flowed, generating songs long into the night. James' terrible voice had no sense of meter even when sober. Tonight the wine spawned awful love songs mocking Joseph's love. Eventually their jaws grew tired from smiling too much, and they fell asleep sitting where they were. In the morning they both woke feeling better than they deserved.

That evening, Joseph and Mary celebrated again, this time merging both families in the joy. Two families that were both anxious for grandchildren. Too many children had died in this harsh time, so Mary and Joseph were their first hope for a future.

Starting the next morning, every day they continued building a home they hoped would soon be filled with the laughter of children. The hours they spent together each day were the happiest times in their lives. Each evening Mary spun or worked on her loom, making clothes for both of them, and she wove small blankets of the softest wool and flax. Small blankets for big dreams.

Silent Song

The roof was not yet completed, so the sky was visible between some beams. In another day or two the roof would be completed. Lit by flickering lamplight, Mary and Joseph shared a meal alone on the dirt floor. Soon this would be their peaceful home. Mary was not full of fire this night, and Joseph was not full of jokes. They were in a quiet place, close to their dreams, and frightened by the sureness.

They had never shared a quieter meal. In the silence each could see their futures in this place. They pictured children crawling, running, and laughing in this room. Babies grew to toddlers in their minds, then into men and women with children of their own. Mary smiled at Joseph with a grandmother's smile, then slid across the floor to lean on his shoulder and chest. Mary stroked his hand, tracing all the little scars of work and kissing them. Kissed his battered fingernails, misshapen from the smashing of wood and hammer. She thought his hands were beautiful; and she imagined again how they would feel when they were free to touch her they way they both desired. She took his hand and placed it on her throat. She loved to feel his warmth flow into her and join hers in this soft place. She rested her hand on top of his and closed her eyes.

They sat in silence for a time. The oil lamps cast dancing shadows on the walls around them. The night wind whistled through the spaces in the roof. The stars shone down on them. Neither spoke, neither needed to.

Mary finally broke the silence. "Will you always sing to me, Joseph? Even when I grow old and fat, my body worn out from all the children I have borne you? Will you still look at me the way you do now? I don't think I could bear it if I saw you look away. If I thought you didn't want to look at me."

Joseph looked at Mary silently; he saw the fear in her eyes. He smiled, and answered her with a song.

> *Since the day you first surprised me*
> *And stopped my blood from flowing to the ground,*
> *You almost stopped my heart from beating*

As my head was spinning 'round,
You have been my only love,
My beauty and my dove.

You are my first thought on waking,
My last dream of every night,
I always want you near me,
Even when you want to fight,
How could you be afraid
I would break the love we've made?

You think the years we share
As we fill our happy home
With children born of purest love . . .

" . . . Oh Mary, that's the best I can do on the spot. Let me just tell you that I love you, I will always love you, and all the wrinkles and scars of time will only make you more beautiful because of all the love we have shared. How could there ever be anyone else for me? It is the one thing in life I am most sure of, and that I can trust you. I know you, and I know your heart."

Mary cried and laughed at the same time, touched by his song, and charmed by the way he gave up trying to create a song on the spot. She could see tears in his eyes, too.

Lifetimes of emotion all struggled for a place to be. Their shadows danced together on the wall from the paired lamp flames. Each saw a dream of the other as old and content; still deeply in love and with grandchildren giggling in play. They each saw a wonderful shared dream in the future.

Mary finally spoke, "That was a terrible song, Joseph, and I loved it." Then they lay back on the floor and let the silent song of their love fill the room and their hearts. And fill the space above them to the stars.

But Joseph saw something in the stars that Mary couldn't see and it frightened him. But he kept it to himself.

Discord

Mary, can't you hear me? Slow down and let me catch up with you! Where are you going in such a hurry?" Joseph ran as hard as he could, but still Mary stayed just out of his reach. "Mary, why won't you turn around?"

She had almost reached the top of the hill when the dazzling light of sunrise made her glow like an angel. At the very top of the hill, Joseph finally grabbed her to turn her around. "Why wouldn't you say anything to me?" As she turned to him, Joseph fell backward to the ground in shock. It was the bloody madman laughing at him, reaching for a grotesque embrace.

"What's the matter, Joseph, don't you love me anymore?"

Joseph jerked awake panting, grateful that this awful dream was over. He had always loved dreams before. Now he desperately searched for the meaning in this nightmare. There would be no more sleep for him this night. And no more peace.

Joseph went to his workshop to lose this painful image in his work. He chose a plane and smoothed the surface of a table, then sanded it for hours. It made him feel normal again to work and smell the comforting reality of wood.

Then he polished it to a shine that reflected his troubled face back to his eyes. He didn't like the face that looked back up at him from the wood. And he didn't like dreams as much as he had before. He was almost afraid to see Mary in the morning. He'd feel better when it was *her* face that greeted him when she turned around. *Is God trying to give me a message? I pray that he is not.*

The gift of "seeing" paired with a curse. Joseph often saw horrible things that made him fear he might be going mad. When some came true, he didn't know if he felt better or worse. If only he could know for sure what these things meant he could use them, but sometimes they were indecipherable and just a slap in his face to get his attention. Just that and then he was left to try to figure it out. But he also saw beauty where no one else could. He didn't know if he'd rather be mad in a beautiful world or sane in a frightening one. He shook his head and whispered, "Oh my poor dear Mary." He struggled to get the awful face out of his mind.

Gift Songs

The creak of heavy-laden wagon wheels and snort of a team of oxen interrupted Joseph's work. He opened the door of his shop to see James leaning against a load of exotic woods – each rare in Galilee. Joseph caressed the grain, consumed the scent of each, as the colors filled his imagination. Still stroking the grain, he turned to see James enjoying his reaction. Nothing brought James more pleasure than giving presents. As a merchant, he had access to things most Galileans would never see. Joseph had mentioned to him once his desire to work with woods that could not grow in this climate. James knew he would turn this lumber into finely crafted art that would bring a great profit from the Romans. It was his way to help his friend start out more secure in his new life.

Mary was thrilled with a package of expensive cloth, dyed in rare rich colors. In return, Mary often baked for James, with cinnamon, raisins and dates that he loved. And Mary tried to bring him something much more valuable. Sometimes she brought her best friend, Miriam, with her to visit Joseph when she knew James would be with him. She was the gift he needed most, she thought.

Miriam's name was the same as Mary's, but she was usually called by this other form of the name because there were so many Mary's in the village. She liked her nickname. Formal people called her Mary, but she liked the murmuring sound of Miriam. It was what she felt inside. *Being known by two names is appropriate,* she thought. She felt sometimes as if she were two people living in one body. One shy and timid, and the other … not.

Miriam felt James was a wonderful man mostly from what Mary had told her. And she loved the way he looked. Shorter than Joseph, and not so muscular, he had a strength of his own. Passionate about his work as a merchant, he had seen much of the world beyond Galilee. Miriam had never been more than a few miles from Nazareth and loved to listen to the stories he told of worlds across the seas. And he was very kind, and funny. Women love a man who can make them laugh. A joke reveals much about the teller, even more about the one who laughs. She knew she could love this man if he would only give her the chance.

James was at his most animated telling stories about his impossible deals. He was a clever man who loved to live on the edge, taking dangerous chances for big profits. He frightened Miriam to hear him speak about tricking tax collectors. He bragged about it too much, she thought. He was always very neat, not like Joseph. James always kept his hair and beard trimmed as neatly as a proper Jew could. His clothes were of the finest cloth, and always very clean. His leather purse was always full. He had taken a Greek name he used in business, but that made him no less a Jew. He was James of Nazareth at home, and Alphaeus to the Romans. Miriam understood having two names and two ways of thinking. She liked that about him, too.

Miriam didn't share Mary's adventurous spirit. She was shy, and thoughtful, but had a laugh like bubbling water and the wind. Miriam imagined she would make a good merchant's wife. She thought she might convince him to live a safer life. But he thrilled with the hunt and was a warrior with his trade. A good sale was like a victorious battle to him. Miriam laughed each time he told another story, even though she could tell he embellished each tale. It is in the nature of all good storytellers to exaggerate. Sometimes a gentle lie tells the story truer.

She loved watching him grow excited while he told his stories; and the way he gestured wildly, painting pictures with his voice. And she loved the way he looked. He was not handsome in the conventional sense, but passionate and alive. But Miriam could sense a touch of the scared little boy in him, too. Something frightened that hid deeply below his bravado. She loved that, too. She imagined most people never saw that in him, but she did. She loved his strength and weakness - she loved all of him.

James had been watching Miriam more than the others knew. He thought she had an appealing face with deep brown eyes and lips as tiny as a child's with a diminutive chin. Her nose was very small, too. In fact, James thought her face was like a lovely child's, almost immature. Her hands were graceful, and restrained. Her movements were subtle, as if she were trying to disappear to avoid being seen by some dangerous animal. But when she did move, it was fluid, but reserved. Subdued like her voice, gentle and soft.

That evening the four of them shared supper in Mary and Joseph's unfinished home. James always seemed to become more animated telling stories when Miriam was in the room. He was performing for her. Mary caught Joseph's eye and winked at him with a nod from James to Miriam. She knew.

Miriam laughed at the story James told, she lowered her head and looked up at him, covering her mouth with the back of her hand as she laughed. James moved closer to her. He sat next to her and whispered in her ear. Miriam touched his arm gently for a moment, then drew her hand back in front of her mouth as if she had done something wrong.They were deeply in love's hesitant first dance.

Joseph smiled at Mary, grinning like a donkey eating cactus.

Miriam's Song

Although Miriam was shy, she knew what she felt. She knew what she wanted. He didn't stand a chance.

Miriam spun flax while Mary wove on her loom. "He is a simple man in many ways, Mary, despite how smart he is. He makes me laugh with his stories, and much as he thinks he is so tricky, he is not so complicated. He only wants to be a successful merchant, with a peaceful family."

"I know, Miriam, he has always been a wonderful friend to Joseph since they were little boys. He doesn't talk about his faith much, but it is simple - and real. James doesn't pretend to be a deep thinker; he just lives a practical life. He is a good man and down to earth and funny. He is a sweet man who has always been kind to me. And he loves Joseph, he would do anything for him, I am sure.

Miriam shook her head. "A simple man in some ways, Mary, but in other ways, he's not. He is pretty stable and secure except for his flirtation with danger with the Romans. That is danger indeed." Miriam worried about things. She worried that the man she loved would be thrown in prison or worse. But she was sure she could convince him to follow a safer way of life. He wouldn't want to lose it all for a prideful game. He would love her so much he would give up all that, she knew. He would want to protect her and their children, that much she knew about this man already.

She conspired with Mary as they made their plans. He would be hers soon, they knew. Mary whispered to her friend, "Men think they make the decisions, but once we make up our minds there is not much they can do. We only let them think they are in control. Unless they get too arrogant, and then we let them know who really is in control."

Our fourth full moon shines on our love, Mary. I love your face in the moonlight. It's a kind light to any face, but beauty like yours becomes angelic beauty."

Mary decided to keep silence and not argue with him.

"Every time I see that light on your face, I remember the first night we walked in the moonlight. I always will. I love the softness of moonlight and the way it kisses your face. It's lovers' light."

They walked the hills again this night, remembering and dreaming. The sheep below them were brighter now; their wool had grown in the passing months. A soft cloud seemed to have settled on the earth below them. The shepherd calmed them with his quiet song that brought them peace against the wolf song in the distance.

An owl added his voice to the harmony. The smaller kind of owl that had a woman's voice, not the deeper bass of the larger owl. They walked in silence. No words were needed this night. Just the song of warmth that flowed between their hands, and the easy way they matched their pace. It was as if they had been together forever, though their love was only a few months old.

They sat on the hill and stared at the moon. The smell of dew on the soil merged with the flowers. And the scent of Mary harmonized with them into a song for his nose. Mary loved the smell of Joseph, too. She rested her head on his chest and smelled the cedar shavings in his beard and the sweet bite of his sweat and the comforting smell that was *him* that always filled his clothes.

Stars brilliant enough to stand the moonlight's challenge spread across the sky. The young couple lay on their backs on the hill and searched for familiar constellations. They whispered, awed by the great expanse of space, awed by the love that had been given them. They whispered because whispering itself drew them closer.

A shooting star fell into the valley, growing dimmer and slower as it fell. It glowed as a gentle light and wobbled like a leaf rocking down from a tree as it struggled against the thick air closer to the ground. It swayed wildly back and forth until it stopped glowing to land as a dark stone from the heavens hidden among the multitude on the ground. Flattened by the burning of the trip, it bounced and slid down the hill. They heard the clink of stone on stone until it came to rest. They thought of trying to find it in the valley below, but they knew it was impossible.

A piece of heaven come to earth, looking just like all the other stones that covered the valley and the surrounding hills. No other eyes saw it this night; they alone knew of this touch from heaven. They took it as a good omen of their new love. God's pebble thrown to get their attention with ripples of sound ... and ripples of love.

Joseph whispered a song written by David about the heavens declaring the glory of God. They returned to the silent stars. The first dew of the night settled around them as they held each other against the chill. It was time for Joseph to bring Mary safely to her home for the night.

They both slept peacefully, alone in secure dreams of a time when soon they would sleep in each other's arms after the passion of love.

Bright blueness woke Mary in the middle of the night. Only light and silence. Light so intense it filled her although her eyelids were still closed. It frightened her. But the light didn't disturb her as much as the silence. Silence so deep it seemed to swallow her thoughts. A voice came from that silence deeper than the earth.

"Chosen one, the Lord is with you."

This frightened her even more, so she kept her eyes tightly closed, hoping this was a merely a dream that would go away.

Then the light calmed her with her name. "Don't be afraid, Mary."

She opened only one eye to peek at a shining angel standing over her. He introduced himself as Gabriel. When he smiled at her, she relaxed a bit. At least as much as someone could relax with a glowing angel over her bed, bearing a life-changing message from God.

He extended his hand toward her. She shrank under the covers a bit. "You please God, Mary. You are the one. You will conceive and bear a son, and you will name him Jesus. He will be great, the son of the Most High, and the Lord God will give him the throne of his ancestor David. *Your* ancestor. He will reign over the house of Jacob forever, and his kingdom will never end. He is the answer to all the promises of God to your ancestors and to you."

Mary wrinkled her brow and said, "No, that can't be, how could it be, since I am a virgin?" Gabriel answered, "The Holy Spirit will overshadow you, in this great light, and it will be. Your cousin Elizabeth is already pregnant in her sixth month, even though she is far too old to bear a child, and has been barren her entire life. God isn't limited by things we expect, but freed by what we believe to create miracles."

Mary sat in stunned silence. Doubting, and very afraid. She was terribly confused. The silence sucked her mind out into it so she could hardly think. *How could there be so much light and so little sound until he spoke, then back to soul-sucking silence again?*

"Do you think anything is too hard for God?" The angel asked, still waiting for her agreement. This was too great a gift to be given unwanted. Too great and too expensive.

Mary argued with herself; she didn't dare argue with him. *What about Joseph? What will I tell him? What if he doesn't believe me? How could he believe me? How could I tell Joseph? What will I say? What is he going to think about me? Will he still want me? Will this mean we never get to have children of our own? But I love him so much, and I want to know him as a wife and lover. What if we cannot? Can he accept that and still want to be with me? What will everyone think about me? What will my father say? But, the Messiah! From me? Why me? I'm not the kind of woman to be mother to the Messiah. Why me? But this is so ... wonderful. How can I say no? But ...*

Gabriel just smiled at her as her silent face frowned and smiled and frowned again as she battled all the Mary's inside her. He had all the time beyond the world.

Finally she told the angel that she agreed. She wanted this gift from God. *How could I say no to something so important? No matter what it costs me.*

Gabriel nodded, smiled at her and disappeared. Her room was dark again. Mary sat in silence. The moon had lowered into the western sky. She remembered Joseph's words about their moon. Mary frowned. *I can't see him yet.* She dressed quickly and packed to leave for Elizabeth's house before dawn. She was overwhelmed and wanted to be with the one person in the world who could possibly understand. *Since Elizabeth had been visited this way a half a year ago, maybe she has some answers on what to do and say.* And she had always been her favorite cousin who had treated her like a daughter. Besides, she didn't know how to tell Joseph, she was afraid he wouldn't believe her. She was afraid he would think she was mad or had been impregnated by another man. This story was hard enough to believe when she had seen the angel in her bedroom. Now that he was gone even *she* started to wonder. *Am I going mad? This is just too strange. I have no idea what to say to anyone.* But mostly, she was afraid of what she might see in Joseph's eyes when she told him.

It would be an awful thing to look in the eyes of the one she loved most in the world and see his disappointed love fading as he began to doubt her. It would be torture to know she was innocent, but not able to prove it. She would have to bear it with grace and patience, and hope that some day he would understand. *Then it will be worth it.* Real love is very patient, Mary knew. She hoped she would think of a way to tell him that he would understand. After all, she had months to think about it. Maybe Elizabeth could help her. *She* knew what it was like to be touched by God to have an impossible baby and have to explain it somehow. Or maybe they could figure it out together. One thing she knew for sure: she had no idea what to say now and wasn't prepared to face him – or anybody.

Her parents loved her, but they often disagreed with her way of doing things and thought she was recklessly independent. She knew they would not believe her. She was overjoyed with the news but frightened about what it might mean to her. The joy and the fear were combined into something that was much bigger than she could comprehend. She needed to be with someone who would just believe her with no doubting, and Elizabeth was the only one.

She had to be gone by dawn. She had to think. She couldn't bear the thought of a doubting look in Joseph's eyes. The fear of the look of love in his eyes not being there anymore terrified her, but still the joy of motherhood – *this* motherhood – filled her. But she didn't know how she could live without him. *Oh, Joseph, poor Joseph – poor me.*

She hoped losing him was not the cost of this blessing from God. But she would bear that price if needed to have this holy child. She would do anything. She had to. The world needed him. Needed him now. He was to save Israel from the Romans, and more. He was to save all of them from the mess they had made of everything. She had to do her part, no matter what it cost.

Mary convinced her father that such an old woman as Elizabeth needed care to deliver safely and she knew she was the one to go. And she had a feeling – a sense – that she had to go right now. It was important that they travel this morning, and she was already packed. He thought she was a little mad, but he was used to her impulsiveness. He would do anything to keep his favorite girl safe. And he knew how stubborn she was when she made up her mind. He knew she would start her journey this morning with or without him. She said she would be back in three or four months after Elizabeth's child was born. Mary told no one about herself, she couldn't take the chance that Joseph would find out she was pregnant. She wanted him to hear it from her lips, but she didn't know how to tell him yet. She didn't know how to tell anyone except Elizabeth, who would understand. She couldn't even take a chance on telling

Miriam. She was afraid Miriam's eyes, if not her tongue, would betray her secret. And, more than that, she needed time to comprehend this mystery she was such a part of. *What will this mean?*

Mary left the healing dove in her younger sister's care while she was gone. The bird would certainly be able to fly by the time she returned. Her groggy father was preparing the donkeys for their two or three day journey. He was glad to be away from the house where her mother was arguing with her. He knew arguing with Mary once she had made up her mind was pointless. Besides, this was his last time to be alone with his little girl.

"Thank you, Father." Mary kissed him on his cheek as they started on the road just as the sun rose. "It's a beautiful sunrise. Thank you again for understanding. It is just something that I know I have to do." *It is a beautiful golden sunrise and my world is new in its light. I wish I could tell him.*

Her father yawned and said, "Even for you, Mary, this is strange behavior. What is really going on? Have you and Joseph had a fight? Are you having second thoughts?"

Mary shook her head. "No, Father, I love him more than ever. It is not him. But to be honest, I do have a lot I want to think about before we get married, and Elizabeth has always had such good advice." *I wish I could tell him, but what if he thinks I am making this up. I hate not being able to tell him everything.*

"Mary you know I love you and I want the best for you. Don't ever forget that. I think Joseph is the finest man I have ever met and I trust him with my baby girl."

"I know, I am lucky to have a man like him love me the way he does. And I love him. But I don't want to see him or Miriam, or anyone for three months. I just need to be alone with Elizabeth right now to take care of her and to prepare myself for marriage. You know I have been a very independent little girl."

Her father snorted and laughed a deep laugh. "Independent, huh? Is that what you call it? I hope Joseph takes this time to get ready for *you*." Mary's father was glad for this inconvenient journey; it gave him some time alone to talk with his daughter before she started life as a married woman. He savored this time on the road. But he would be very glad to get off the donkey and rest at Elizabeth's house, and he could see it in the distance. But Mary had another surprise in store.

"Father, I have another big favor to ask of you."

"Certainly, Mary, what is it?"

"Don't come in to talk with Elizabeth, just let me off here so I can see her by myself."

"You can't be serious, we've been on the road for days and I need rest."

"Please. It is very important to me. I'll explain later, but I need to greet her alone. Please, father."

"This makes no sense, have pity on your poor exhausted father."

"I can't explain now, just trust me. I hate to do this to you but I have to and I cannot explain."

"What is up with you and all this mystery all of a sudden? Have you lost your mind? All right, get off here and have it your way. Just give your father a kiss and tell me I'll see you soon."

"Thank you. I promise I'll return as soon as Elizabeth gives birth and can get around again. That will be in three months." Then she kissed him and watched him start the long journey home. Mary took a moment to prepare herself then walked to Elizabeth's door. *How will I tell her what has happened? I haven't told anyone and already it is starting to feel like it was just a dream. Am I mad?*

She didn't need to worry. Her cousin could feel it already somehow. When Elizabeth came to the door, Mary was greeted with a song about how blessed she was of God and John danced in his mother's womb at the presence of the growing Messiah.

Mary answered with her own song of the miracle growing inside her. Joseph had taught her how to make her own song. She sang as a woman touched by God with the life of life.

Nocturne

Joseph patiently watched the moon shrink from full to disappear, then grow back to full again. *Still no word from Mary. She didn't even say goodbye, just left a vague message for me with her father. She said she needed to be alone with Elizabeth for three or four months because she had a lot to think and pray about. What does that mean? She doesn't want to see me until after Elizabeth has given birth. There hasn't been a day we haven't seen each other since we met and now this? But I know her and I trust her. I know she loves me.* Joseph acquiesced to her difficult request. He loved her. He didn't understand, but he was patient - and he knew better than to rush love. God had given him a lot of grace. He would need every bit of it. But doubt grows like a seed in the dark and his life had been very dark in her silence. This night as the moon was growing to its brightest, his soul was shadowed in the deepest darkness.

The full moon drew him outside to feed on its nourishing light. He remembered the first night they walked together in this light. The night he *knew*. The night before the day he first asked her to marry him. The night he whispered his dream to the moon before he dared to ask her. Low in the east, the moon promised a long night of light. Light enough to travel *She's breaking my heart. It's been more than a month since she has disappeared. Something is up. I have to go and see what this is all about. I have to know if she still loves me.*

He went home and gathered food and a cloak for his journey. Even though he knew she didn't want to see him, he went anyway. He would decide along the way. If he decided not to see her, he could always turn around. If he determined he had to see her, he would be close to her by the time he knew. He journeyed through the night, arguing with himself. What *will I say to her? What if she tells me to go away? Why has she pulled away from me? Why is she making this painful demand without so much as a word of explanation? But, don't I trust her? I'm afraid. I'm afraid that maybe I don't. But I do. Except... this is so strange...*

Joseph argued with himself all night, yet his love was stronger than fears or questions or the unknown. Since they fell in love there had never been a day they had not spoken until now, until this month of maddening silence. He thought she would at least send him a message. *Has she lost her love for me? I am just a simple carpenter, and she is so beautiful. Is there another man with more money and a handsome face? Is there someone who can give her a better future? Do you still love me, Mary? Are you having doubts?*

The moon was directly overhead now and lit the road clearly. A wolf howled from the hill above him, answered by another muted by great distance. Owls joined the moonsong, both kinds of owls with their songs like a woman's voice and a man's.

Summer flowers filled the air, the soprano notes in the song of smell, the chords completed by the bass of damp earth, and the mid-tone notes of cedar and oak. He recognized some trees by his nose alone while they still stood uncut. The subtle smell rose to crescendo each time his saw ripped through the wood. He knew each kind of tree like a friend. He could tell the sound of leaves that was the voice of each. Joseph paused in his journey and closed his eyes.

The gentle wind whispered like a soft harp through the cedars around him. The clatter of a thousand tiny hanging branches sang from willows near the stream. The incense of the healing sap that oozed from the cedar's wounds dominated this song to his nose, his ears. Eyes still closed, he walked with arms outstretched until the prickly cushion of the cedar touched his fingers. He loved the contradiction of this soft pain that made him itch for an hour afterwards. It was good to be alive.

Joseph broke off a small piece of cedar and touched it to his tongue. It stuck him like needles. He bit down and chewed. It numbed him as it bit him back. Bitter and sweet at the same time. Spicy aroma filled him. He had never known the taste of this tree before. He wanted to know everything; he wanted to know *life*. He had never felt so alive.

The taste faded. His tongue throbbed a little. His eyes still closed, he listened to the whisper of the cedar like a voice inside his head. *Cedars speak Hebrew, Aramaic, Greek, and Latin. I can hear them all.* He felt the stones under his sandals, the dust between his toes, the wind that blew his hair against his shoulder, and his fingers that had unconsciously rested over his mouth as if he were silencing himself to listen to this moment.

He opened his eyes to new brilliance that surprised him. The moonlight seemed much stronger now, lighting his journey to his love. *Oh Mary, I love you. I miss you. What are you doing this night? Are you sleeping peacefully, or has this moon drawn you outside, too? I know you love this light as much as I do.*

His legs ached already, but he still had far to go. He drank from his wineskin and tasted cedar mixing with the grape. *A new taste.* Not good, but new. *New wakes me up inside and tells me I am alive.* Moonlight silvered the cedars surrounding him. The wind pushed them into ocean waves of silver dancing. He felt the pang of wishing he could share this sight with Mary.

He broke off a piece of bread, he drank one more sip of wine, remembering Mary's face and the times they had shared a meal. He prayed they would share a lifetime of cheerful meals. Joseph smiled. A wolf howled, distracting him from his dream. He shivered with a fear that Mary might not love him anymore. He hurried on, he had to know.

The moon fell low in the west while gleaming planets arranged themselves in the east. They had been gradually moving closer together until they gathered tightly just over a month ago. Now they danced, slowly arcing farther apart as they rushed toward disappearing below the horizon in the light of the dawn. These bright patterns drew his eye and fed his curiosity. He didn't understand the sky; he understood the earth. But something about this sign spoke to him, comforted him.

The sun rose as the moon fell, twin orbs balanced on the opposite sides of the horizon. Exhausted, Joseph slept on the ground until the sun was high overhead. It was a long journey still ahead for him. He would arrive this night. He walked until the sun set and the full moon rose and arced across the sky as he travelled. Wolves worried his mind with their cry that sounded like doubt tonight. The moon lit the trail and teased him, comforted him, and set his mind free to imagine a thousand different things in the lonely light.

He arrived as the moon hung low above the horizon. He rested on the hill above Zechariah and Elizabeth's home. He leaned against an old oak and rough bark massaged his back. *Now what? Now what am I supposed to do, now that I am here? Do I go down and knock on the door and wake them up? Surprise, Mary! I got tired of waiting! I want to know what is going on!* Joseph chuckled at himself and this absurd situation. He still didn't know what to do. He had thought he would understand by the time he arrived. He removed his sandals and rubbed his feet. His head scraped against the textured bark. He sighed at the dark windows below. He whispered, "Mary, I love you." A face lit by moonlight lightened the window and looked up to the hill.

Joseph started to jump up to run to her barefoot, then stopped himself. *She left me the message to stay away. If she is ready to see me, she will send me another message. Wait, you idiot, just wait. Oh, Mary, I miss you. What should I do? I miss your face, I miss your voice, I miss your song, I miss the way you touch my face. I miss the way you scowl and laugh as you try to smooth my impossible hair.* He hid behind the tree. His throat cramped - desperate to call out to her, but frozen in the battle of wills inside of him. Joseph's voice couldn't understand why it wasn't allowed to call her name.

Mary disappeared from the window. Joseph realized he had been holding his breath. An owl broke the silence with three hoots that gave a voice to his unspoken words he wished she could hear. Then the door opened. Mary stood outside. She stared up at the hill, then turned slowly, searching for something. Joseph wondered if she could sense his presence. He knew she hadn't seen him, or she wouldn't have been looking around. He felt his heart pounding, he wanted to run down the hill to hold her, kiss her, hear her voice. But he didn't.

He watched her from a distance, aching with longing at the way she moved. She looked like she was dancing every time she turned. He closed his eyes and kissed her in his mind. He opened them and she was there, safe and healthy. He could relax. He knew he shouldn't be with her yet. They would have the rest of their lives. He filled his eyes with her. He filled his heart and fed his dreams. Mary stood and stared directly at where he was hidden, but couldn't see him. Yet she stared at the spot, thinking of him. Something inside her could feel him. She whispered his name. Finally, she went inside. Joseph closed his eyes. *"I'll see you soon, my love, when you are ready."* He gathered a few stones to arrange at the base of the oak as his secret message she would probably never see. A simple line of stones - not enough to be obvious, but one too many to be an accidental grouping. It was a way he could leave a message she might see and wonder about, but not know. Like his visit. Someday, she would know.

The sky was growing blue; the stars were fading. The eastern sky was like a rose unfolding. The sun would rise soon. He had to leave before he could be seen. *What would she think if some neighbor said a strange man was hiding, watching her?*

He started his long journey home. The sun rose as the moon fell, twin orbs balanced again. The balance was just off from one day. The moon was already falling behind.

When he arrived home his father asked him where he had been. Joseph told him he had been walking and thinking about Mary. His father wisely gave him time and didn't ask further. He was worried, too. Something didn't make sense and the whole village whispered.

Joseph collapsed into bed and swam in hopeful dreams.

Joseph filled his loneliness with work for the next two months. He was busy making furniture for many in Nazareth, finishing up promised work. He completed presents for Mary. He prayed and sang as he worked, but his songs became sadder as the months drew on. He began to sing the lonely psalms. Then he noticed a disturbing distance in his neighbors' eyes. They looked away from him too often. Sometimes he could hear them whispering; then grow quiet as he approached. It was as if there was a secret he was part of, but didn't know. *Mary, why haven't you at least sent me a message?*

He threw himself into his work, both work for money and work on the home they would share. He traveled into the hills to harvest two more trees. The solitude sustained him. He spent time with James, but his friend became uncomfortable talking about Mary. James thought Joseph should go to see her anyway; it had been over three months since they had seen each other. But Joseph knew it wouldn't be much longer.

When he heard that Elizabeth had delivered her son, John, Joseph sang with joy. *Mary will be home in a few days at last!* He sang with anticipation for a week; then the next weeks passed. His songs faded, his worry returned. Then her younger sister came for him. She said Mary was waiting for him in her parents' home. This little girl who usually jabbered happily seemed secretive, and ran away as soon as she had delivered her message. He wondered why Mary hadn't come to him herself. Joseph began to imagine the worst as he walked to see the woman that he loved more than life. His pace slowed instead of quickening as he approached her home. He was afraid.

He carried a large bag of gifts he had made for her during the months she was gone. He picked flowers along the way, taking the time to try to calm himself. *Something is wrong, something is very wrong. Is there someone else? None of this makes sense.* When Mary's parents met him at the door, they looked like mourners at a funeral. They had always been glad to see him before. His heart sank. He asked them what was wrong. They only looked down and said, "Mary is waiting for you in back." He shook. He trembled, afraid of what might be waiting for him. Four months of waiting patiently without a loving word had taken its toll on him. The little clues had added up, he couldn't pretend there wasn't a problem anymore.

When he walked through the door, Mary ran across the room to him. She threw her arms around him and trembled in his arms. "I love you Joseph, I've missed you. I've missed you so much!" He felt heavy tears plop on his shoulder like rain after a drought. "I've missed you, too, Mary. I love you." He let out a sigh of relief. *Everything is still good. I shouldn't have been afraid. She still loves me, that hasn't changed.* But when he drew back to look at her, he saw fear in Mary's eyes. An awful fear. She looked away; then pulled him tightly to hold him close. She didn't want to look in his eyes yet. He thought she looked like she had gained weight, he felt her swollen belly pressing into him. She was still a tiny woman, but ... he dropped his hand to her feel her stomach. The bulge was firm. "No. Oh, no. Mary, *no.*"

He pulled back from her to look. He pushed the flowers into her arms that were still waiting for the return of his embrace. He had no embrace for her now. He dropped the heavy bag of gifts on top of them, crushing them. Her arms were full, but not with him. He stumbled away from her, staggering under the heavy weight that suddenly overpowered him, pulling him toward the floor. He was a strong man, but he had to grab the doorframe to keep from falling. His ears were ringing. He couldn't breathe. Mary was saying something, but he couldn't hear her words. He closed his eyes for a moment. Before he opened them again, he whispered from his darkness. "Why? Who?" He swallowed hard, he was afraid he would be sick. "How could you do this? So this is why you hid with Elizabeth. You told me you loved me. Whose baby is this? I trusted you."

Mary clung to his arms and looked into his eyes. "Joseph, you don't understand. I'm still a virgin. I love you, Joseph, *only* you. This is from God. An angel came to tell me I am chosen to have the child of God. I have *never* slept with a man, I promise you, Joseph. You are the only one I love, the only man I will ever love, that hasn't changed."

He wanted to believe her, but her belly spoke more loudly than her words. But her eyes, her tears - they told a story, too. Nothing made sense. He pulled himself loose from her grip, turned and walked away. Mary cried his name as he rushed down the street. People turned their eyes away from him. The gossip had already spread. His friends pitied him. Most people loved Joseph; he was a good man. They couldn't understand how Mary could have done this to them. And to make matters worse, this incredible story.

Joseph heard her voice fade in the distance. *She says that God made her pregnant! Lies, and blasphemy as well as adultery!* It would be adultery, because they were betrothed, so almost married. *In the eyes of the law she could already be stoned to death for adultery.* His face turned pale at the thought of the vindictive self-righteous ones gathering around her, slowly breaking her bones until she was a dying heap under the pile. There always was one who threw the first stone, and then the others joined in.

Always one who made the first move to end a human life. Always one secretly glad for the excuse to feel the thrill of killing. Sometimes no one would join him, and it would be just a stone or two causing a bruise. Sometimes a defender would cry out and block the stones until they stopped. Other times the crowd moved on in their purpose, relentless as a sandstorm.

Joseph had seen it before, and he always tried to stop it. It was a horribly slow way to die. Smothered and broken. Inevitable. The terrible suffering finally ended by the merciful or cruel. Finished by whoever decided it had gone on long enough and used a heavier stone to crush the skull. If not, life and pain could linger helplessly for too long to imagine. Joseph remembered the pleading eyes he had seen. He didn't have it in him to ever speed their release. Cruel kindness came from someone else, if at all. He could never forget those pleading eyes. He felt guilty that he couldn't stop the crowds, or even end the suffering. Now he saw Mary's eyes looking at him in his mind from a pile of stones. He saw her lips form the words, "Joseph, please, if you love me, finish this." He shuddered. He knew he would do anything he could to protect her, but she had added insane blasphemy to her sins. Not just saying she had seen God, but that he had made her pregnant! This is how the pagan Romans saw their gods, as rapists. He prayed this town would remember how good a woman she had been and how kind she had always been to those in need.

Joseph had never felt so empty in his life. He couldn't go home. Just walking kept him from going anywhere. There was no "where" to go to. He walked the streets of Nazareth until he ran into the last thing he wanted to see that night ... the naked madman muttering to himself as he walked jerkily down the streets. It was as if his arms and legs never listened to each other as he moved, they moved without sense or connection, but always fast. He had no destination, but he was always in a hurry to get nowhere. *He's just like me, I understand his walking now - he's going to the same nowhere as me.*

Joseph looked at the man in a new way now. Long hair and beard hung matted and tangled, wild as his mind. He was covered with scabs and scratches from running through the thorns. He smelled like a wild desert animal. Kind people fed him, gave him clothes; but when it was warm he threw them away, preferring to go naked. He said he didn't need clothes, like Adam and Eve before they had sinned. He was like them, sinless in the Eden of his mind. Most people avoided him, believing he was possessed by an evil spirit. He yelled at God. He yelled at everything. He yelled at things no one else could see. He yelled at stones and trees.

The madman's words chilled Joseph's heart like ice. "The Son of God is here! I'm the one! Don't listen to the lies! Don't believe her!"

Joseph felt himself flush with fresh embarrassment. *Even he knew before I found out! What an idiot I am! Am I the last to know? What a cuckolded fool.*

Joseph knew he couldn't handle more insanity this day, so he slipped away before the madman could see him. He ran out of town, and retraced the steps he and Mary had taken that perfect day he had asked her to marry him. He saw the hills that had been touched with sunrise. They were somber gray today. He turned around to face the other hills that had been painted with the last rays of that day. He remembered the echo of beauty. He sat where they had rested, where she had danced for him, only him. He remembered her promise to love him forever. He sat until the stars came out. He waited for the world to get better. It didn't. The more he thought, the worse everything became.

Joseph closed his eyes. *It's over.* He knew he would have to divorce her to break the legal bond, but he didn't want her to have to undergo any more shame or danger. *I want it to be quiet and private.* She had enough to deal with. *Poor Mary,* he thought, as he wondered what she would do. *Will the father marry her and provide for her? Will she have to stay with her parents forever? Who would have her now? Why did she do this?* He realized he still loved her. *What a mess. How will she ever recover from this tragedy? What about this poor child, born a bastard? What will happen to the child? Poor, innocent child.*

He pitied Mary, she either was mad or a liar. He didn't know which he hoped was true. If she were mad, would she descend as deeply into madness as the naked man who showed all of Nazareth where the twisted path to madness ended? *Everyone has taken a step or two into madness, when life has pushed them past their limit.* He felt himself at that point now. *Everyone has had a glimpse into the gaping maw that waits to swallow anyone without the grace of God.* Our world is difficult, and he knew some take the ghastly easy route instead of fighting the hell that hides inside a frightened mind. He cried for her. He sighed for himself and the child.

He wondered if he should still marry her anyway. He loved her. If she would simply tell him the truth, somehow they might be able to overcome this. He loved her that much. But, if she wasn't able to be honest with him, there was no hope. And if she believed she was innocent, that *God* had impregnated her; then she was mad. He wondered if he could live that hell that would spread out from her mind to swallow both of them. He had seen it before. Madness often found a home in this country occupied by invaders. In this place where there was no hope. When hope is gone, madness waits to fill the vacant space. He wanted a simple life with a woman he loved whom he could trust. He had never loved before like this. He didn't think he ever would again. But this could never work unless she released this madness that seemed so dear to her. Eventually it would destroy both of them. He didn't want to come to hate her. He loved her too much for that.

He was cold, inside and out, and exhausted from the most horrible day of his life. He started home a dozen times, then turned away, reluctant to find the nothing that waited for him. When he was so tired he could hardly stand, he let the numbness lead him back. He returned to the lonely place he had built for them to share, and winced at the echo of the door closing on an empty house that could have been a home.

Echo

Dawn glow woke Joseph in a moment of peace until he remembered that his world had ended yesterday. Ice clutched his heart with its cruel grip of reality. *Am I going mad? There's not room enough in my mind for the two realities warring in here. I know Mary and know I can trust what she says. How could she be lying with those eyes? I know my Mary. She loves me, I am sure at least of that. But if she is not lying, is she mad? Or am I? What really happened?*

He found no joy in his work anymore. He lost himself temporarily in the familiar motions but without song. The sound of his saw was now just noise. The rasp was only an annoying sound like someone clearing his throat continually to break your concentration while you try to think.

I don't want to think about anything. I want all these thoughts to end. There is no solution. All I know is that the woman I love carries another man's child. That is pretty real - and awful.

He desperately wanted to lose these thoughts in mindless work, but they kept coming back. His knuckles bled; he scraped them more than usual. His hands bled so much he had to stop. He was staining the wood and making it unclean. As he went for a cloth to wrap around his hand, he froze- remembering the day Mary first surprised him. The day she cleaned and bound his wound. He had thought she would always heal his wounds, not cause them like this. Joseph looked at the scar on his left hand. It was jagged and paled. The redness had faded with time, their time. It was a hard ghost of a scar now. Like their love.

New blood clotted over the old scar. Joseph cried. He would do no more work today. He took his cloak off the hook on the wall and closed his workshop. The argument in his head wouldn't stop, so he tried to distract himself in the hills. He saw abstract beauty in the skies, on the ground. Beauty couldn't touch him inside anymore. He envied the freedom of the hawks that soared effortlessly in the sky. He wished he could fly with them away from Nazareth. He wished he were a hawk. He wished he were almost anything but himself today. He couldn't imagine what she said was true, and he couldn't imagine not loving her.

If I walk long enough, will I find the Mary I used to know? Maybe that Mary is hiding in those hills. Maybe she is still there. The Mary who wasn't pregnant. The Mary who didn't lie. The Mary I thought I knew. He went to places they had shared together in carefree times. He wondered if he believed he could find her there, and wake from this to find it just a long bad dream. It made no sense, he knew, but nothing else made sense, either. He knew there was no hope.

But hope is the friend of madness, and the enemy. He knew a somewhat mad belief in the impossible is the only way things have ever changed in this world. He knew the stories of his ancestors and their belief in the impossible. He prayed. He prayed to the God who gave an impossible child to Abraham and Sarah. He prayed to the God who gave love to Isaac and Rebecca. He prayed to the God who used cheaters and liars and murderers and prostitutes and adulterers to show what faith could make from a failed man or woman. He prayed to a God of transforming love. He prayed to a God who used the scarred people of the world like Joseph used scarred wood to make something beautiful.

He wished his love could let her go. He wished he could be free of the torment. He wished he could wander the desert like the madman he feared might have a companion waiting here inside of himself. *"Maybe we could wander naked together out here. Maybe this is what happened to him long ago, maybe this is how madness comes."* Joseph laughed for the first time at the thought of joining with that nameless man. A joyless laugh. No one knew where he came from or who his family was. He never used a name, only called himself a king and a son of God. *Wouldn't we be a pair? Madmen talking all day about God's child. I'm afraid I'd get cold going naked, though. Is this sort of pain what happened to him? Did he once have a Mary who broke his heart and mind?*

Joseph walked the familiar path out of town and into the hills – their hills. He walked for hours until his legs ached as much as his heart. Finally, too exhausted to continue, he stopped to rest. Only after he sat down did he realize where he was. His mindless wandering had brought him to this place. He had thought he was better, but now he broke down and sobbed. The emptiness of the picture before his eyes and the memory of the love that had filled this place before made the emptiness deeper than he could bear. He sobbed until he had no more tears inside. He yelled so loudly the hills answered him. Then silence. Then he yelled again. The echo and the silence paired as his pain bounced until it disappeared. He screamed from his silence several more times. Purged, he crawled into the silence; felt the rawness of his throat, so unaccustomed to screaming.

The world was rearranging itself inside of him. A world without song.

Echo Answered

James searched Nazareth for Joseph. No one knew where he went, but everyone heard what had happened. Miriam wept when she told James the story. They couldn't understand; it made no sense. Then Mary came to his door, her eyes red from the tears that had never stopped since Joseph walked away. She was afraid for him. She knew she had devastated him. James finally heard the whole story from her trembling mouth. He just listened, using all his skills to parse the truth from her words. He could tell when a person was lying to him - he had to in his job. He pitied Joseph for the first time in his life, and Mary even more.

James was no outdoorsman, but he loved his friend and thought he knew where he might go. James searched he hills around Nazareth that were filled with dozens of blind valleys and caves where a man could hide. There were miles to search, but James had one clue. Joseph had told him about a place that the two of them often played when they were children. Joseph had told him he had taken Mary there. He thought he might revisit that place in his pain, looking for comfort. Looking for things lost.

Years of filling his head with numbers had dimmed James' memory of childhood explorations. He never walked in the hills alone anymore, the way Joseph still did. But he remembered the general direction. After three hours he saw what might be Joseph in the distance. The tiny figure in the distance first paced back and forth, swinging his arms wildly, then a distant shout echoed through the hills. Another. Several more. Then silence. The figure sat immobile for the half-hour it took James to finally reach him. It was growing dark.

James was afraid to shout; afraid Joseph would flee from him if he knew he was coming. He knew he was at the point of breaking. Joseph had withdrawn from everyone, including his closest friend. James didn't know what he could do, but knew he had to do something. Joseph was immobile, staring into space. James had no idea what he should say when he finally reached him; he'd rehearsed a dozen possible things to say. When he finally arrived, he used none of them. He sat silently and waited. He knew the best thing he could do was just be with him to let Joseph feel his presence. His words were not important, but Joseph's would be when they came. He knew that he would need to let those words flow to let the poison out.

A long ten minutes passed before Joseph spoke, almost whispering. "I thought I knew her. I thought I could trust her. I thought God had brought me the greatest gift he has ever given a man. I still love her, James, and that's the pity of it. I don't know who she is anymore, I guess I never did. What a fool, what an idiot I am."

James remained silent. He knew he should let Joseph speak without any outside influence. His pain needed to flow freely to form itself enough to be removed. Joseph continued. "I don't know if she is mad or a liar. I don't know who the bastard comes from. A Roman soldier, or one of the men in town who have been smirking at me, thinking I am a fool. I am. They are right. What a damned fool I am. How could she do this? How could she do this to us? How could she do this to me? She told me she loved me. How could she do this to herself? Why would she sleep with someone else? It makes no sense. I think I know her – this is not … or was she raped and doesn't remember? Or seduced and cannot allow herself to acknowledge it now. Is that why she imagines this fantastic story? If somebody has hurt her this way, I want to know. I love her and want to stand by her. Even if she was raped by a Roman soldier, half the child is still *her*. I love her, and that child is part of her. Or is she playing me for a fool? Or could she possibly... Oh, now I am becoming mad, too." Joseph sat in silence for a minute, squirming in his pain. "I need to know, and I cannot. I need to know, James. I need the truth, whatever it is. Tell me what to do. You know how to see the real world. I can't think clearly. My head is spinning. There are no good thoughts. No good thought at all."

James waited to see if Joseph had finished. He didn't want to stop this flow of pain that was saving his friend. There was too much to stay inside without doing great damage. He also waited because he had no idea what to say. He opened up his bag and gave Joseph food and wine. They both drank before James finally spoke, "I don't know what to say. I have never claimed to understand women, and this one is more difficult to understand than most. What I see makes no sense, but I have to listen to my heart. The heart is wiser than the mind. I have seen her with you and I have never seen a woman more in love with a man. She sometimes asks me about you in private to help her understand you more. She asks me about things you might like so she can surprise you."

"She certainly surprised me with this." They both laughed. A bitter, beautiful laugh. If ever a laugh was needed, it was now. James asked for the wineskin. He needed to give himself time to think about what to say next. He was afraid of saying the wrong thing, but he was more afraid of not trying to help. "She loves you, Joseph, I'm sure of that. I don't know what to say about the rest of this - the angel, the baby, the Messiah..." He lifted his hand and let it drop helplessly into his lap. "It disturbs me that she left for almost four months without telling you goodbye. That bothers me. That didn't seem like her, but I imagine she didn't know what to say and was afraid you would know something was wrong. Maybe she needed to take time to concoct this amazing excuse. Or... maybe it *is* true. Those are all the options, and for the life of me I don't know which is more unlikely. I've never seen an angel; but I know Mary, and this kind of elaborate deceit isn't like her. I know people, Joseph. I live by reading the truth people try to hide. My greatest strength as a merchant is that I know when I am being lied to. She came to me today to ask me to try to help you understand. I didn't feel a lie in her. And I looked. I looked hard and I know how to find a lie. Whatever it is, she believes it. God help us all. She may be mad, but she loves you. I don't envy your position anymore. I always knew you two had a special kind of love. This isn't what I expected, though."

Joseph sighed, took another long drink of wine, and asked, "So... what should I do? Can I live with a woman who may be mad? Is she just hiding the truth from herself for now until she will be able to accept it eventually?" Joseph darkened and looked off in the distance for a moment of silence. He didn't look afraid; he looked numb. "Or will she descend rapidly into the awful world that pitiful one lives in, you know, the one that occasionally runs naked through the streets of Nazareth screaming about being the son of God. Is that what awaits my Mary? Eating raw hares and praying with their guts spread between the trees?" Joseph searched the horizon, as if he expected to see her running wild out there.

"Or is it true? Or am I mad to even consider that? I know God can do miracles, but this doesn't feel right to me. This isn't the way a Messiah would come. In shame. Shame and hiding for four months." Joseph sighed and shook his head. "Why did she run away and hide? What was she trying to hide? Why didn't she tell me? Why didn't she trust me? And, even if she is mad, should I desert her? If she were sick I would stay with her and nurse her back to health if I could. Or stay with her until the end if I couldn't. I *love* her, James! I wouldn't leave her alone if she were sick. She says she loves me, wants me. But why did she disappear? Was she hoping the father would still take her? Did he reject her, and so now she is settling for me? Has there been someone else all along? Is this merely an attempt at an excuse, is she lying to me? Is she mad, and will her madness take me, too? I'm half way there already! If what she says is true, wouldn't God have done things differently?"

Joseph calmed and sat silently. James was wise enough to just wait beside him. He knew he wasn't done. Joseph clenched his fists and stood up letting more hurt and anger out.

"Why did she run away and leave me alone to wonder without a word? Then this surprise! This is no way to tell me – with a swollen belly." Joseph continued in a falsetto, "Oh, yes, by the way, Joseph, I forgot to tell you … ummm … I'm pregnant, but I didn't think that was important enough to tell you." Joseph spat on the ground and roared, "Is this the way God works? It doesn't sound like God to me!"

Joseph let the silence fill him, and when he had calmed he continued, "But, still … I love her. I told her I would always love her, and I mean it."

James still waited, just listening. Joseph had more to say. " Nothing makes sense. I can't think clearly. Maybe thinking doesn't make any sense with things like this. The more I try to understand the less I do. This isn't right, if this is how our life together starts, what will happen later? Will it get worse? Much worse? Will she deceive me about everything? Will I never be able to trust her and relax? Will I always wonder what will happen next? Will she leave me someday for the father of her child, or someone else? Will she love me and be faithful, but be mad, and dangerous to herself and the child? I never saw a sign of this before. What happened to her? How can I help her, help her heal? What should I do? I love her, James, I know I will always love her."

James put his arm around Joseph and said, "I don't know. Joseph, I don't know. All I know is I am your friend and will do whatever you want me to do. I wish I could make this all easier for you. You don't need to decide today, take your time and be sure. Sleep is good."

"And dreams." Joseph shook his head, afraid of dreams now, not loving them anymore.

It was getting hard to see, so they started home. Joseph looked forward to working with wood. Something he knew; something he could understand.

Kaddish

Each day fewer children came to play in Joseph's shop. Finally even Suzanna and Daniel stayed away. Few friends spoke with him on the street; most avoided him. Even his work no longer brought him pleasure. He stopped singing. The only song came from the tools, and now they sounded like a Kaddish dirge. His saw sang a new song.

Yit'gadal v'yit' kaddash sh'mei raba ...

He felt it was chanting his own funeral. His favorite saw was mocking him. Then the congregational response *Amein* repeated over and over. It was as if the whole village was mourning him and the death of his love. As he continued to saw, he heard the next line. *In the world that he created as he willed.* Joseph shook his head. *Is this the world that you will? It isn't a very happy world.* When the next line repeated from his sad memory, *May he give reign to his kingship in your lifetimes and in your days,* he threw the saw to the ground. *Mary knew these words as well as I do. She's using our hope for a Messiah against me!* He bent and picked up his saw to continue. He gripped it tightly and felt the teeth biting into his hand. He gripped harder; this pain took his mind away from his deeper pain.

He knew what he had to do, but he couldn't bring himself to do it. He had to tell Mary he was divorcing her. But he loved her, and didn't want to hurt her, but he knew he would. He couldn't bear the look on her face he kept imagining. *What else can I do? What did she expect? I wish this was all only a bad dream. I want to wake up back in our beautiful world before this nightmare. That world is dead. She destroyed it.* He pushed the saw faster in anger and the noise grew louder. But the smell of pine comforted him. Sawing this fast brought the smell of fire.

He couldn't put it off forever; this baby wouldn't wait. The child was coming, no matter what. He had to tell her he was divorcing her tomorrow. It would be kinder to do it as soon as possible, so they could go on with their lives in whatever way they still could. *Kinder? What am I thinking? Kinder? How can I ... how can I see her eyes when I tell her this? I could never hurt her ... but ... what can I do? Maybe I should just go visit my cousin for a few months and let her figure it all out. She likes to do things that way, doesn't she?* Joseph slammed his hand down on the wood, then calmed again. He continued sawing because it helped him think. *No, that is a bitter thought I don't really mean, but I am so angry and frustrated and ... cornered. Cornered like an animal in this mess of her making. She never even let me know what was going on. That is no way to start a marriage.* The loud thump of the cut piece of wood falling into the sawdust punctuated his thought. Joseph put down his saw. *I have to do what is right, as right as anything can be now. I can't pretend that this isn't a horrible mess I don't want to be part of.*

Joseph left his shop to walk the hills they had walked together again, but this night he walked alone. *I need to get used to being alone. There are a lot worse things than being alone.* Joseph cried. He missed her. He had gotten used to missing her for almost four months, but then he had always known they would be together soon. He thought he knew, and that was the hardest part, he still *knew* inside. It made him crazy, he believed her despite everything in some little place inside that was wiser than his mind.

But he had made up his mind no matter what his heart said. What else could he do? He would tell her in the morning, even if it broke both of their hearts. He could live without love, but he couldn't live with madness or lies.

Dreamsong

Joseph lay awake for hours, dreading the morning. Exhaustion finally brought relief and dreams. Troubled dreams at first, like those he had endured since Mary returned two weeks ago. Then Gabriel made his third visit as God's messenger.

Bright blue light filled his dream. And silence that pulled the earth away until the angel spoke.

"Joseph, son of David, follow your heart. Mary is not lying to you, as impossible as it seems. She loves you and has been faithful to you, and she always will be."

The light was blinding, but comforting somehow. Gabriel frightened him but made him feel safe at the same time. "Marry her, because this child has indeed come from God. Name him Jesus, because he will save his people from their sadness, from their hopelessness, from their weakness and foolishness. He will bring them freedom and hope and peace."

Joseph rubbed his eyes and sat up. This was not his imagination. This was not just a dream. The light in a dream doesn't hurt your closed eyes. Or was it? *Is this just a dream of the answer I hoped for so I wouldn't have to hurt her? Is this the only way we could be together, so I worked it out in my dream to convince my waking self? Or was this dream real? Can I trust a dream with my life? Am I going mad with this hallucination?* He always feared madness, he felt it was all around and looking for him. *But this feels real. But wouldn't it feel real if I were mad? Maybe I have snapped and ...*

He ran his fingers through his hair and sawdust fell in front of him. It always did. That was the same. *Can I hope that Mary is still the same? Or does it matter? I still love her. Is this dream just my way out of my conflict? A way that I can tell myself that I believe her at last – the only way that we could go on?*

He hated the insubstantiality of dreams. He was man of dreams, but he hated them now. He hated that they weren't concrete but left things to interpretation. He had spent his lifetime so far learning the language of dreams and how to parse out the real from the symbolic. Dreams had spoken to him as long as he could remember. But

… how to see what was just a dream and what was real was always just beyond him. They never gave enough information to know for sure. They were not of the mind, but of the heart. And the heart can lead one astray. But more so the mind, he thought. *Reasoning was good when you have all the facts, but when has that ever happened?*

In the end he had his answer. *I'd rather be mad with Mary than sane alone. I believe her.*

Joseph couldn't wait until morning. He couldn't leave his Mary suffering in sleepless pain one more hour. He ran to her, he pounded on the door and woke everybody up. He shouted, "I need to see her now!" They tried to keep him away, to protect her from what they thought was this gentle man's anger finally burst free out of his control into blind rage. But Mary knew. She came running to him. He held her close. He struggled to speak, in breathless phrases. "I love you. I'm sorry I doubted you. Please forgive me. I understand now. I am so sorry I hurt you. Let's complete our marriage ceremony as soon as possible. I want to be with you for the rest of our lives, with you and this holy child." Mary covered his hands and face with kisses and tears.

Refrain

The carpentry shop sang again. New songs of deeper love and hope. Joseph's work was joyful again and with more purpose than any man had ever had before. The awesome responsibility focused him. *I will raise the Messiah. I'll be step father to God's Son. A God who chose to give up his power to become helpless and be dependent on a simple man and his wife. A God who wants to know us this well – from the inside.*

God chose me to be his father. What will this mean? Will God surround us with protecting angels, and make our life easy? That would be nice, but I don't think so. What would be the sense of that? Why come at all unless it is real, a real experience of what it means to be human. To be frail and helpless as a baby. To have to struggle to learn, and work for your survival. And to be mortal? Could God die? Even in human form, that's unthinkable. But, what would God feel when he began to grow old? When his body began to wear out? Would he simply heal himself, or leave to go back to heaven before that, when he had decided he had learned enough about what it meant to be human? How much would be enough for God to know? How much of our pain will be enough? Will he learn what it means to be old and helpless and frail?

What does it mean to be human? Joseph pondered the ultimate question asked by philosophers and ordinary people throughout the centuries. *To live with limitations, to live with struggle, to live with hope. And to love - definitely that. When God breathed life into Adam's clay and he became a living soul, what was that breath but love?* Joseph was beginning to understand love. Love that believes and hopes. Love that is steadfast despite the obstacles and fears. Love that is stronger than even fear. Love is what lets us become more than just dead clay.

If God is going to let himself experience real human life, and is not going to make it too easy, what is this going to mean for Mary and me? He put down his plane and walked to the window. He watched the shadows of clouds stretching and slanting over the hills in the distance and then disappear. He was beginning to understand. God, the all-powerful, was entrusting his Son's life in their hands. *He would be watching, his angels helping a little, but not too much. They were not alone.* There might be many faithful humans who would help, but what about the others? There were bad people in the world; there were those who were consumed with evil. *Evil wouldn't want this miracle in the world. What will this mean for us? Will the angels protect us from all the powers of evil, or will we be left alone to battle them?* Joseph had to sit down. He stared at the wall for a minute, then walked outside into the bigger world.

He saw the people in the village in a new way. He felt a new threat from strangers. He even wondered about his well-known neighbors. When he looked into another's eyes, he tried to get a sense of who they were. Joseph realized this fear could drive him mad. He had to get back to living in faith of God's protection, or he would lose himself and all he was and not be any use at all to Mary and her son. Always though, in the back of his mind he would be on guard.

He saw the way people looked at him, he saw them laughing behind his back. He knew they thought he was a cuckolded fool that chose to believe Mary's unbelievable story. Or some thought they had made up this outrageous lie together to try to cover up their sin. Most of the rest thought they were just crazy. Yet, a few hoped secretly behind their smirks that this might be the Messiah come to save them from the occupying Romans; and to save them from themselves, the harder occupying force from which to be freed.

These thoughts dammed up the flow of his songs for a time, but soon he remembered Mary and their love. In a few days they would complete their marriage and she would move into the house he had crafted with care. Every detail was imbued with love as he worked. Each piece of wood finished lovingly, each tree chosen carefully. He had even traveled far to gather dead limbs from the tree they had sat below on that perfect day. He had an important use for it to frame the words of a prayer. A prayer and a desperate hope that would always be by the door where they would remember it as they went out and when they came in to the safety of home. Somewhere in the wood there lived memories he knew. Memories he sang to as he worked the wood into something useful, something elegant, something pure.

After the ceremony, they entered their home and closed the door. Alone at last as husband and wife who were passionately attracted to each other. But this is no ordinary love story. This is no ordinary love song.

At home in each other's arms, they held each other through the night chastely. Each woke in the middle of the night surprised by the comfort of their beloved next to them. The sleeping face of the beloved is the gentlest assurance in the world. They began life together with a child inside of her they loved that wasn't his. But Joseph loved him as if he were his own. He understood the honor and the responsibility. And this Son of God was also son of the woman he loved. He was Mary's child and of her flesh, her smile, her laugh, her spirit. Mary took his hand and kissed it, kissed the scar, kissed each finger as she told him how much she loved him.

Mary took his hand and placed it on her belly. "He is here, Joseph, the Messiah is here inside me. I wonder what he will be like?" Joseph could feel her happiness at the thought of this baby who would soon be in their arms. He loved babies, he would love this one more than all the others he had ever held. Already imagining toys he could make for him, he realized that soon he would teach him how to work with wood and read the holy words. *Imagine teaching God the words he had given us. Such a great emptying to become like us.*

His hand still in hers, resting on her belly where the light of God grew in this world's dark time, he kissed this mother of all mothers who loved him with the purest love that was.

He was human, and part of him wished this wedding night they were making love to create a child that was fully theirs. His love wanted to be expressed, released, returned. But he knew how important this child was for the world and for all time. He lay awake now as Mary slept a peaceful sleep. He kept his hand in hers on him – the One.

He had hoped to live a normal loving life, all he wanted was a family. God had chosen a different life for Joseph, and he was afraid of what it would mean. He knew of the neighbors gossip; he felt the stares, the mocking eyes. He missed the simple life that could have been. But, he chose this difficult life, just like Mary chose. A life like no other man had ever lived. He prayed for protection for Mary and her child, he prayed for strength and wisdom to guard them. He prayed he would never make a serious mistake, he prayed for grace. He thanked God for the love of the woman sleeping next to him, and prayed that there might be a time when they might be free to love each other fully at last. He was a man. He loved.

Sometimes he wondered if the visit from Gabriel was only a dream. Only an excuse he made to be with Mary and believe her story. Sometimes in the silence he was afraid he was wrong, and married to a dangerous madwoman. Afraid he was mad himself. But his love was stronger than his doubts. And if this was madness, it wasn't so bad.

He looked around at the home he had built for them lit only by the moonlight coming in the window. It was a good house, solid and built with love. A house built by dreams. A house built for dreams. He remembered all the moments thinking of her as he fit the wood together and made it much stronger than it needed to be. He thought of the trees he used to make their bed, he remembered his dreams of what their first night in this bed would be like. Not like this. And yet, the love was just like this. The two of them and the promise of a holy child.

J oseph woke to the smell of breakfast and the sound of an angel singing a love song to him. She kissed his forehead. "Hello, husband. Are you hungry?" They ate sweet bread with dates and raisins together in bed and held each other in this safe place. She kissed him on the lips, and told him how much she loved him. "I'm sorry, Joseph. I'm sorry last night was not the wedding night we had dreamed of. I hope you are not..."

"No, Mary, I'm not disappointed, or angry, or sad. I am with the woman I love and she is carrying the Messiah we all have dreamed would come one day. That is a lot to be happy for."

"But will you... do you still want me that way after this? Do you still find me pleasant to look at? I'm all swollen up like a house. This is all so confusing. I love you more than ever, but here I am with child before we could ever be..." Mary said, fighting back her tears that finally would not be restrained.

"I've never wanted you more, Mary. You've never been more appealing to me. I will always love you." Joseph held her as she sobbed. His tears joined hers. "You are right, though, this isn't what I imagined our life would be like, it is better. Come walk with me to my workshop, I want to show you what I am making, and I want to show off my spectacular young bride to all the world."

Mary sat up with fear in her eyes. "I can't go out, everyone is staring at me and laughing at me, they think I'm crazy or worse. I want to stay in here."

Joseph took her hand, and kissed her cheek. "Mary, you can't hide in here forever. People have always loved you. You know the truth and soon they will, too. The quicker you begin going out again the sooner things will get better. You aren't ashamed to be carrying God's child are you? Have you done anything wrong?"

He was right, but so was she. It wasn't easy bearing the stares and whispers of the people they had lived with their whole lives. Everything had changed. It was a difficult walk at first, but it got easier along the way. A neighbor talked with them, and that helped them relax, until the naked madman appeared, singing his mocking song directly to them.

"You are liars, you are liars claiming to have God's son. That's only the product of your sinful fun. Who do you think you are fooling? I am the one. I am God's true son. You are liars pretending you didn't have the fun. Look at you, you love in secret, and are pretending you are pure. Your sinful fun! Everybody knows. Everybody knows. Everybody knows."

He pranced around sticking his belly out and waddling as he chanted. He poked his finger obscenely at them and laughed. And then shook his genitals and thrust his hips repeatedly toward them.

"Everybody knows, everybody knows, everybody knows. That's why a baby grows in your big belly."

Mary froze like a statue. There was nothing she could do.

"That's just the product of your fun, I am the one, I am the one, I am God's true son."

The people of Nazareth gathered around this spectacle, laughing at them all. "This madman speaks the truth. This is some show, all these mad ones gathered together in one place, claiming God's parentage. Who would have thought Nazareth would be so full of God's children at one time?"

Mary wanted to die. She cried while Joseph tried to comfort her. Then without warning, the madman screamed and lunged at Mary. "I am the Messiah, not that lie in your belly!" He tried to kick her stomach hard, but Joseph grabbed his leg and deflected it, then pushed him to the ground before he could connect. He used his carpenter's strength to subdue him as other men in the crowd came to hold the swearing man down. The women circled to protect Mary. They formed a wall between her and the threat. No mother can stand to see another's baby threatened.

The madman soon calmed, so they released him. He ran a short distance; then taunted them again with his song. He thrust his hips forward and repeated. "Just your fun, just your fun. Look at what your fun has made!" Mary sobbed, humiliated and terrified. Then she ran to the safety of Joseph's shop.

Her first trip outside hadn't helped her fears. And Joseph realized no angel had come to protect the child. If *he* hadn't stopped this madman, he would have kicked her in the belly with all his force. His foot came within inches of the baby. Joseph knew he would always have to stay alert to danger from now on. He looked to heaven but saw no tardy angels apologizing.

Song of the Turtledove

I f the dove were ever to fly again, she should be able to by now. She felt like part of their family, as her voice combined with theirs every day. But her sweetest sad song joined a voice that often came from close outside the window. Her song wrapped together with the notes of another gentle dove. Wrapped into chords of sad beauty.

Mary felt trapped inside this house for safety, but she hoped the dove could fly free outside. It was time. At dawn, they took her outside to join the song that came from the tree above. His song silenced as two couples waited to see. She tested her out of practice wings. Mary whispered, "You can do it. Go, fly to be with him and sing. *Sing for me.*" She rose to the tree and sang for them all, celebrating their reunion after six months.

Joseph and Mary hugged, bathed in the light and song. Joseph kissed his wife and said, "I have a gift for you inside." He had hidden a piece of parchment that he had mounted in a frame. He didn't speak a word. He didn't hand it to her, but simply drove a nail into the wall and hung it by the door. Mary read it out loud:

God grant that in this home
May only words of love be spoken.
May only peace live here
And understanding.

God grant that all feel his presence here,
Protecting those sheltered by this roof.
May his love fill this space
Like laughter and song.

God grant that there always be food on the table,
Joy in each heart,
Peaceful sleep and hopeful waking,
And his light fill the rooms with love.

Nesting Song

Like the doves nesting in the tree, Mary sang as she prepared a home for their baby who would join them within weeks. She repeated the lullaby Joseph sang for her last night to help her sleep. *He is so dear, but he is struggling every day. He used to have more work than he could handle because of his craftsmanship. Now people are avoiding him and making excuses. This strange situation we are in makes other people uncomfortable. They don't know what to think, so they just avoid him. They know this story couldn't be true. I can't blame them. Poor Joseph!*

But there were a few who tried to believe that possibly this might be real. No one dared to share such a wild hope out loud. Much as they wanted to believe in the Messiah, this was little Mary and Joseph from Nazareth, not the powerful royalty they expected to produce a king. Besides, Mary had acted so strangely by running away. Even their own parents were skeptical, but tried to believe for their sakes.

Anne knew her daughter couldn't lie to her about something like this, and she knew how much she loved Joseph. And he believed her, or at least pretended to and made up a story about another angel visiting him in his dream. Anne knew his love was strong enough to do something like that. She was grateful it was Joseph in this situation, what other man would bear it so well? Mary's mother couldn't imagine how her daughter could have had intercourse with any other man when she was so much in love with him. It didn't make sense. None of it made sense. She wondered if Mary had been raped, and the experience been so awful she blocked it out of her memory with this fantasy excuse. *Or maybe it was true.* Mary was as good a woman as could be. *Even if I am her mother, she is the best child I have ever known. Her heart is big enough to love the entire world, God couldn't have chosen better anywhere,* her mother thought. *I hope it is true. I want it to be.*

Mary's belly was swelling larger every day. She rested her arms on the windowsill to listen to the hungry staccato of baby doves when each parent returned to feed them. Mary cradled her belly in her arms, and rocked from side to side. She smiled at the thought of his hungry cry and the joy she would feel when he lay at her breast, satisfied into sleep. *A man can never know what it is like to carry life this way, and then nourish it from yourself.* Mary hummed to her boy.

86

Joseph was worried. He needed to provide for them. He kept himself busy making things they would need, but he needed more money to come in. He wondered why God didn't seem to be providing like he did before Mary was pregnant, when everyone was congratulating him on their betrothal. *Before all this I had plenty of work. God, if you have given me the job of taking care of them, please help me do it. Why are you making everything so hard? Why is it so hard if it is so important? I don't understand, this was not my idea. Why choose us and then make it impossible?*

But Joseph knew he could provide somehow, he was creative and versatile. He knew if nothing else, at least the Romans were always building. It was an affront to him, the way these arrogant conquerors built huge buildings in their own style no matter how they clashed with whatever existed around them. Romans were not like the Greeks, he thought, their culture was only built on power and war. Their gods were scattered everywhere in appalling idolatry. Worse, they had created more harlots than idols everywhere they occupied. Innocent virgins were seduced or raped. *Is that what the people of Nazareth thought had happened to Mary, and that she was trying to protect her child from a life of shame?*

Joseph was exhausted from a day of rejection, asking those who had eagerly sought him out before for any scrap of work now. He hadn't changed, and if anything, his work was better now. His neighbors said they didn't need anything now, but they would let him know when they did. But he saw the work that others were still doing for them. All of it was inferior work to his. He had to find something to do. He loved his work - he needed it for his soul as much as the money. But now he had to borrow to keep them fed. He had worried himself out of songs.

He called on the Roman occupiers; they had no problem with his work. He was just another Jew to them. They didn't know about his situation, and they didn't care. His craftsmanship impressed them, but he had a hard time putting his spirit in his work. He made furniture, too, first he made a new design of chair to ease his Mary's aching back. Soon others wanted this comfort for their own. There were a lot of aching backs that were eased by the kind of chair he made. Mary loved hers - she realized his love had given him an idea of a way to comfort her. She knew what was eating away at his soul. She watched him struggle without a bitter word. Her man had grace and patience. She couldn't imagine what her life would be like without him in it. She loved to comfort him at night and touch this man she loved. She loved the way he smelled and the way he warmed her bed. In this difficult time he loved it when she rubbed his sore back and touched his face. They were two teenagers in the bloom of complicated love.

Joseph massaged Mary's aching back. Pregnancy had strained her young body. He loved her body, and she loved his. They looked forward to the day when they might be able to finally share what they felt completely. She wanted to give him a child that was fully his own someday. He deserved it; she knew how much he wanted a child of his own.

They followed the religious laws about proper contact between husband and wife when a woman was carrying a child. He was human, he wanted to express his love - it made him a little crazy at times. But he was patient, and they had the kind of love that could endure almost anything. They played like children, and made up silly games. And they prepared in whatever way they could for the birth of their child.

One day Joseph returned from his work for the Romans without his usual songs. Mary could tell he was upset. She rubbed his shoulders and sang to him until he relaxed. "What's troubling you today, my love?"

Joseph sighed and shook his head. "The Romans wanted me to build some of their accursed execution crosses. I told them I couldn't do it. I can't use my skills to make a thing that would kill our people in such a horrible way. And how could I choose a tree that would be used this way? It's the only form of execution I've ever heard of that is more slow and painful than stoning death." He shivered when he remembered imagining that fate for Mary. "It is too inhuman for me to think about, a horrible way to die." He looked in Mary's eyes with deep pain. "What kind of monster can dream up that sort of death?"

Mary held his hand. She felt her stomach turning at the memory of those times she couldn't avoid seeing Jewish victims slowly dying. Part of the purpose of this tortured death was to be the most visible horror the Romans could arrange. Mary remembered the victim's sharp cries with each hammer thud, then the gradually weakening screams and moans until the days-long agony eventually ended. Often it took three days or more of struggling for breath before they finally died. It was intended to be slow. Often the bodies would be left hanging until they rotted for more dramatic effect. Sometimes this punishment was for a minor crime when they wanted to make a point. She hoped the Romans would be long gone before her son was old enough to have to hear or see something so terrible around him. She didn't want him exposed to that horror. She hoped he'd never have to see a crucifixion. It was a terrible thing to watch. No one deserved a death like that, no matter how bad his crime.

The pair of doves began their evening song, distracting Mary and Joseph from their dark thoughts. Joseph stood behind his wife with his arms around her. Their fingers were intertwined on her growing belly as they looked out the window. They listened to the familiar song from their friends in the tree. Then Mary brought supper. Joseph closed his eyes and breathed in the aroma of the spices Mary used to make a simple meal a feast. She was an artist with food, an artist for the nose and tongue. Joseph journeyed on the spice trail in his mouth. He discovered new scenery he had never tasted before. They ate to the music of the same peaceful song David heard when he was an innocent shepherd boy. The well practiced harmony of the pair of doves. Joseph joined and sang about the dove compared to his gentle love from Solomon's Song of Songs. Joseph was from Solomon's line, from the powerful tragic love of David and Bathsheba. Mary was from Nathan, his full brother. The illicit love that caused so much pain and death before it had been redeemed led to these two lovers joined in a holy bond. A millennium later, these children of David's line bore the final shame in innocence. They bore the shame with grace in innocence. They finished it forever as people mocked them even as their purity made a place for God to be born into the world. The last of David's sin was paid for, and left room for the last of David's love to grow into the child who would save this world from itself.

Joseph, I feel like I am waddling with an armload of heavy stones out in front of me. I used to be graceful, but look at me staggering out of balance with this huge belly. I used to be pretty." Mary began crying while Joseph struggled for the right thing to say. He had learned to be very careful with his words when she was like this, so he waited for her to continue. "Now my swollen legs look like palm tree trunks, and I'm carrying water around like a camel with his humps. Except these two humps are in front." Joseph was relieved that she was able to joke through her tears, so he spoke.

"Mary, you're still just as beautiful as the first time you danced for me. You'll be lighter soon and dancing again, and swinging our baby around as the three of us dance together."

Mary eased into the comforting chair Joseph had created. "It's almost time, Joseph. It *can't* be much longer or I'll explode." Joseph knelt in front of her and removed her sandals to massage her feet.

"Oh, that feels good. Poor little feet to have such a big woman riding on top of them all day!" Mary closed her eyes and smiled. "You are so good to me, such a good husband. Massaging my feet while I relax in this wonderful chair you made to make my aching back feel better. All under this strong roof in this solid house you made for us. You are a good man, my dear Joseph, and I love you. He will, too."

"I love you too, Mary. But just try to take a nap while I finish the carvings on the cradle. I want you both to be comfortable and safe here in our home. Everything is almost ready for you." He pointed to her belly, nodding his head. Then he hummed a lullaby to them as he carved the last intricate designs into the wood of the cradle. It was a labor of love. As he carved, he pictured the baby's fingers exploring the curves, and his teeth exploring, as they began to arrive. He imagined his son's little carvings from his teething adding to the texture of the design.

Her time had almost come. She would be safe here, in this world that he had made for them. Their baby would be born in as much security as he could provide.

And their friends and relatives were nearby. Now they waited for the day this child would choose.

It was not to be. The Empire had other plans. Far away in Rome, bureaucrats decided they needed a census of the colonies to be able to plan their budgets properly. A date was chosen with the enforcing power of Imperial soldiers behind it. Since people moved around in these colonies, everyone would have to return to their ancestors' appointed town, so no one would be missed. Now. No waiting for babies to be born at home.

Mary was almost ready to deliver, but it didn't matter, there were to be no exceptions allowed. Joseph knew what Roman understanding and mercy looked like. So they left the safety of their home and traveled to David's ancient home. Bethlehem was a long journey for a woman ready to give birth, so Joseph made it as easy as he could. He was afraid she would go into labor before they could reach their destination, so they traveled slowly, alone. Mary rode his gentle donkey. Their friends had other destinations required, and their parents were too old and would be represented by the younger members of the family.

It was the fourth day of their journey. Mary was brave, but she cried. She cried not so much out of pain, but for fear of the danger to her baby. Joseph wondered why God asked this of them now. Why this unreasonable journey, so dangerous for a pregnant woman? If he was supposed to protect them, why was God making it so difficult? He didn't know all of this was just to get them to Bethlehem to fulfill some obscure prophecy.

"Don't you care?" He looked to the sky. *"Don't you care about them at all? Where are your angels? Are they too busy doing something more important, like delivering messages?"*

He sighed like the desert wind, "I guess it's just you and me," he whispered into the donkey's hairy ear, and caressed his sweaty neck. "We're the only angels that will get them safely there. Funny, I always thought angels smelled better than we do, and weren't so covered in dust. I had hoped it would be easier, that there would be angels. I guess that wouldn't be authentic human life for him. Just two human parents and a donkey loving him, protecting him the way two loving parents do. Angels have their place, and so do we."

"You'd be surprised if he answered you like Balaam's ass." Mary interrupted his whispered talk with God via the donkey, "Really, Joseph, I'd prefer it if you didn't go mad on me out here in the desert carrying on conversations with donkeys and trees and leave me to deliver this baby alone. I'm in sort of an awkward situation right now, have you noticed? Can we stop for a while, please? I'm afraid this little one is being shaken to bits inside of me, and I need to feel something still beneath me for a minute, I'm getting sick to my stomach. I know this dear animal is doing his best." She scratched the donkey behind his ears and gave his head a gentle pat. "I think he might enjoy getting my huge belly off his back for a few minutes, too. I know my two feet get tired of carrying this weight."

Joseph lifted her off the donkey and helped her to the ground. "The baby has dropped lower, Joseph, and the bones of my hips have spread apart, feel how low he is now."

Joseph touched her belly and realized there was little time left. He held her close, but as he looked over her shoulder to the sun getting low in the west, he became angry with God and frustrated. *Help them! Help us get to a safe place! They could die out here, is that what this has all been for? This baby who has changed our lives stillborn in this desert and his mother dead behind him?* They were still far from Bethlehem, and there were no buildings in sight. Sunset was coming much too soon. They needed to find a place to spend the night. He decided they had traveled almost as far as he dared; he couldn't let her get more exhausted. Joseph saw a stream in the valley below. "Mary, can you ride a little longer? Look down there. We can be there in an hour, safe in the shelter of that valley and trees and with plenty of fresh water if you can take this just a little longer."

Mary squeezed his hand. "That sounds wonderful to me, Joseph, just help me back up on this donkey."

When they reached the stream he made the softest bed for her he could with branches from the palms and cedars. While she and the donkey rested, he caught three small fish. He made a simple meal and gathered dry wood for a fire to keep back the chill of the evening. Even in the middle of the summer the desert quickly grew cold at night. The golden sunset faded through the blues into velvet black. The stars watched over them. Joseph saw no angels, just the constant stars. Joseph wanted useful angels.

The vivid stars were actually the planets Venus and Jupiter. They had watched them move closer to each other for weeks until they almost touched now, combining their light. They each were the brightest stars in the sky alone, but now they combined their light. Two fiery stars intimately close and powerful, becoming one. Tonight they almost vibrated with the narrow distance between them as the atmosphere made them shimmer back and forth between looking like two stars or one. It was a hypnotic effect. Before the moon rose, these two stars were brighter than anything else in the sky. He imagined tomorrow night they would merge. He wondered what would happen then, and what did it mean? He remembered many months ago when they were close together as morning stars – now they were here as evening stars after hiding behind the sun for a time. They performed an amazing dance in the sky back then just before Mary disappeared for months. When their lives started this incredible journey he could never have imagined. Mary cuddled closer in her sleep, an angelic smile on her face in the blue light of only stars.

Dreamless sleep ate their exhaustion. They held each other close, for comfort as much as warmth in this lonely valley. He watched her face in the faint blue light that came from only stars and moon, since the fire behind her had burned to glowing coals. He added more wood to the fire to keep her warm. He had warmed her other side. Together they sheltered the child between them. The baby moved while Mary slept on. Joseph felt him moving, felt this new life. He loved him already. *Please wait, Jesus. Please wait until we are safely in Bethlehem. Just rest, you'll have plenty of time to stretch, and walk and run soon. If you will just please wait until it is safe.* Joseph felt the wetness on his cheek cool in the night air. He was afraid for them. Joseph rolled on his back for a time, watching the stars. He talked to God, he prayed for their safety. He prayed that this baby would wait until they were safe in a comfortable inn with women to help him. Women who knew what they were doing. He knew he certainly didn't. He prayed: *Please, for them,* over and over until he fell asleep again.

The cry of a wolf woke him. Their two stars had set and now the moon ruled the sky. He added more wood to the fire. He prayed again until he fell back asleep.

At sunrise, they left the valley and when they had climbed the next hill, first viewed Bethlehem in the blue haze. Mary squeezed his hand with hope now seen. "We'll rest safely there tonight, my love," she said. He kissed her on the cheek. He hoped she was right, because he was afraid a sixth day of this would kill her. He prayed this fifth day didn't.

It was a long day's journey but they arrived in time to register their names in the census before the sun went down. The city was crowded - David's children had been fruitful indeed from the crowd of travelers he saw. *The eleventh commandment of God, and the only one most people faithfully follow*, Joseph thought with a chuckle. *Be fruitful and multiply*. David's city was full. There was not a vacant room in town. After their seventh rejection, Mary's water broke, soaking the donkey's back. Exhausted from the journey, and desperate, Joseph begged for his wife. Finally one innkeeper offered them the only shelter he had left, his stable full of travelers' donkeys and some cattle. The stalls were full, but there was room for them with the stored hay. Joseph was frantic, he knew his wife needed a better place than that to give birth, and she was in labor already. It was this or no shelter at all.

They were alone and Joseph was afraid. It shattered him to see his love in pain with nothing he could do to help. He had never even watched a baby being born before, that duty belonged to the world of women in Nazareth and men were always kept away. But they were alone this night. Mary instructed him in what to do, but he was afraid she was dying. Death in childbirth is all too common, he knew. Mary had assisted in a dozen births, and she knew what to do. But she was in pain and full of fear with no experienced woman to help her. She fought against her fear, for both of them. She stroked his comforting hand; her fingers traced the scar she loved. "Joseph, God wouldn't let this child die, or me. He needs his mother. I don't understand why all of this had to be so much more difficult than … oh. I don't know, but there must be a reason we just don't understand. It will be fine. Together we will be fine. I feel safe with you here with me, and God."

Joseph was afraid to leave her long enough to try to beg for someone to help. All had refused so far. There was no help anyway in a place that didn't care enough to make room for a woman in labor who was left alone in a stable with animals and their smelly excrement. No help from men or angels, they were on their own and Joseph was terrified watching his Mary in birth pain. He was surprised when his petite wife squeezed hard enough to hurt his carpenter's hand. She was soaked in sweat and panting now, exhausted and shivering. *What kind of baby would God's son be? Would he be huge? Would he glow like an angel? Would he be born able to talk? That's crazy, he's a baby, what am I thinking? How will he be different? Or is this all some fantasy of Mary's and this some stranger's child?*

Her screams brought him back to her needs. He loved her, but he was helpless to ease her pain. Mary was bleeding, and the bones of her hips had separated farther.

Joseph had to watch the painful contractions squeeze her. They took over, out of her control. She shivered and struggled and pushed until she collapsed for a moment of rest before the hardest part began. She was not allowed to rest for long; her body took over and surprised her. It knew what to do. She tried to hold back, but it hurt too much to fight it. Joseph saw a look like terror in her eyes.

"I'm scared, Joseph." He was terrified himself. He thought he might soon be the only survivor of this night with mother and baby both dead. But when Joseph saw his son's black hair as he crowned, he yelled to tell her.

Between gasps, Mary told him his son was coming *now*. After this long struggle it was over soon once the baby's head was seen. Joseph gathered the slippery child in his arms. He caught him in his rough hands, first grayish-blue then suddenly changing to red with his first cry that brought the breath of life into his lungs. Joseph was worried about the shape of his head, still compressed from his journey into the light. The baby blinked and squinted in the dim oil-lamp light, as the light he himself had created first touched his eyes. Light met light.

Joseph thought he looked confused, bewildered by the way his world had changed. It was cold and bright and hard now, he liked it better where he had been. God's Son was welcomed to this world by a stable full of animals. Their donkey sang in his dear awful voice. Joseph cut the cord, and lay him in his mother's arms. She rested there awhile before the afterbirth began to come.

It was a calm moment for them to greet the new life that had joined them. His mother dried him and rubbed him with salt, then quickly wrapped her son in clean white cloth she had woven from flax. It was the softest thing she had. His father laid the tiny king in a manger he had filled with fresh sweet-smelling hay to cover the splinters on the side. It was the best he had. Simple gifts from poor humans to the one who owned everything. But they brought one precious gift. Their love. He was born into a loving family. Jesus went to sleep while Joseph tended his wife as she delivered the afterbirth. It was surprisingly more painful than the child had been, but mercifully short. When it was done, he cleaned her, kissed her, and brought her baby back to her arms again. He never would forget the look on her face as she held her son. It was a memory that would make him smile the rest of his life. He would replay it often as he worked with wood, or as he lay in that private moment before sleep took him to his world of dreams. Mary talked to her son in that language mothers always discover inside themselves when they speak their first words to their child.

Mary had wrapped the baby in swaddling clothes. It was as if he were being returned to the restriction of the womb without the warmth. His arms and legs had only been free to move for a few minutes before they were bound. It was the accepted cruel comfort.First, it reminded babies of the only world they had known, and mothers were taught that if a baby were to grow tall with straight arms and legs, he needed to be wrapped into immobility. The fingers he had not yet discovered were hidden from Jesus again. His toes would have to wait for days to be known. God was tightly bound, so he couldn't move. But it reminded him of the only world he had known, the tight world where he could hardly move. He stopped crying, and focused all his attention to his eyes and ears. His world was still upside down and senseless; it would take time for Light to know light again.

Gabriel was busy elsewhere, a few miles away above the hillside, announcing to shepherds the wonder of this night. They left their sheep and somehow found him, after checking dozens of stables looking for a baby in the feed troughs, as they were told. That night many in Bethlehem laughed at crazy shepherds looking for a baby in a manger. They thought there was madness in their absurd quest. Madness with their excited tale of angels and a Messiah who would free them from the Romans and much more. Madness to believe the prophecy was real, but in such a humble way. These excited shepherds who were thought mad were the first visitors who came to worship him. They found him in a manger, as rough a throne that has ever served a king. While the shepherds gathered around his wife and the baby, Joseph took this moment to write down the words to a song that was forming in his heart.

Out of the darkness
Out of the silence
Came the bright light and cry of life
That entered the world unknowing
Fragile as a whispered wing
Nine months growing in the darkness
Blind and deaf
Light saw and sang from fragile flesh
Suspended between heaven and earth
Before the first breath of spirit shared
Returned into itself.

Simeon's Song

After the census, the crowds in Bethlehem thinned. Mary and the baby were not ready for the long journey home, so Joseph found a place for them to stay that was better than the stable. Eight days after his birth, Jesus was circumcised and officially given his name. The name that had first been given to Joseph by an angel in a dream. Forty days later, they took the short journey to Jerusalem for the purification after birth. They could only afford the offering of the poor, a pair of doves. Mary cried as they handed a small cage to the priest; these were not her doves, but the thought of their innocent sacrifice still made her cry. One for Jesus, and one for her. It was an unnecessary sacrifice for one born without sin. But it was the religious law. She thought about the lovely song, the graceful flight of these, her favorite birds. Song and freedom traded for the law. Soon just blood and silence.

When Simeon, an old man in the Temple, asked to hold the baby in his arms, he raised his eyes to heaven and sang: "Master, now may your servant go in peace, according to your word. For my eyes have seen your salvation which you have prepared in the presence of all peoples, a light for revelation to the Gentiles and for glory to your people Israel."

He had long known that he would not die until he saw the Messiah with his own eyes; it had been told to him in a dream long ago. He was another who believed in dreams. Simeon blessed them all, then said to Mary, "This child is destined for the falling and the rising of many in Israel, and to be a sign that will be opposed so that the inner thoughts of many will be revealed - and a sword will pierce your own soul too." After the word "sword," Joseph pulled his son away from the old man. Mary and Joseph didn't know what all that meant, but it didn't sound like a very easy road lay ahead of them. They began to be afraid. This Messiah was not the Messiah they had imagined. Like most Jews in this occupied land, they imagined a mighty leader who would destroy their enemies and make them free. Jesus gurgled and spit up. Mary wiped his chin.

After Simeon spoke, an eighty-four year old widow approached the child. She had served at the Temple day and night since she had lost her husband as a young wife after only seven years. She had served in the Temple for over sixty years. She told everyone she saw about this child who would be the deliverance of Jerusalem. She started people talking, but most dismissed it as the ravings of a strange old woman, who had never seen the fruits of her own life. Maybe she put all her unfulfilled dreams into this child. This baby was here on earth about unfulfilled dreams.

Mary and Joseph wondered what would be next as they journeyed back to Bethlehem. Joseph had not had a dream or a visit from an angel in some time now, and he was struggling to decide what he needed to do next. For now, he was desperately struggling to keep his family fed in a strange villiage. He'd be glad when they got back to Nazareth, but they weren't ready for that long a journey with a baby yet. They would stay in David's city a little while longer as Mary and the baby grew stronger. Soon he hoped they would be home and the grandparents and James and Miriam could see their beautiful son. And in Nazareth they all would be safe in the home he built for them.

A lifetime of observing the stars and reading the omens the heavens displayed had never shown these sages anything like this before. These Magi directed the royal courts in Babylon by what they read from the night sky. These stars told them the world was changing, that a baby would be born and nothing would ever be the same. These men who lived in the abstract world of the sky had never traveled, but this time they needed to see what had come from sky to earth. They were ill equipped for travel. Too old to start a life of adventure now, still they had to see with their own eyes. And their king wanted to offer gifts to this one heralded by the eternal skies.

Their wealth bought everything they needed for this journey but youth and strength. Their great desire was strong enough to overcome their weakness. They had patience learned from lifetimes watching the slow movement of the stars and planets. Camels were much less stubborn then these old men. The desert sands were small compared to the span of space. Navigation was no problem to these men whose minds lived in the complex interwoven paths of the stars.

They abandoned the court; the royalty would have to make decisions on their own for a short time. Everyone in the palace was anxious to hear what they would find. These wise men had never become as excited about anything before. Gold came from the royal treasury, and incense. Expensive gifts for a king too young to understand. But toys seemed inappropriate even for a baby king. And they knew he was more than just a king.

The wandering star directed them, writing a story they knew how to read. They traveled to the palace in Jerusalem. They assumed they weren't the only ones who knew; surely the king in Israel would know. They expected it to be the king's son, of course. But this birth was a surprise to him, and not a pleasant one. King Herod hid his intentions, and called his scribes to search for clues for the place this infant king would be born. They searched the scriptures and found a prophet had written that the Messiah would be born in Bethlehem, David's home as a child. He told the Magi to come back when they found the child so he could pay homage, too. But Herod had already had his own sons put to death so they could be no threat to his jealous throne.

He knew no mercy. He asked the astronomers exactly when this star had appeared, so he could know the age of this tiny usurper.

So the Magi followed the star and rushed to the village of Bethlehem. The star led them until it stopped above where the child was sleeping, where the cosmic trail led to a humble place. Mary and Joseph had left the stable for a better place, but still it was no palace. This king was hidden in obscurity. They knelt before him and offered their gifts. Mary and Joseph wondered what would come next. It seemed he actually was something more than just a baby; others seemed to recognize him for who he was. But to them he was just their son, a helpless precious baby, and the focus of their love.

The astronomers left Jesus and began the short trip to Jerusalem. Exhausted from their journey, they slept before they could arrive with the directions requested by Herod. An angel came to them in their dreams and warned them of Herod's lie. Avoiding Jerusalem, they returned home a different way. The angels were still watching, just keeping their distance. Joseph would have preferred them in the same room, one to the left and one to the right.

The same night the wise men left, Joseph received another warning in his dream by the angel he had come to recognize as Gabriel. He was told to take the child and his mother far away from Herod's reach immediately. They were to go to Egypt and wait until Herod was dead. This monster would not stop searching his kingdom for the child who was a threat to his throne.

When Herod realized the wise men were not returning, his rage ordered a terrible decree, an echo of one in Egypt a millennium before.

Slaughter Dirge

In all the villages around Bethlehem, pairs of Roman soldiers marched from home to home pulling babies from their mother's arms. All male babies under the age of two were ordered destroyed. The one soldier held the parents back with his sword while the other killed the child any way he could. Some ways were too horrible to repeat. If the parents fought, the soldiers found a more gruesome method. The word spread to comply or the baby's death would be slow and terrible. Death would come, their only choice was quick or not. The Romans were efficient and practical in their cruelty. No empire ever grew by compassion.

The screams of babies and mothers echoed through the streets. Many parents died at first in failed attempts to save their children. Soon the word spread that the only hope was for their other children. The wailing song of mourning faded slowly, days after the soldiers' inhuman work was done. This was not what they were trained for, and most of them hated it, but knew a horrible death was waiting for them if they didn't follow orders.

There was no glory here, no bravery, no honor. After killing a dozen babies or more, each soldier became numb to his job. The cries no longer moved them. The sound of soft flesh tearing no longer shocked them. These soldiers were stationed at the farthest reaches of an over-extended Empire. They occupied a country full of zealots anxious to make them leave. They were far from a home that was beginning to have internal problems itself. A soldier's job wasn't easy here in a land where he was hated. After this abomination, they were hated even more.

Joseph and Mary traveled quickly back to Nazareth to prepare for the long journey to Egypt and explain what they were doing. They needed to say goodbye and share their baby with their parents. Joseph rested in the corner, enjoying the scene. Jesus was entertaining his grandparents with his smile. Tiny bubbles and gurgling sounds made the grandparents laugh and prompted more from Jesus. Joseph laughed at the way this baby turned the grandparents into joyful fools, celebrating drool. James and Miriam played with the child overjoyed and fearful for their friends. Even they wondered what the truth was inside this complicated mess that sounded like madness. But love is stronger than fear of madness.

After two days rest, they had collected what they would need for a long time away. Joseph gathered the tools he would need to work in a foreign land. He spoke the universal language of craftsmanship he knew would be understood. They didn't know how long they would be gone until it was safe to return. They said goodbye to family and home and any sense of safety. They wished they could wait for the grandparents get to know their baby more. None of this seemed fair.

Dawn found them already on the trail with Nazareth hidden behind the mountains again. Joseph wished the angel hadn't told him they had to go to Egypt. But Gabriel had been right before. *But was it just a dream? This stuff can make you mad. Dreams. Nazerth is pretty safe, hidden in a bowl behind the ring of hills. Travellers on the trail below may not even know there is a village hidden next to the trail; but I guess I shouldn't argue with an angel. Or is it just my dream?* Joseph looked at Mary and the baby and knew he couldn't take the chance.

Days into the journey, they began to hear stories from other travelers of the horror chasing them. The slaughter of the innocents. Two years of sons gone from a village and all the other villages surrounding it. A king's fears soured into the deaths of babies. Hundreds of innocents murdered. Hundreds of parents' dreams gone. Bloody baby bodies growing cold in mothers' arms and fathers helpless in curdled rage.

Mary cried at the thought that they were responsible for the deaths. If the wise men hadn't told Herod about the baby, all these innocents would still be alive. *It's my fault. How could this be part of God's great plan? How could he allow this horrible sacrifice?*

Joseph remembered the angel's warning, and rushed to get farther along the road, staying far away from Bethlehem on the way to Egypt. The danger of a journey alone among the robbers was less dangerous than traveling with anyone who knew who they were. Any mention of a messiah even in mocking jest could bring death.

"Mary, Egypt. *Egypt.* So strange to go to Egypt like the Joseph I was named after, to the Egypt where, a millennium before, another slaughter of innocent boy babies left only one survivor. Moses survived to lead his people to freedom in the promised land and now we are fleeing back to Egypt for safety for this little one."

"I'd rather not spend forty years on this donkey getting there, if you don't mind, dear husband. Please find a more direct route than Moses did." It was their first laugh of the journey. They couldn't stop feeling responsible for so many parents' sorrow.

They prayed there would be no more. This baby brought a lot of blood into the world already - and they had expected this Messiah to make things better. The way God seemed to be working his plan was full of pain and sorrow and death. And fear, lots of fear. Here was the Son of God with only these two protecting him and running from armies and madmen and who knew what else. Joseph had a lot of time to think while he walked. *Why was there no help for something so important? Or was it their imagination and had they lost their minds in all this struggle? What kind of god has this kind of plan painted with the blood of babies?*

The whole land of Israel shared the song of mourning. Mothers wailed with the sound of doves. Mary held Jesus close to her breast as Nazareth grew small behind them. A strange land and language waited before them with dangers they would face alone. This was a time when they needed friends if they ever did. They were afraid to tell anyone where they were going, lest they be followed. James gave them money, but they wouldn't tell him where they were going. It wasn't safe. They prayed God would take care of them.

Joseph talked to his old donkey again, and the others he had purchased for this trip. The gold the wise men gave them wouldn't last forever.

"Dear faithful friend, what is Egypt like? Can the other donkeys help you with the Egyptian language? Do the donkeys in Egypt at least speak donkey like you do? Maybe you can translate for me? I'm afraid I don't know a word of Egyptian, just a few phrases in donkey."

Mary sighed. "It's starting early on this trip."

The donkey didn't have an answer for him, and the angels weren't forthcoming with miraculous help. So he talked to himself. *You never know what you are getting in for when you fall in love. This certainly isn't what I imagined my life would be like.*

The safe route was the long route to Egypt. Joseph was grateful that the wise men had brought expensive gifts. Incense and gold took up little space for the trip, and the incense was even more valuable than gold. The caravan routes were watched by robbers looking for valuable cargo. But thieves didn't have a lot of use for carpenter's tools, so Joseph had hollowed out hiding places inside them. If the wise men hadn't brought their gifts, he didn't know how they would have saved their son from Herod's executioners. Once again they were away from home but this time farther and they didn't know for how long. Maybe forever. The angel wasn't specific. These angels were helpful but exasperating. They didn't understand the limitations of human life. They didn't understand uncertainty and frustration. They didn't understand time.

The baby's cry was swallowed by the desert. A voice gets lost in that much sky. Mary sang comforting lullabies to ease him through the journey. She kept him covered so his baby skin would not be burned by the sun. Two weeks went by in the wilderness. Dangerous days alternating with frightening nights.

Joseph saw danger in every shimmering mirage of dancing layers of blue. Sometimes a movement in the corner of his eye would shock him to attention with a feeling like a kink deep in his intestines – a warning from some invisible muscle that was a left-over ancient signal bringing danger to his attention. It always made his heart pump hard and put him on alert. He was getting tired of this.

A caravan rose into the sky and quavered before resolving itself on the sand behind them on the horizon, solidifying. They were closing on them fast in the practiced efficiency of merchants. Soon the sound of clanking metal pans and the snorts of camels filled the air. Closer, the camel bells shook the rhythm as the higher notes could be heard. Joseph and his family moved like a tortoise as the caravan overtook them. A voice called out. "Are you on your way to Alexandria?"

Joseph answered that they were, while Mary hid the baby in the folds of her robe. He lied. There were far too many Jews in Alexandria, so they didn't dare take the chance. Instead, they were headed for the heart of ancient Egypt that was the center long before the Greeks and Romans diluted the culture. They were headed for the Nile that snaked into a wide head where the flood plain spread into the sea. No one would look for them there, and this was where the first Joseph had seen the cities grow.

Five more days they journeyed as the sun arced across the sky. Five more nights stars chased each other into the western sea of sand. Each sunrise lit the sky in reds and golds as the family followed the arcing sun again. Each morning's trail was erased by the wind, and only hints remained. The tide of wind in ebb and flow sculpted an ocean of frozen waves of sand rippled in memory. Weeks after they started, one mirage finally shimmered into something that stood still. Joseph sighed with relief when he saw it, since their water was running low.

"Joseph, what are those strange mountains, pale blue in the distance? They look too perfect to be real. I thought they were a mirage at first. I've never seen mountains that were that regular."

"I have heard tales about them, Mary, but they are much larger than I imagined. They must be the pyramids."

The next day they enjoyed the green lushness surrounding the Nile. The pyramids were blinding white here in the area of Memphis and Giza. The strangeness of this world enveloped them, making them feel they were not on this world anymore. Everything was different. A strange language chattered around them as foreign as a bunch of birds. Their writing was alien and alluring, carved into the idols and statues along the streets. The market was full of fruit they had never seen before. The blinding white limestone pyramids gave everything a surreal look. They cast a soft light like a second sun. Their scale was too huge for anything man-made.

Mary and Joseph sat in the shade, holding their baby up to see the pyramids against the deep blue sky. They were as mesmerizing to a baby's eye as the full moon shining in the blackness. Such early wonders fill a little mind. Jesus looked around as if he understood, and would speak if he could, but hadn't learned how to yet. When he could finally speak, he would have a lot to say, like all babies, all God's children who are new in this world

Odd sailboats made of reeds moved slowly against the current, tacking to make headway. Mary tasted one of the new fruits of this exotic land and handed it to her husband to try. They enjoyed the moment of peace, far from Herod in a land where the angel had assured them they would be safe. Now what? They didn't speak a word of the language in this land where their ancestors had been slaves.

Mary touched his hand and said, "The first Joseph came to power in Egypt because of dreams, and his honor and integrity, but mostly through the inscrutable hand of God. Like us, he just found himself here. But he came here in chains as a slave to ultimately become the salvation of his people. And here we are now in this strange place where Joseph lived most of his life."

"Mary, we wouldn't be alive today if he hadn't saved our ancestors from starving during the worst famine in history. God has strange workings to accomplish his plans; I'm beginning to understand just how strange. That Joseph listened to dreams, and it saved our people. I try to pay attention, too."

"Where will we find a place to live, and how, Joseph? I'm tired, and the baby needs to rest in shelter. He has traveled way too much for such a little one."

"And it has to have room for my work, assuming I can find a way to sell it here. And those palm trees are tall and straight, but their wood is worthless to my work. I'll have to find a way to get real wood in a land where they make their boats from reeds. Maybe that will make my work more valuable, too."

"Joseph, we're safe from Herod here, but I wonder how long we will need to hide here until he isn't a threat anymore. How far will his war against babies spread? Would he try to kill all the male babies in all of Israel? Would he kill John? He's that age. I made sure Elizabeth was warned."

"Surely that monster Herod would stop with the area near Bethlehem, Mary. You need to stop thinking about it. It is not our fault."

"But I feel so guilty and responsible for all those babies killed because of us. *Why?* Why did this horror have to happen? How could this horror possibly be part of God's plan? Surely the screams of dying babies and their helpless mothers must reach God's ears. I can't imagine the grief those mothers felt as soldiers killed their children. How awful it must be to stand helpless and watch someone kill your child." Mary shivered as she cradled her child in her arms, protecting him from her fears. She couldn't protect herself, though, and her tears fell on her baby's face. Jesus looked up at her with a worried look on his baby brow. He sensed she was troubled.

Joseph wiped her tears. He held her and promised her he would protect them with everything he was, and God had plans for this baby that no Roman army could prevent.

After they had rested, they searched until they found a temporary place to stay and settled in to wait out Herod's storm. They had been drawn to the city where craftsmen were honored under the protection of Ptah the Egyptian god of craftsmanship. Joseph and his craft were welcomed here. A new style to this city had a market here. Memphis spread from the Nile to the pyramids of Giza and the river brought shipments of exotic wood from Africa. Soon the music inside this wood and Joseph's cheerful song would fill the baby's ears, as Joseph's father had filled his ears when he was young. This country valued craftsmanship and style. The sculpture and the architecture and even the language all had a soul of beauty and strength. It became part of his art.

They made a home there. Mary put the first gift Joseph had given her on the table to remind them of that night when the full moon first shone off the polished wood. It would remind them of the time when their love was new and life was simple. The box rested on linen she had woven, next to the rough ugly clay tableware they had formed around pieces of the wise men's gold while they were still in Bethlehem. Baked inside these plates and bowls too ugly for anyone to want to steal was the money they would need during their exile.

Jesus grew.

Joseph was a consummate craftsman, playing the native beauty in the wood like music from an instrument. His style was simple, subordinate to the pattern of the grain. Surrounded by intricate carving in Egypt, he experimented with new carved patterns as he incorporated Egyptian designs into his work. He observed the symbols but changed them to make them his own. His papyrus theme flowed with a foreign curve, adding movement to the static Egyptian stiffness.

He finally started selling his sturdy chairs and tables to Egyptians who were attracted to foreign styles. He shared ideas with an Egyptian carpenter he met at the market, and they became friends. Joseph wondered if their ancestors had been enemies in the time of Moses, or if both had suffered under Pharaoh. He wondered if they had been friends in the time of Joseph and if their descendants would be friends far into the future. Egypt and Israel were bound in a repeating cycle of friendship and enmity.

Wadji was dark, with short-cropped curly black hair. Powerful ropes of muscles covered his wiry body. He rarely wore a covering over the top of his body since his skin usually glistened with sweat in the hot Egyptian sun. His laugh reminded Joseph of his friend James. They struggled with the languages, but the language of carpentry joined them. They taught each other their own skills, and each became a better craftsman because of it. They also shared the universal language of music.

Joseph didn't know how long they would need to stay in Egypt. As always, God expected him to act in faith and wait. Lots of waiting always. He was becoming a very patient man. This exile was expensive; they sold the frankincense and myrrh to pay for a more permanent place to stay and for food.

As the months passed, Wadji helped them bargain and found a more comfortable home for them near his. As the months passed they learned more of each other's language so they could communicate more freely. Joseph told him about his land and God and when his people lived here before. Trust had grown betweeen the two friends. Trust that let him take a chance with part of the truth. He told him about the slaughter of the innocents, and their escape that brought them here to safety. They were just an ordinary family with a baby here, not the one that Herod sought. It was a plausible story, and true enough. Who wouldn't run to save their child if they could?

Wadji told them stories passed down from his ancestors of a horrible time of plagues that ended in the slaughter of all the Egyptian first-born. It was an obscure story, the details had been fogged in time, but Joseph recognized it. It was Joseph's God who sent the angel of death with such a gruesome plague to free his ancestors. The story of Passover sounded differently to Joseph now, hearing it from the other side.

Wailing Song

They were settled in Egypt for a few months when new Jewish refugees arrived with news from their home. The slaughter of the innocents had enraged the zealots in Galilee and had driven some to attempt a rebellion against impossible odds. As retribution the Empire attacked and burned Sepphoris just four miles from Nazareth and enslaved the survivors. Then they sought out those responsible for the revolt around the countryside and crucified over two thousand rebels and innocent victims. Some moaned on the crosses for over a week before they finally died. Thousands of widows and mothers suffered as their husbands and sons were tortured before their eyes, just out of their reach. To make their point more graphic, the Romans would not allow the bodies to be removed after they died. They left them hanging to bloat and rot and be eaten by birds. Their loved ones had to watch this horror. The stench of two thousand bodies was inescapable. Guards killed anyone who tried to remove a body for burial. Another rebellion was unthinkable. How would they punish an additional attempt? Something worse?

Mary and Joseph knew they were responsible for the chain of events that had caused so much suffering and death already. *Two thousand more horrible deaths, how many more before this is done?* Joseph shivered. He didn't want to know what Mary was thinking; she had a horrible expression on her face. They both felt horrible guilt about what was happening because of them. But they were glad they were here, far away from Herod. The Romans ruled Egypt, too, of course, like the rest of the known world, but this was a more civilized place to the Empire. It knew how to behave and so it had favored treatment as a colony. The child would be safe here, far from Herod's reach. Unless a spy found out and took word to him so he could send an assassin.

Wadji and Joseph shared some of the work of carpentry that was almost impossible to do alone. Joseph learned Egyptian quickly; both had an ear for languages. Mary and Wadji's wife, Marba, shared their very different ways of cooking. Marba showed Mary how to cook the new foods that grew here. And Marba loved to play with Jesus as she practiced for the child of her own who would be here soon. Mary thought her friend looked regal with her long neck and delicate features. She had long fingers that danced in the air as she talked. Mary didn't have a gift for learning languages, but she was very intuitive and read faces and gestures well.

The marketplace was their playground. Marba guided her through the booths to find fair prices. The smell of exotic foods and spices excited her with ideas to surprise Joseph with new tastes. Now that they were finally safe, she could begin to think of this as an adventure. But she missed home and her parents. She wished they could get to know Jesus while he was still this baby with wise eyes. Joseph showed his son off here where no one was looking for the King of the Jews to kill. Here he was a baby a long way from home. A very long way from home indeed.

Joseph and Mary loved to watch the sun move from face to face of the pyramids as the day went on. There was a time each day when the face aligned toward them on each in the row of pyramids brightened like the sun, then faded into shadow. It was like a lighthouse beacon of the day that marked the movement of time.

Wadji was a musician too, and in the evenings he and Joseph shared their music, adding to the possibilities each owned to make a richer sound. The soft wailing rise and quavering fall of Wadji's music carried the listener's emotions on a journey to their deepest unexplored soul. Joseph's sense of rhythm and the feel of carpentry in his music resonated with Wadji like his heartbeat. Once they were familiar with each other's style they improvised into complex interwoven melodies.

Music can be a polite language; they waited for each other to finish their solo part when the music told them what was called for. They added harmonies and countermelodies when that part of the conversation came. The courtesy of the music came naturally as it took them into the surprising accidents of sound. Like a lover's caress in an ear, it was creative play with frequency and time. They closed their eyes and didn't need to look at each other for clues, the music told them what to do and when. Joseph shared music from his ancestors as did Wadji. They sensed the roots they had in common from the first Joseph's time in Egypt. This music had returned to the place it first combined.

Those generations of visitors who became slaves shared music and left that part of their soul in the land. And the melodies of the Nile traveled with them through the desert to the Promised Land. Joseph recognized some of the music he had learned from his father from these parallel melodies from Wadjii's flute. Songs of slavery and songs of the burning heat and songs of longing, and songs that touched something ancient.

Joseph knew the communication musicians feel at this deep level that is almost like lovers' intimacy without touching. It is not sexual, but is the same sort of play. The coupled dance through frequencies and time, and intervals and chords transports souls into angels' song. Listeners can appreciate it, but never know it fully. One has to lose himself to the larger music with another to understand. It is an ecstatic experience, transcendent, holy.

Joseph and Wadji understood each other beyond the handicap of language. Mary and Marba enjoyed the music, and more the happiness it brought their husbands. They felt the music draw them like the current of a river and hummed along as they swayed to the flow. Soon their bodies wanted to take part and they tapped on cooking pots and furniture. The subtle drumming and the hollowness filled in the spaces with a new layer. The music became richer and more connected. It fed upon them all and fed them, too. Friends fill the soul, especially when so far from home.

I t was the best part of every day. Joseph had put down his tools and washed off the dirt from his work. Before they ate, Mary inspected his hands for splinters. She always found some, it was part of doing work with wood. He had learned to ignore them as he worked, but they needed to be removed. She hummed a song like she had hummed that first day when she held his injured hand.

"Hold still, my love, I'm afraid this one is going to hurt, it's very deep." Mary probed with a pin to loosen the splinter to pull it free.

"I'm pretty used to them, Mary. But it is so much easier when you do it. I used to make such a mess, and have to gouge myself pretty deeply to get them out. Or else miss them and wait until they became infected and pushed themselves out with the yuck."

Mary shook her head. She loved his hands and all they did. His strong hands made her feel safe. She looked at the web of scars that had grown across them from his work. Many more than when they had first met less than two years ago. She kissed his hand for all the time they shared.

Life in Egypt was easier, it was almost home to them now. But there was no Temple here, no synagogue, and they were afraid to travel to Alexandria where there were many Jews and a thriving synagogue. It was not safe to call attention to themselves. Herod had long arms and an idle word could get back to him. They couldn't take the chance of being recognized. No one knew where they had gone. So they quietly practiced their faith with candles on the Sabbath and private prayers and reading. They were Jews in silence in this world. Their friends were all Egyptians; it was best to stay away from other Jews for now, and certainly the Romans.

But the ritual of the splinters and the quiet talk always gave them time to draw near and bring another day to a peaceful close. It was their private time to touch souls and share their days with the old dreams and the new.

After almost a year in Egypt, Gabriel lit Joseph's dreams again. It was time to travel back to Nazareth since those who had been trying to kill the baby were dead. It wasn't the best time of year to travel, but he had learned to listen to angels. They would miss Wadji and Marba. They would miss those dazzling perfect mountains that watched over them, as they had watched over generations of all the children of Israel long ago as they grew from a family into a nation. He said goodbye to Joseph's city, the other Joseph of dreams. They were going home. They were anxious for the grandparents to play with their big boy. Jesus watched the pyramids grow faint into the haze of their journey. In his child's mind he wondered why they were disappearing. They had always been in his world as long as he could remember, since he was only a few months old. He would never see them again. The journey home seemed much quicker than the trip away. Soon the familiar landscape welcomed them.

Mary's father, Heli, saw them first as they came home unannounced. He called to his wife, Anne, and together they ran to meet them on the way. Mary's mother took her grandson in her arms. "Oh, Mary how handsome he is, and look how much he has grown!"

Mary glowed with that pride a mother feels when her own mother holds her child. Joseph unloaded as the grandparents played with the grandchild they had barely seen before they disappeared, perhaps forever. They hadn't known if they would ever see each other again.

They rested with Mary's parents while they cleaned the house Joseph had built for them. They celebrated with Joseph's family. Everyone wanted to see how much the child had grown.

He had perceptive eyes. He took in his new world and smelled the strange smells. He liked the smell of his grandmother's cooking. Life became normal at last.

E xile had stolen the baby from them; he was bigger now. His grandparents had missed too much time, and were making up for it. Mary was radiant. She sat with Joseph to watch the show.

James and Miriam waited on the edge of a wall of grandparents and aunts and uncles. Miriam called over her shoulder to Mary, telling her how gorgeous her baby was. Miriam's hands were on her cheeks and she was bent at the waist, hanging in for a closer look. Then her arms stretched forward unconsciously reaching to hold the baby. She wanted one of her own. But for now she wanted to hold this one. Mary noticed, and nudged Joseph and whispered in his ear. "James better get ready, a mother has just decided to be."

Joseph smiled as James put his arm around Miriam. Mary smiled at Joseph and he shook his head silently. *I wish you as much joy as I have, my friend, but a tenth the trouble.* It was easy to imagine things being easier for James. He had lots of money and didn't have the problems of dealing with *this* child. Nobody else did.

Sometimes Joseph wished he had a normal marriage with an ordinary child, but he realized how important this was. In the middle of the difficulties of daily life, even the miraculous can be lost in the mundane. This baby didn't look like God. He didn't act any differently from any other child. Sometimes Joseph wondered if he was wrong, and his dreams had been only dreams. He thought of the other Joseph who knew about dreams, and followed them to painful greatness. *Painful greatness, a blessing and a curse. Angels, stars, wise men, searching shepherds, a virgin birth . . . maybe all this was merely our dreams and madness. Jesus seems to be such an ordinary child.*

Mary could always sense Joseph's moods, and took his hand in hers. She didn't say a word, just traced the line of the scar on the back of his hand with her index finger. She looked at him without a word and kissed him.

Life was comfortingly normal at last. Time passed. Jesus grew.

Jesus crawled into everything as he explored. He pulled himself up higher every day. He loved to take unsteady steps with his father holding both his hands. His mother cheered his wobbling, then swung him up in her arms. Soon he would take his first steps alone. Then, like every toddler, he would own the world.

Joseph made up a song for him about his pretty feet and where they would carry him. About strong feet that would never get tired. His parents played with his perfect toes, each one tiny in their fingers. Baby feet, soft before the walking hardened them.

One morning, Mary woke Joseph with a shake and whispered to him to hurry to see their son. Jesus sat in the golden light, straining to push himself up. He was on all fours, but struggling to stand, serious about it this time. They wanted to praise and cheer him on, but they didn't want to distract him. Mary held her hand over her mouth, and Joseph wrapped his arms around her from behind. God on earth struggled to rise in the sunlight to stand alone for the first time.

Now he could look out the window at what he was trying to see - two doves in song on a nearby branch. He giggled and cooed along with them. His parents knelt and kissed his head from both sides, and told him how proud they were of him. Then sang the song of baby feet together with the doves.

Love Song

Jesus was weaned now, and sleeping in his own bed. He had grown to be a big boy since they had settled in at Nazareth. This cool night Mary and Joseph spent a peaceful evening talking about all the unexpected adventures they had experienced in the years since they fell in love. They had lived through more difficult times than they would have chosen for a peaceful life. She kissed the scar on his hand, and traced it with her finger as she leaned against his shoulder.

"I remember the afternoon when you got this scar, I was standing outside the door for quite some time watching you with the children, Joseph. I was thinking how good you were with them, and how much they loved you, and you loved them. I fell in love with you then. I thought about what a good father you would be, and how much I wanted to have children with you. You *are* a wonderful father, Joseph. There couldn't be a better father for our child. But I want to give you children of your own now. You have been so patient. So very patient. I want to make you happy. Please come to bed with me."

After so much time together and all that they had been through, they trusted each other more than any other two humans ever had. She knew she could trust him fully; he had been there for her through things that would have been too much for most men. He did it all with grace and the strength that reveals itself in gentleness. Oh, he was human, and often all this was too much for him, she knew, but his love was strong, it bonded him to her no matter what.

Even when he had thought she was lying or crazy, he still acted with love and restraint, trying to protect her as best he could. But then the angel told him the unbelievable was real. She knew he would never desert her; she knew he would protect her and love her as long as he had breath. He had wondered if part of the difficult job he had been given to be guardian for God's son meant that he would never be allowed to make love with the woman he loved. He wondered if chaste caring was all there would be, with no children of his own to detract their focus from Jesus. He had decided he loved Mary so much that he could do even that, if that was what God required. He was glad it wasn't. When he awoke this morning, he had no idea this was the day that would change.

Mary knew he had waited years for her, but love is always timid. Love always fears the loss of something so precious that it feels fragile. She lowered her eyes and whispered, "Joseph, do you still find me pleasant to look at? I'm not the girl you fell in love with, and I have had a child. I'm not a girl anymore."

Joseph held her face in his calloused hands, and raised it up to his. She was comforted by the familiar roughness of his hands. He looked into her eyes. "Mary, you are the most beautiful woman in the world. I love you. I have ever since that day in my shop. I always will. I love the way you laugh; I love the way you cry. I love the way you are with our son. I love the way you look at me, I love the way you laugh at my jokes no matter how bad they are. I love your angel's voice. I love the way you move. I love your face maybe most of all - I could look at it for the rest of my life. Do I find you pleasant to look at? Oh, Mary, you know."

Two gentle lovers free at last, blessed by God with a love deepened by trials and proof. This is no ordinary love story.

J udean and Galilean tax collectors were appointed by the Empire with firm quotas to fill that rose regularly as the local governors demanded more. Rome needed more to maintain the struggling giant it had become. The economy was choking here in the provinces and at home. These tax collectors enjoyed the incentive of permission to pocket everything they collected in excess of their quota. The people had no way of knowing. They only knew they were being cheated; they didn't know how much. These tax collectors had the authority of Rome behind them since they were the ones who kept the Empire alive. They were universally hated by those they bled.

The drain of the occupation and taxes sucked almost everyone to the edge of poverty or beyond. Joseph and Mary struggled. The wise men's gold was long gone. Joseph's business suffered. On top of this, many avoided him because the village was sure he was either crazy or a fool. Their story of Jesus' virgin birth made them the object of jokes and whispers. They were avoided and other carpenters were used instead.

Joseph worked hard, and cheaper. The little that he made was often consumed in taxes. The only way he could feed his family was to borrow from family and friends, and try to sell them more furniture than they could use. It was made with fine craftsmanship, but it was piling up without a market. It was hard to work with the shop filled with unsold furniture. It was driving Joseph mad. His friends were struggling, too, but not like him. This double handicap was draining him as he tried to imagine every way he could to make money. People were becoming annoyed with him when he appeared at their doors carrying chairs and wooden toys begging for anything he could get for them to feed his family and keep his house. Even people who liked him and his work began to resent his desperation. The sarcasm became more pointed. His family would starve if he didn't find some way to make enough.

The last time the tax collector came, he told Joseph he could no longer accept furniture for his payment; his great house was full of them. He told Joseph how much money he had to come up with in a month, or he would lose his home. He didn't have it, and he didn't know how he could get it. And now it was down to days. *Days* before the end when they would be on the street and penniless after the tax collector seized everything to sell for the debt, including the home he had built. *Days.* And they would take everything his parents had, too, and her parents.

Cold panic gripped Joseph. It started in his belly and spread until he could no longer think. He felt himself breathing fast, but he couldn't seem to get enough air no matter how fast he gulped it. His ears began to ring and he felt himself struggling inside looking for a place to run like a chicken struggling to get away from the axe headed for its neck. But he felt the necks of his whole family held in the grip of Rome; and the axe was in the air, ready to fall. His old mother and father on the street with them. Rome was cruel. *Days.*

Joseph prayed. He begged God for help. He knew the God he trusted wouldn't let this happen to Mary and his son. But he couldn't sleep at night. He grew impatient with God, and his prayers burned with the fire of his frustration. He hadn't chosen this life. All he wanted was a simple life with a loving wife and children. Honest hard work should make a simple life possible. *Why all these impossibilities? Is this what it means to be chosen by God?*

One night Mary realized he wasn't hearing a word she said. He lived in some dark place that frightened her and she couldn't pull him from it with her love. He told her he had to walk to think and pray. The pain on his face terrified her. She asked him to stop and kiss her first. She held him tightly and stroked his back as she told him that she loved him. Then she held him as she told him everything it was about him that she loved. But he was numb and couldn't feel her love tonight. One by one she told him each thing she loved, holding him there; then kissed him and told him one more time how glad she was he had chosen her. "God will take care of us," she said. "We'll see."

She put his warm cloak on his shoulders. She hugged him for a very long time, almost too long. She knew how difficult not being able to bring his family the security they needed was to him; it was tearing him apart. She knew he had started questioning God. She knew because she was, too. She knew they might soon lose their home and end up beggars on the street. She knew how many hours she had prayed for God to take care of them since he had chosen to give them this responsibility. She just wanted God to be fair. She wanted her husband to have a little relief. She knew how hard it was for him to have to ask family and friends for money to keep his family alive. And how it hurt him when they looked at him with disappointment. When they wanted to avoid him. When they looked at him as a fool and a failure. He never made enough to pay them back, he was just sinking deeper in debt. The taxes broke his spirit every time he thought he had a chance of catching up. The rules changed constantly outside of his control. It seemed the only ones who prospered were the selfish, evil ones. *Why would they be rewarded, and not those who tried to live by love toward everyone?* Joseph hung his head and walked into the night.

Mary ran after him. She caught him by his sleeve and pulled him around. She pushed him against a tree, held his shoulders tightly and kissed him hard. "Listen, Joseph, I love you. We will work this out somehow. We have friends, and God will not desert us, he is only testing us. These Romans won't be here forever, and then everything will be better. We will make it. You are smart and strong, and you can do anything you want to. I believe in you."

Joseph touched her face. His fingers lingered on the cheek he loved. He said, "I know. I just don't know how yet. I want to walk until I do." Then he kissed her and hugged her.

"Go in out of the cold, I'll be back soon. I just need to do this and try to find some part of me I must have lost."

Mary was afraid. *He looked at me too long, like he was saying goodbye.*

She believed in him more than he believed in himself. Mary knew how much he needed to hear that tonight, and to feel her lips and arms. She went inside to pray for him, for them. She ached for him like he was gone forever. It frightened her.

Joseph's breath clouded before him in the moonlight. *I'm walking too fast for night.* He didn't know where he was going except out of Nazareth. He had always loved his hometown, but now he wondered if he was supposed to take his family somewhere else. *Is it time for another dream or angel visit? Is it time for more instructions, or is this just the subtle way you are telling me to go? An angel would have been much kinder, or is that too much trouble to waste on us - do they have more important things to do? Should I take them to a bigger city, like Jerusalem? Or back to Egypt? Or to a smaller village? Somewhere where no one laughs at us behind our backs. Where people don't think we are insane. Where people don't think Mary lied to me and I am a fool. I don't know what to do.*

As he left the streets of Nazareth behind, he realized some trace of Mary's warmth and scent still lingered. He could still feel her warmth from her hug. But the cold night was stealing that from him. He stopped and pulled a handful of his cloak up to his nose and savored the smell of Mary one more time. He remembered the smell from her hair that seemed a lifetime ago when he still had dreams. When he had hope. Movement flickered in the shadows. He thought he saw something frightening there. Soon he would be deep in the shadow of night where he would not be able to see these little shadows anymore. That was the comfort of deep darkness for him. He would enter Shadow's home where dim light could sing.

He moved on. Soon all that surrounded him was sky and hills. Moon and stars lit his way. He looked to one particular group of stars and laughed despite his mood. It was not entirely a bitter laugh - there was a seed of something else. Since he was a child, he had pretended this was where God lived. It helped him to have a place to picture the Almighty. It made the idea small enough for him to wrap his mind around. Somehow that felt more real. He knew the stars he loved most, he knew the winter stars that lit the night. Orion and the Pleiades, Sirius and the Bear. The full moon visited Orion tonight as it always did this coldest time of year. It was like a glowing lantern held above his head as he went hunting or off to war, lighting the world below him. Orion always hunted in the winter and then hid in the summer sun's glare, out of view.

Night sucked his warmth out of him, and all his strength, so Joseph found a large rock to rest on. He wrapped his cloak around him, and stared at the night sky. Antares burned fiery red like Betelgeuse. Sirius was more intense, almost green in comparison. He looked down at the hills, lit gently blue. Huddled sheep seemed to glow against the brown winter grass. But there was no white in this moonlight; they were blue sheep to his eye. He thought of nothing for some minutes. He just let the beauty of this night flow in. Beauty always was a comfort. Beauty always eased the pain. But there was no music in this night.

He closed his eyes and smelled the earth, the trees, the distant smell of wool sleeping damp in the dew. This quiet night he heard an owl, and once a lonely wolf that never got an answer. He could still taste Mary on his lips.

He surprised himself with the loudness of his sigh. He remembered why he was here this night. He talked to God, although now he doubted if he was listening, or even there. He picked the spot in the heavens where he pretended he might be, and stared there as he demanded answers. He was soft at first, then angry, then he cried out loud.

"I am doing everything I can, why don't you help? Do you want us to die after all this? Why did you trust me with your son only to make things impossible? What? What am I supposed to do? Am I being punished for my secret sins? Are all of us being punished for my doubts? Help them, at least. If you are a God of love, why don't you? I would, don't you care as much about them as I do? Or is all of this just madness, madness, madness all of us? Are you just part of our madness, too?"

There was no meteor flash across the sky. No trumpets from the angels. *Silent Gabriel must not care, either. He only cared to get things started and trap us here.* Only the silent moon and stars burned on in silence the way they always did even on the nights they were hidden by the clouds. Joseph sat, thoughtless at last, waiting in that dead place come to rest his mind. He had no more to make a decision with now than he had before. Silence. *I guess I shouldn't have been so honest. I guess I shouldn't have given so much away to those who needed help. I should have charged more. I should have not worked so hard to make things perfect. I should have cheated those I could. That's what makes people prosper, isn't it God? Those are the ones you reward. Those who take care of themselves.*

"Am I just talking to the empty sky? Answer me! I trusted you!" This voice from his silence shocked him. It was as if the words of another screamed from his throat and evaporated into the size of the night. But he was not embarrassed, he was angry.

He waited as that silence deepened, swallowing him the way it had swallowed his words. The only answers were inside himself. God was silent if he was listening at all. He searched his heart. He knew the woman waiting for him loved him with the kind of love he had always hoped for. He knew he loved her and trusted her. He loved his son. He loved his craft. He was good at it. If he couldn't sell it anymore, he would find some other way to make a living as a farmer or a shepherd or merchant or another occupation he couldn't even imagine yet. He could change. He would find a way. For now he would live with the humiliation, and feed his family whatever way he could. Tomorrow he would talk with James who understood money and the twisted way this occupied world worked. But for now he would return to the warmth of Mary's love waiting for him as it always would.

James' hearty hug welcomed Joseph into his home. He sensed Joseph was troubled. Joseph sat at a table had made, on a chair of his handiwork. He caressed the wood, enjoying the grain and smooth finish of his finest work. He remembered the weeks he worked on it, making it perfect for his friend. James entered the room with wine, cheese and bread.

Joseph surveyed the craftsmanship surrounding him in his friend's home. Rare things from far away lands. Expensive things. Joseph had never cared about these things before, but today he realized that merely one of these things could take care of his family for months or a year.

The wine made him feel better. The cheese was substantial and filled him, but he wanted to save most of it to take home. He was embarrassed to ask. They spoke of casual things at first; he told him how Jesus was growing. There were uncomfortable silences. Finally, James asked him what was wrong.

"I'm not making it, James." Joseph sighed, resting his head on his hands on the table. After a moment he continued. "I am no businessman. I am a craftsman, and I work hard, but I am not making it. These taxes, and the struggle that we all have in this occupation is killing me. And, to be honest, a lot of people are avoiding me; they think Mary and I are mad, or worse. I hear the things they say about little Jesus. Every time I think I am beginning to get a little ahead, the tax collector raises the amount I owe. There is no way. None. I have tried selling my furniture every way I can, but now people are getting annoyed with me. They are tired of my begging for work. James, the taxes are due at the end of the month, more than I can possibly make. We will lose our home. I don't know how I can feed my family - they can't eat wood. I wish they could, I have plenty of good furniture I cannot sell. I have not worked on a house for a very long time. I have borrowed everything I can from my family and Mary's to try to keep going, but they don't have any to spare now, either. It disturbed me to have to ask them, but I didn't know what else to do. I knew they were struggling, almost as much as we are. But this double burden that came with Jesus … I never dreamed this hard time would last so long. I used to be able to make money easily with my craftsmanship. But now ... I don't know what to do. You seem to know how to make money, tell me what to do."

James always knew when to listen and let the flow of words and what lay behind the words flow free when it needed to be set free. He waited until the silence had time.

James held Joseph's arm. "Relax, friend, I won't let that happen to you, you are my brother, my mother never gave me one. These Romans have made it hard for all of us, but you have even more against you. Sometimes I think you are too honest and generous for your own good. First, I can help you through this crisis; then I can show you how to use the Romans the way I do. I'll introduce you to them. They appreciate craftsmanship like yours and they are the ones who have the money to buy it. It is our money. It is only fair that you should get some of it back from them."

Joseph sighed, relieved and embarrassed. He hated to ask this of his friend, but he would do anything for Mary and Jesus. And he would do anything for James, too, if he could. He looked down at the table – gratefully lost in the pattern of the grain, not wanting to look his friend in the eye. He felt like a broken failure, a beggar. *How could one who worked so hard and was such a craftsman be reduced to this?*

James did what he could to help him feel better. It started with wine and a plan. "I'll He teach you what money truly means and how to grow it like a garden. Most people have no idea what money really is. It's simple, a lot easier than carpentry." Joseph began to relax for the first time in months. James was enjoying himself as he taught his secret philosophy.

"These taxes steal our profits, and drain us. It is impossible to pay all they demand, so if you are to survive you have to not let them know about everything you sell. I just don't tell them everything, and pay them what they ask for what they know about. That is the first thing to do, like stopping the bleeding from a wound. Next, use them. Make friends with the Romans and flatter them and convince them the value of your work. It is easier than you think. I'll help you. I can brag to them about your craftsmanship, and get their attention with small gifts. I will buy some of your work to give them first. It will help both of us. I need to keep them satisfied. They are the market for my finer things, and often I can keep these sales secret from the tax collectors. A sale without these taxes makes twice as much or more. I'll show you. But you have to be careful, these collectors need to feel they aren't being cheated or they can make things rough for you. But these Romans need me. I am able to bring them the things they want. I have made friends who can get these fine things. They will protect me, because they wouldn't want to lose their supply of all these luxuries. They are isolated out here so far from their home. They like their comforts. And, some of them have truly become my friends. But you are not as safe as I am here, remember to be careful, they can be rough."

Joseph felt his brow wrinkling. *Rough?* He knew how *rough* Roman punishment could be. He was frightened. *How could I dare to take that kind of chance? I would be no help at all to Mary and Jesus if I were caught, then what would they do? But do I have any choice? I have to find a way to survive in this impossible world. I will be careful. I will take as few chances as I can. I will tell no one, not even Mary.*

"Wait a minute, I have this wheel of cheese that someone gave me and I am afraid it will spoil before I could eat it, and I know Mary has loved it before. Please take it to her for me." James always had a way with words and gifts.

Joseph walked home that day with enough money to pay the taxes, and some left over. Plenty left over, in fact. For the first time he didn't worry if money would come in time. He brought James the pieces that he would use as gifts, and then went to work making more. He wanted to be prepared to sell them as soon as James was ready. And James was always ready to make a sale.

Sawdust Song

Jesus often napped in his father's shop, lulled to sleep by the song of the saw and plane, and his father's voice. He liked to play with the piles of sawdust and the curls of wood that had spiraled off the plane. He loved the smells, he could tell you what kind of tree each smell came from before he knew many other words. His father taught him as he answered all his questions and made everything a game.

Joseph made him every kind of toy he could imagine. Slowly the shop began to fill up again with other children who shared his toys and were each given some of their own. The shop was full of song again. He would have another child soon; Jesus needed to know what a family was like. It was an important part of being human. Joseph taught the children to sing with the rhythm of the saw. They played with words and built the songs together. The shop was full of laughter as a dozen children sang playing with their toys in the sawdust, making winding trails. They spread interweaving intricate designs together. Little handprints and footprints added to the trails creating a beautiful carpet that always changed; more intricate than an oriental rug. Joseph bent down and smoothed an area blank then drew in the sawdust with a stick.

"Here's your name," he told his son. "Here is a *yod*, this littlest letter in the alphabet to start your name, then here to the left is the next letter, that looks like a house, a *hey*. Then this long skinny letter like a staff, called a *vav*. Then the prettiest letter, that looks a little like a bush, called a *shin*, and finally, this funny letter that looks like a tree that is bent in the wind, an *ayin*. This is what your name looks like."

The letters seemed to fit into the design on the floor. Jesus struggled to copy the letters in the dust while his father went back to work. Finally he gave up and joined in the songs.

Mary stood at the door watching her husband sing as he planed and drew songs from the children like purpose from the wood. Jesus sang along as he smoothed the wood that was his *big person's* job. Mary watched her husband as she had that first day years ago. She had known he would be a wonderful father. She felt his baby move in her. She closed her eyes and caressed her stomach. She listened to the plane, the voices, the little voices struggling to keep up with the rhythm. She smiled the smile of a contented woman, full of life and full of love.

J oseph came in the door with something moving around inside his cloak. Jesus wondered what was going on. When he saw the smile on his father's face, he got excited.

"Abba, what's in there?" Jesus was jumping up to see, his little hands up in the air.

Joseph kneeled down as a wet nose snuffled out of his cloak, followed by a pair of eyes and a whimper.

"A puppy!" Jesus reached out with both arms and took the puppy, hugging him, and resting his cheek on the puppy's head. Jesus ran to his mother while the dog's ears flapped with each step and he looked around at his new home. His feet flopped like a rag doll, but his tail wagged steadily and fast.

Mary kneeled down by her son and scratched the puppy's head. She kissed Jesus and said, "You're a big boy now - can you take care of him?"

Jesus said, "Oh I will! I love him. Look at his ears!" A long tongue licked Jesus' cheeks until he laughed so hard he had to put the puppy down. The dog jumped on Jesus, knocked him on his back and licked his face into uncontrollable laughter. "He likes me! Look Amma! He's so soft and furry!" The thump of his tail against the table leg was amplified by the tabletop like a drum. Both ends of the puppy equally showed how happy he was with his boy as a playmate.

Mary told Joseph, "So you found a great one already, dear. I thought it would take longer." Mary rubbed his back and felt his soft fur. " He's really cute. What should we call him? Have you thought of a name for this sweet boy yet?"

Joseph smiled and said, "Caleb. I thought Caleb would be nice."

"How very original of you, Joseph. Did you stay up all night thinking up the word 'dog'?" Mary grinned.

Joseph smirked and crossed his arms over his chest, "Sometimes simple is better, dear. Besides, Caleb was brave and faithful when everyone else except his buddy Joshua was afraid to go into the Promised Land. He wasn't afraid of giants, just like little David. This is the kind of dog I want loving and protecting Jesus. Caleb, the courageous. Caleb the faithful. Caleb the cute."

Joseph knew the madman might appear again and it was clear the angels were not on guard the way he had hoped. If he was the one responsible, he wanted the most help here he could get. He wanted a dog's keen ears guarding his son for an early warning of danger. And a dog's love can give the boy a taste of that love which is like no other. The love one species can have for another. So different yet so much the same. But a different kind of love that shows how love is more than just human.

Joseph wanted the security a dog could bring to a home, a warning so they could sleep in peace. And he never knew when someone might slip up behind him. And long before the dog would be able to protect them, there would be the wonderful puppy time. And like there is no love like a dog's faithful love, there is no play like a puppy's play. Caleb squealed loudly and Jesus let go of his ear. Mary kneeled next to him and rubbed Caleb's belly as she said, "You have to be gentle with him, honey. He is small and his ears are very sensitive to pulling."

Jesus started petting his head and told the dog, "I'm sorry Caleb, I didn't mean to hurt you. I pwomise I will be more careful." Then they started playing stick, Caleb fetching the little stick Jesus threw. But he was having too much fun growling and playing tug of war with it to give it back for another throw until Jesus finally worked it loose.

Soon the puppy was following his instincts and herding Jesus, and keeping him out of danger like a serious little shepherd doing his job.

Heart Song

Mary was growing large again. Joseph's son grew in her and Jesus would have a brother soon. Tonight, Joseph and Jesus both rested their ears on her stomach, listening to the fast heartbeat inside, counterpoint to Mary's slower beat. They could feel him move. The cheerful family was growing. Family prayers were sung together. They made up songs about everything. Silly songs sometimes they could never finish without laughing.

Most of their married life she had been pregnant, it seemed. Joseph loved the way she looked - she glowed. Jesus spent more time with his father in his shop now that he was getting old enough to help. Jesus loved smoothing wood with rough stones, and sand and cloth. He liked to feel the surface of the wood grow smoother; he had learned the testing touch from his father. Jesus loved to blow the fine wood dust off the piece with a puff of breath that made a little cloud. He liked oiling the wood and waxing it to make the surface shine when he polished it with a cloth. Mostly he liked to finish the toys his father started for him, so he felt he had made them, too.

Jesus helped with the toys they gave to other children, he learned the satisfying feeling of making a personal gift to give to someone you care about. He especially liked helping his father with gifts for his mother and grandparents. Mary helped him make gifts for Joseph, too, so he wasn't left out. Gifts of love that were tangible things to show the way this family felt. Sometimes a gift is a song.

Working Song

The summer was long gone and now it was the coldest part of the winter, when the north wind found ways through the most solid walls. Jesus curled up like a cat close to the fire in the workshop. The scraps of wood kept a warm glow in the corner. The comforting sound of the saw that accompanied his father's song brought him peaceful dreams. He rocked with the music of the saw that brought a peaceful smile to his sleep. He yawned and stretched and called with closed eyes for "Abba," a child's word for "Daddy." It was a simple sound for little lips to form. Jesus was growing, and loved learning to talk with his father. They made words a game they played everyday. They played with the sounds of words, and rhymes, and twisted the meanings into silly jokes. Words were a wonderful game.

Once he knew he was safe and his father was in the room, he smiled and re-curled into his dreams. Joseph watched his son sleeping peacefully near the fire. *"He will be a great man someday, the Messiah, this little one. He will free us from the Romans. Hard to imagine how he will do it"*. For now he was just a child learning to talk, learning how to do simple things to help his father. He was the most intelligent child Joseph had ever seen, and the best, there wasn't any bad in this child at all. *"He really is God's Son. I forget in the normalness of every day."*

Joseph was up to his responsibility. Not only did he do everything he could to keep his family safe and provided for, he knew he was responsible for teaching him everything he needed to learn here on earth. He taught him what it meant to be a man, to be a loving son, to love the world and all the magnificent things in it. He taught him to love song, and humor, and craftsmanship. He showed him by his example how a loving husband treats his wife and son. He taught him about God, and the word of God that filled their lives. He sat on his father's lap in the synagogue and swayed with him to the rhythms of the chanted words, the song of God's voice. Sometimes Joseph felt self-conscious teaching him the words that, if all this were true, came from him originally. *Forgotten, by choice in the great emptying he allowed so he could be like us, a man without all knowledge and all power. He was just a baby. I don't know what I expected, but after angels and a virgin birth, and wise men and prophets in the*

Temple ... to see my son sleeping by the fire next to his puppy... I thought it would be different somehow.

Jesus opened his eyes and smiled at his father. He rose, sucking his thumb, dragging his blanket through the sawdust. He wanted a hug.

T he song of the saw sliced through a log and the cut piece fell into the sawdust with a soft thud. "Come here, Jesus, want to show you something." Joseph rubbed the cross-section of the tree with sandstone to make it smooth as they talked about growing trees.

"Look at the rings that make up this tree." Joseph brushed the sawdust off then rubbed oil into the cut piece of wood to make the rings stand out more clearly.

"Let's take a trip through time together." Joseph counted the rings back through the years.

"Here's the year you were born." He pointed at a wide ring.

Jesus asked, "Why is that year so wide, when some are smaller?" Joseph closed his eyes, remembering. "The year before you were born and that first year of your life were both good years for the trees. There was a lot of rain and sunshine --both the foods that trees eat to grow fast and strong. Before that there had been a lot of bad years, a long drought that made these narrow rings you can see here. Caleb sniffed the wood, confused. There was no food here. *What's all the fuss about?* He thought, and settled back down with an awkward thump and a disappointed sigh.

Joseph continued, "But let's go farther back, deeper into this tree." Joseph counted out loud sixteen years, smiling as he pointed them out. "This is the year your mother was born, a very good year as you can see."

"Show me the year you were born, Abba." Jesus was rubbing the wood, feeling the ridges of the rings. "Here, just a few more rings inside, this one. This was my first year on earth. It must have been a drier year."

"How about your father, Abba, where is his ring?" Jesus stared at the concentric circles going back in time.

Joseph thought a moment and then counted much farther back into the heart of the tree. "Here it is, this one, and your Grandmother's ring is here, just back toward mine four rings."

"So this tree is just a little older than they are?" Jesus hoped he understood what his father was teaching him.

"That's right, just one, two, three, four …six… eight … ten … eleven years older than my father."

"That's a long, long time. Look at all the rings!" Jesus whistled. "Show me where donkey's ring is, Abba."

Joseph closed his eyes for a few seconds, counting in his memory. "No, Jesus, you show me. I'll take you part way there and then you count out the last three. Here is the place for you to start sixteen years ago. Now, you count the rings back three more years and show me when he was born."

Jesus was very proud to count three rings and figure out for himself when the donkey was born. It was a very big thing to do. Then he asked his Abba, "Why are there rings?"

Joseph answered, "When spring comes with the rain and sun and the tree grows fast and there is this wide space, then when it gets dry and then winter comes and the tree slows and sleeps there is this darker one."

The sound of the rain outside stopped suddenly, and Jesus went to the doorway. "I love the smell of rain on the mud. It makes me feel good."

The birds celebrated in song for this time when the worms would rise up to make their lunch-hunting easier. Jesus giggled and played in the puddles, splashing his feet and spinning with his arms outstretched. Caleb splashed with him, and barked. Jesus cried out "I'm having f…u…n!" with the word fun held long and bounced in his mouth as he spun and spun in the gentle light after the rain. Then he stopped and pointed at the sky.

"What is that? It's pretty, Abba. It glows. Colors."

"That's a rainbow, son. Sometimes after a rain we are blessed with one. Like the one Noah saw."

Jesus said, "I've never seen one of those before."

Mary's time had come, but this time they were safe at home, with her mother and her sister to help her. Joseph was relieved, she had done well before in difficult circumstances, and for once he wasn't responsible for everything. Grateful and relieved when the women took charge, he took Jesus for a walk; he had things to say that Jesus needed to hear.

"You're going to have a little brother or sister soon. You'll have someone to play with all the time. You know you'll always be my big boy, and the big brother."

Jesus squeezed his hand, "My brother will be fun to play with, I know that."

Joseph asked him, "What if it's a little sister?"

"I know he is a brother, I can feel him." Joseph saw the certainty in his eyes and realized he knew.

"You know when you have a brother it will mean we have more of us to love each other in our family." Joseph stopped and pointed. "Look at this tree, Jesus, and tell me what you see."

"It is tall and straight and it's the kind that is green all year. It smells good, like incense. And I know it makes my hands sticky with the sap and it is hard to get them clean."

"That's right. All trees have a use. All the straight trees and the crooked trees have their place. The differences of the trees give us different things we can make. Sometimes we need straight poles and sometimes something else. Some woods are hard and some are not so strong."

"Like the oak and the terebinth that are strong and the pine and willow that are soft and easy to work?"

"Yes Jesus, that's right. You are learning to be a good carpenter. Every tree, everything in God's creation has its perfect place and use. And you are a big help to me with the wood. You know how to sand and polish really well."

The sun was growing low and golden, Joseph raised his son up in his arms and carried him home; he was tired at last.

In the middle of the night James was born, named for Joseph's friend. He would be Jesus' devoted brother and best friend. He had been right, of course. At his birth cry, Jesus awoke, and came to see his brother in his mother's arms. He kissed him, and felt his tiny fingers, and wondered at the miracle of life. *So this is how a person starts.* Jesus thought as he watched this new life take his first look at the world.

Joseph held Jesus, and talked with him about all the fun he would have playing with his little brother, then took him back to his bed and sang to him until he fell asleep. Then Joseph sat with Mary, and kissed her.

Mary gestured toward Jesus and said, "He loves his little brother. They look good together."

Joseph smoothed her hair back from her face. "Thank you, dear, he's beautiful, and so are you."

Mary whispered to Joseph. "I have to tell you, husband, this was a lot easier here in bed than on a donkey ride to a stable far from home. I'm glad I was younger then."

James was growing sleepy, so Joseph held his new son, rocking him until the tiny baby felt like he grew much heavier as he fell asleep. Joseph sang a new song for this son that shared his best friend's name.

The Song of James and James

J ames cradled his namesake in his arms. He was good with numbers, but awkward with a baby. He held him like he was a very large and fragile egg. He acted like he was terrified that he would drop him. James was proud of the great honor, and delighted for his friend who finally had a son of his own blood. He knew Joseph wouldn't love Jesus any less, he was his firstborn, and they were very close. Jesus was the child Joseph experienced everything with first. First steps, first words, first baby vomit in his beard. First of everything except the knowing that this one had come from him, and of the physical love he shared with Mary. And he had missed the first four months of Mary's pregnancy with Jesus. But that time there had been that awful time of doubt. That horrible time when his love for Mary and his disbelief of what she had said had pulled him apart until he knew.

This baby grew in their love and closeness from the start. There was no separation from their family and friends, no army chasing them. And Joseph had the opportunity to choose a name to honor his best friend. No angel appeared to announce a name this time. Mary gave her husband the greatest gift a woman can. It gave her a joy she had never imagined.

James babbled strange baby-talk sounds to little James. Joseph smirked until Mary poked him in the ribs. Miriam hovered close, with one hand on big James's shoulder, the other playing with baby James's toes. James sang. He sang along with the baby's burbles. He sang with his cries. He calmed him like he had watched Joseph calm Jesus. His terrible voice sang a delightfully stupid song. James and Miriam knew. In three months they would be married.

Silly Song

Joseph sang even more as he worked now. But at this moment he was distracted. Jesus held the plank as his father sawed it to fit. When they placed it in position, Jesus realized it was cut too short, and told his father. Joseph sighed and said, "Thank goodness! I can always glue another piece on, but I don't know what I would do if I had cut it too long!" Jesus looked puzzled, and then when his father started to laugh, joined him.

They spent the rest of the morning working while singing the silliest songs that could be made up by a new father and a three year old. Mary brought them lunch, and stood outside the door with James in her arms, listening to the songs and jokes. She remembered the first time she stood outside this door. She looked at his baby asleep in her arms, and smiled the smile of the most satisfied woman in the world.

"You are a silly, silly man. But I love you, and I'm grateful you love me." She knew she could always trust him and his humor had helped them through some terrible times.

When they started another song that she knew, she joined in and added her soprano voice. James cuddled up to her full of their silly song. Caleb howled in time. The donkey outside added his voice. They were getting loud. Then Joseph stopped to tell Jesus a story.

"You know, Jesus, when that old donkey of ours was first born, I could pick it up easily, it was so light. Then each day it got a little heavier, but ... each day my muscles got a little stronger as I lifted it. Through the years, he just kept on getting heavier, while I kept getting stronger, until today ... why, I could go out there right now and pick that heavy beast up over my head if I wanted to!"

Mary groaned, "Jooo-seph! Stop it! You are terrible!" Then they all laughed and laughed again as they ate. Jesus kept repeating the joke he had just heard in a three-year-old's versions, the distorted reflection of humor as a child slowly begins to learn the essence and the subtlety. "I can still pick up that tree over there! Ha ha ha!" Then he ran to Mary and grabbed her by the legs and struggled as he said, "I can still pick you up, Amma, ha ha ha!"

It was a wonderful silly day they would remember as long as they lived.

Once the children were asleep, Mary and Joseph sat by the fire. Joseph respected the silence with a whisper. "I wonder what we should expect next from Jesus? Things have been blessedly quiet, with no angels for a long time now."

"I don't know about you, Joseph, but I like it this way." Mary took his hand, absently caressing his scar. It made her feel safe to feel it. As it faded with time, their love grew stronger. She remembered the first day when she practiced her smile before she first used it on him. She knew she could make him love her like she already loved him. The saw just gave her an excuse, besides she cared about him and wanted to take care of his hand. She loved his hands. She loved the way he touched her.

Life was as normal as it would ever be for them now. Sometimes they heard the neighbors sarcastically joke about this *child of God* that was born of a *virgin*, but mostly the details of his birth were forgotten. Even their parents were undecided, only cousin Elizabeth and her husband were sure, of all their relatives. Jesus seemed exactly like a normal child to everyone. But Mary and Joseph knew. It was good to finally be living a hidden normal life. Jesus needed to know what human life was actually like. God had chosen the perfect parents for him. But they were tired. It hadn't been an easy job.

The wise men's gifts had been used up long ago. Joseph earned a living with his work now that James had helped him learn the craft of selling. People treated him the way they had before, for the most part. A few still made fun of them, but everyone thought they were good people, even if some thought they were a little strange.

They *were* a little strange; all this might make someone crazy. But they were as sane as anyone who was touched by God. They thought things would be easier, they thought somehow angels would protect them and him. They thought that people would support them as they raised the Messiah. They thought at least they would get respect, not sneers. It was not God's plan. God didn't use the easy way they imagined. What would be the sense? Why bother at all with coming to Earth if it were not real? Earth is as real as it can get. It is a battleground of body and mind and spirit. It is the place where spirit dances with flesh. It is the place in the universe where angels watch, holding their breath.

"I love you, Mary," Joseph said, and kissed his wife. "I love you, too." she said, and whispered her secret name for him in his ear. It made him smile, it always did.

Obbligato

Mary was curled up next to Joseph, enjoying his warmth in this peaceful night. The only light was a half-moon through the window. Everyone was sound asleep, deep in dreams. The only sound was a soft creek as the madman opened the door to slip into the house, heading for Jesus.

He was standing over the boy's bed, reaching his hands down to choke him when he heard a soft growl behind him. Before he could even turn around, Caleb's teeth were already deeply into his leg. He screamed, and then fell to the ground where Caleb released him long enough to sink his teeth into his arm. And then he shook him, tearing deeply into his flesh, his loud growls drowned out by the screams.

Joseph was above them now, ready to jump in, but it was clear that Caleb had the situation under control. So Joseph lifted Jesus, to make sure he was not harmed. Jesus stared at the screaming man in the soft moonlight and saw his gentle Caleb shaking him. "Abba, what's going on?" Mary brought a lamp and set it on the table. The flickering light let them recognize the madman. Joseph put his son in Mary's arms as she took in the scene. She hugged him tightly and whispered, "Shhhh ... everything is all right. We'll talk about it later."

Joseph had dropped to one knee and patted Caleb's back. "Good boy, good boy. You can let him go now. I have him. Good boy, Caleb." He kept patting his back until he finally let go. The man was covered with blood from his arm and his leg. His screaming turned to cursing and his usual claims of divinity. Joseph threatened to let the dog loose again if he didn't shut up. He did. He wasn't *that* mad.

Silence returned to the home. Joseph pulled the man up, and dragged him to the door by his hair. Caleb growled and convinced him it was time to leave. He wasn't insane enough to run. He limped away, clutching his bleeding arm. Joseph kneeled and rubbed Caleb's head, then took him in his arms as he thanked him for protecting them. Caleb wagged his tail, but still growled and kept his eyes on the threat as he disappeared.

Jesus asked, "Why did that man want to hurt me, Abba?"

Joseph looked at Mary, and they both waited for the other to say something. But neither had an answer they thought he was ready to hear.

But Caleb knew what to do. He walked to Jesus and licked his face and received his well-deserved hug.

He was gone. There was no warning. Jacob was singing in the workshop one day and that night he died in his sleep. Early in the morning Joseph was already at work with Jesus and James when his mother, Ruth, came from the house next door crying. He knew immediately what had happened, but held her as she talked. He wanted Jesus and James to hear what she had to say and he needed to prepare himself.

"When I woke he was next to me with a relaxed look on his face, almost a smile, but when I touched him he was cold, not hot like he always has been. I tried to wake him, but he was gone. Gone peacefully, in his sleep. I didn't get to say goodbye. Now I am alone. He's always been there since I was a girl."

Joseph hugged his mother as she cried more deeply. He looked over her shoulder to Jesus and James who both stood with their arms hanging down, not knowing what to do. He silently gestured to them to join him holding his mother. One hugged from either side.

"My good little grandchildren, my big boys, how he loved you." The past tense coming out of her mouth triggered a new wave of crying for all of them to join in.

Joseph had a moment for his own grief. His father had always been there in his life, at home and working in the shop. Everything he knew about being a man and a craftsman came from him and his grandfather. While embracing, through his tears, Joseph surveyed the workshop and the table his father was working on yesterday afternoon. All that it needed to be complete was sanding and the finish. He could still hear the whisper of his father working with the plane yesterday. The gentle sound like a breeze as the fine curls of wood spiraled out. Those last curls were still on the floor below the table just where they fell – where his hand had brushed them off the surface of the table.

Joseph said his goodbye then before he went next door to do the duty of a son for his dead father. He wanted to remember him as he last saw him yesterday. He looked around at all the tools they shared, the tools his father and his grandfather had made. Then he looked at Jesus and James and knew these tools would be used with the skills he had passed on already. *Goodbye, my Abba, Shalom.*

Another Joseph Song

Mary knew she was carrying another boy. This baby's personality was quiet and strong inside her. Mary would give her husband a gift beyond all gifts. This one they would name after him, to carry on his name. He certainly deserved it, if anyone ever did. *I hope you'll be exactly like your father - this world could use another generation with that gift.* And Joseph needed new life in the family to fill the void from his father's death.

He came quietly into the world with barely a cry. He just gulped for air and started living without wanting to disturb anyone. He looked around to gather in the room. His brothers held him, kissed him on the forehead, and welcomed him to the family.

His father wrapped him in a blanket to keep him warm outside as he showed him the stars. He whispered a song of the mysteries that waited. Joseph and his three sons stared into the sky as the women tended Mary. Joseph could see the stars reflected in his three sons' eyes. The winter stars, the stars that had more room to roam.

Two seasons passed as the boys grew. Mealtimes overflowed with love and laughter as the boys competed for the silliest song. Mary shook her head and sighed. "Joseph, look what you have started." There were songs about the bread, songs about the fruit, songs about the fish who used to swim, and soon would again in their bellies. Joseph was worse than the kids.

Mary stopped eating and leaned back to enjoy the larger meal. Little Joseph was grinning as he tried to sing along with his big brothers. His face was smeared with food from ear to ear. Food was on his forehead and on his feet, yet somehow some found its way into his mouth.

Joseph hooked a finger full of food from his son's face and brought it to his lips. He smacked his lips and said it tasted sweeter now with little Joseph's sweetness added. Mary groaned with Jesus and James. The little guy scraped his cheek and tasted it to see if his father was right. He looked puzzled as everyone laughed. Joseph picked him up and hugged him and kissed his slimy face. Then he carried him with his outstretched arms, and aimed for Mary. He rubbed his messy face all over hers as everybody laughed.

Then Jesus put a dab of food on his nose, and James spread a bit on his forehead. Joseph and Mary had plenty on them already, and little Joseph was already a mess. There was a knock on the door from a neighbor come to borrow some oil. She looked at all the faces covered with food, but didn't say a word. Everyone kept quiet as Mary got the oil. It was an awkward silence with the muffled sound of stifled laughter while everyone pretended seriousness.

As soon as she left and the door was closed, the room erupted with laughter. Everyone knew Joseph's family was a little strange, but now one more story would spread from this night with their faces covered with food, playing like babies. They loved life, and this kind of fun was the best part of it.

Caleb has been gone all day, now it's becoming dark. This isn't like him." Joseph stood at the door looking and calling him again. "Mary, he always stays close to home so he can protect his family. Something is wrong." Joseph lit a lantern to search. He was afraid a soldier had become annoyed and pushed his spear through him. Caleb barked when they clanked past with their armor's unnatural sounds disturbing the day. Joseph always tried to stifle his barks. He was afraid what might have happened when he wasn't around to hold his mouth closed and protect him from himself.

Joseph searched the alleys and everywhere a dog might enjoy. Dogs live in their noses so Joseph used his to search for the most exotic odors he could find, no matter how foul to his human nose. There was no sign of him. He hated to go home and tell the children he couldn't find Caleb, but it was better than bringing his lifeless body back. He didn't want to fill his home with tears. It seemed empty already without the dog who was always there.

Then he heard a frightening song of wildness. It was a howling like their cousins the wolves made on lonely nights. A pack of wild dogs was howling to the full moon rising in the east. It was a howl of gratitude and praise to the hunter's light that they would use this night. A pack of hungry wild dogs is as dangerous as a pack of wolves to a man alone. But Joseph thought he heard Caleb's voice among the pack. He wished he had brought a staff with him, or an axe. All he had was his light. *If I go back, the pack will move on and I might never see Caleb again.* He loved his dog.

Caleb was intoxicated by the connection with his genetic family. He was a dog and running with his pack seemed normal. And exciting. He had smelled the kill now and the thrill of running down wild animals with the teamwork of the pack. A pack could use strategy to run down even a faster prey. It made him feel powerful. It made him feel smart. The rising full moon filled him with memories older than himself. *I've never felt so alive, with my pack. I can run all day and all night and go wherever I want. And nobody can tell me what to do.* He howled a different howl than he had ever heard come out of himself before. It gave him a shiver. It felt good.

Joseph headed into the wilderness after them.

The pack was on the scent of something larger. Caleb was excited. They were sniffing now, making sense of the complex trail. It was not clear which way to go, since the prey had crossed back and forth and spent time in this area. Caleb was salivating and yelping with the others. *This is what my nose is for! It's been wasted until now.* Caleb howled and was answered by the pack that had been strangers this morning. He was not the leader, of course, but had been accepted after they had settled by wrestling for position. He would follow this dog who was strong and wise in the ways of the wild. Old memories awoke, memories past dogs had left in his blood. But now some noise was disturbing the pack, something was threatening them. Something was pulling his mind away from his celebration. It was ... his human name. He was angry to be pulled from this good place in his mind. And the pack had turned and was growling at a man.

Joseph called to Caleb, and it threatened the pack. Every eye was on him, a lone figure far from the village. They started toward him; the pack splitting so some could circle around from behind. Caleb moved with the pack, facing this threat to them. Facing this threat that could be prey. *Why are you doing this?* He thought. *Why are you chasing my pack?* Caleb was angry that Joseph had put him in this dilemma. But his other family, his other pack came back to his mind. But he loved what he was discovering today. He loved the wildness of it.

The growls had changed to angry barks and the pack moved closer to Joseph, circling him. Joseph was afraid, but he called out again to Caleb. "Caleb, come home. We miss you!" This yell triggered the dogs to bark angrily and start to run at the man. Caleb ran faster and got to Joseph first and turned and growled against his pack, defending him. The pack stopped. Slowly the leader of the pack walked up to Caleb and faced him with a snarl. His teeth were bared halfway back into his jaw. Caleb knew this dog alone could kill him in a fight. It had been established already. But he stood his ground and growled. The bigger dog stopped. He looked in Caleb's eye and saw the pack-love fade into a disappointing new wildness that was other. The dog turned and the pack ran off, gone forever. Caleb would never be welcome again. He had chosen another pack.

Play Song

Joseph's shop was crowded with children, more than ever. His three sons had many friends to play with. Silly songs and children's laughter filled the air. A large box of wooden toys was in the corner, and a smaller box of flutes and drums. Nazareth was filled with children's songs again.

Moshe started a song. Jesus played a flute. James and Daniel banged a drum. Martha and Leah played more flutes. Rebecca clapped her hands. Susanna sang with her beautiful voice. Joseph set the rhythm with the saw, a rhythm that lurched with the children's disconnected pace. Caleb howled in time. It was awful, and wonderful.

Joseph gave up with his saw and focused his full attention on their song. He reminded the children of the verses to the song he had made for each of them, and led them all in turn. They struggled with their instruments, but kept better time as they sang.

There were two new children who didn't have a song yet, and Joseph made sure there was a verse for each before they left. Every perfect child was known. Each song was a verse of the larger song of a generation of Nazareth. Joseph knew how much this meant to them. And how much this meant to him.

Jesus watched his father care for each of them and he learned how a man shows love. He saw how caring eyes could try to understand the secrets of each little dreamer's dream. Jesus never would forget that day and what he learned. He saw his father gathering the shy and making them feel whole. He saw a sad child brighten, a sickly child get stronger, and a troubled child find peace - each in a song built just for him. He saw the innocent power of children to build a kingdom of hope on earth.

The family was gathered around dinner when a strange wailing started outside the front door. It was a sound that twisted like a serpent in a beautiful turning note that changed without the corners of stopping places. It just went on and on.

Joseph shouted as he jumped up. "Wadji!" All the children looked to each other for an answer, then to their smiling mother who was right behind Joseph on the way to the door.

A smiling dark-skinned man with a flute leaned against the doorpost playing this beautiful melody and smiling with his eyes. Wadji and Marba hugged Joseph and Mary and they held up their little girl. Their boy was with them and jumping up to hug Mary, too.

Jesus and the other children were up now trying to understand who these strange-sounding people were. Wadji kneeled down and hugged Jesus. "You've grown into a handsome little man. We've missed you all."

Joseph was holding their little boy he hadn't seen for years. "What brings you to Nazareth, Wadji, and how did you find us?"

"It is not hard to find the best carpenter in a village, all you have to do is ask. Once we were in Nazareth, it was easy. And *what brings us here* is you. I think you left some of your dreaming skills with me. You keep coming to me in my dreams, and your boy there, so we just had to come to see you."

Mary broke in, "Let's talk about that later, come sit down after your journey and have something to eat."

Later that night after the other children were all asleep, Jesus got up and secretly watched the adults from the shadows. They were happy and laughing until Joseph asked about the dreams. Then Wadji grew quiet and everyone became serious. Jesus couldn't hear what they were saying except something about Wadji loving Joseph's God and somehow Jesus was part of it.

Jesus wondered what he could possibly mean.

It was a week of song and happiness until they left to go home to Egypt. When Wadji was leaving, he held Jesus in his arms and told him he would see him again some day, he was sure of that.

The family was growing. Mary's belly was huge again. She loved being pregnant. She loved the way it made her feel, except toward the end. Her three sons were anxious to have this mystery of life enter again. They wondered if they would have another brother to play with. Or maybe a sister would join their family. Each birth was a little easier for Mary, she was getting used to this. She loved babies, and she loved giving the man she loved this gift that brought him so much joy. Mary knew this would be another son, but with some of the gentleness of a woman in him, a sensitive soul. She could feel his personality growing, almost talking with her. This one didn't kick, he moved slowly around in her, gently. She would name him after her uncle who had been so kind to her as a child.

Joseph had asked Jesus to occupy his brothers in his shop making toys for the little one who was coming. They all worked happily, each in whatever way he could, depending on his age. They finished precious gifts they would bring like three wise men to this new baby. Jesus, James, and Joseph.

Joseph was too young to do anything but rub the wax awkwardly into a shine. He put his heart into it, though. He wanted to be like his big brothers and his father. One more son would join them today. Mary's five boys. Four children and Joseph. She lived in a house of men. It wasn't easy for her, but she had been her father's favorite little girl, and she understood men.

Time passed as the children grew and Joseph and Mary's love started another life growing in her. A different kind of baby to join the family.

A Daughter's Song

Mary had already borne four sons. More years had passed and now their fifth child was coming tonight. They were all good boys, Jesus, James, Joseph and Judas. They loved each other and were the best of friends. Joseph wondered what tonight's child would be like. Healthy like the others, he prayed. This child was smaller. Mary had been huge with all the others, but this one felt different. The birth went quickly, and Joseph was surprised with a daughter.

He loved his boys, but this little girl who looked so much like her mother touched his heart in a different way. She was pink and tiny but filled the room with her healthy cry. She would be a singer, he was sure. She was still wet from birth as he sang his first new song to her. Mary laughed at the bliss she saw on her husband's face. He wanted her to be called Mary, like her mother. He hoped she would be exactly like her, he said. Mary wanted to name her after her friend, so this first daughter was the Miriam form of the name.

Joseph loved his little girl. Mary thought she would never get to hold her daughter if she weren't the only one who could nurse her. Joseph held his wife in his arms as she nursed Miriam, and sang a new lullaby to them both.

Song of the Two-Man Saw

Joseph needed to select and cut down two trees for his future work. His seasoned wood supply was dwindling. Jesus loved these trips with his father now that he was old enough. There were two trees they needed to find on this trip. One tall and straight, but the other tree needed to be a gnarled and twisted survivor. They journeyed up into the hills with the donkey cart and saws and axes. Joseph found a tall tree that would do well. It was time to show his son the song of the two-man saw.

It took Jesus some time to get the rhythm, but soon they sang and moved the saw like two dancing to music, When two move together at the proper speed, the saw slides through the wood easily. But out of time, it bucks and bends and kinks. It was like learning to dance with a partner. Jesus loved this dance, he felt it throughout his body, it pushed his muscles to their limit, it made him feel like a man. He felt like his father's partner for the first time, not like a child doing a child's work.

Joseph watched his eyes and knew what he was thinking. He was as proud of his son as he had been on the day when he watched Jesus stand alone the first time. Joseph started a new song, praising him, as he was becoming a man. It took them most of the day to fell the tree and cut it to the lengths they needed. They rested and ate a meal as they watched hawks fly overhead.

Then Joseph asked his son to look for a smaller tree that could stand a lot of strain, one that had proved itself already in its life. Jesus searched the hills with his eyes until he saw one that might do. It was high up in a rugged spot where the wind had twisted it for many decades. Jesus said he would go up alone and bring it back down while his father rested. He took a handsaw and rope and climbed like a goat up the cliff. Caleb followed him as far as he could, then waited at the bottom of the cliff for him to return. Eventually he rested on the ground, but his eyes never left him.

His father watched him too, with a mixture of concern and pride. This was a precious gift his son was giving him. He looked forward to telling Mary every detail of this day. Jesus struggled and sweated for hours to finish the job and drag the small tree down. It was a perfect choice. He had a feel for the character of the wood. He had a feel for people, too.

154

Joseph caressed the familiar comfort of the axe in his hand. His grandfather had made it and passed it on to Joseph's father. Now it was in his hands. *Soon Jesus will own this family axe and pass it on to his son, and his son until time wears it away.* Joseph tried to feel the unborn generations touching this tool that had been so much a part of his life. He tried, but he couldn't feel them, and it puzzled him. He just felt yesterday and today in the wood. He wanted his grandfather's axe to be important for generations more. This axe was important, it was history, and it was future.

Jesus lowered the tree down the cliff, then climbed down after it with the saw tied to his back. His bright eyes showed the pride he felt in this gift that proved himself a man.

After Joseph examined the tree his son had brought him, he pointed out all the good features of his choice. He showed Jesus how perfect it was for his needs. Then they performed the ritual they always did when they harvested trees. Joseph handed Jesus the bag that was full of seeds.

"Choose three, as usual, for every tree we harvested. Make sure there is at least one seed of the same kind of both trees we took." Joseph smiled at his son as he spoke.

"Why are planting these seeds, Abba? It will take fifty years for these acorns to grow into trees large enough to harvest, and almost as long for this cedar?" Jesus knew the answer, he had heard his father tell the reason many times. But he wanted to hear it again this day, this first day he felt full partner with his father in their work. This first day he understood from sweat. Sweat equal to his father in their work. The first time he felt what the planting meant in time. The first day he could imagine his own grandchildren, and what this planting would mean for them. *My descendants will hear stories of the great craftsman, Jesus. They will see my work in their homes as they grow up.*

"You know, son. These trees are for the generations after us, like the trees we harvest were planted by my grandfather and those of his generation. And by those who planted long before they were born. We are part of the legacy."

They carefully chose locations where the seeds would have the best chance of survival. They planted them tenderly and shared the precious water on this hot day. They planted with a prayer for each, and marked the spots so they could return to water them until they were strong enough to survive on their own. Joseph put his arm around his son as they celebrated a fine day's work.

The sun had set before they started home, but a full moon lit their way. They sang the funniest songs they knew as two hard -working men on their way back from a rewarding day's labor. Jesus babbled excitedly, and when they arrived home, he told his mother all about their day. Joseph praised him, and told her everything he had done so well. The storytellers entertained her, warmed her mother's soul.

Jesus almost fell asleep at the dinner table. When he had gone to bed, and his little brothers, too, Joseph and Mary sat up and talked about their boy well into the night. He would be a great leader, they knew. He would lead with gentleness and strength. They hoped he'd find a way of peace. They couldn't imagine their boy leading an army to kill the Romans - they knew he'd find another way.

W-w-what are y-you making there? I c-can't t-tell w-w-what that is f-for."

James winked at Joseph from behind Agabus and said, "Joseph is making a frangulus."

"W-w-what's a f-frang-frangulus? I've never heard of one."

"Oh, it's something the Romans prize; it's something only the most elite Romans even know about. It's a secret among only the most sophisticated." James affected his most serious expression. Joseph gave his friend half a scowl, half a grin.

"W-what's it do?" Agabus asked, clearly interested in this exotic item in front of him. He took it and touched it gently as he turned it over and over for close inspection, handling it as if it were made of fragile gold. James immediately took it back to place it carefully on top of some soft cloth so it would not be scratched. Agabus opened his pouched and started filing his nails frantically.

"That's the heck of it. We don't even know. Joseph just got some secret plans from a Roman and he is following them."

"H-how mu-much w-wo-would you ch-charge me to make one f-for me?"

"Oh, we couldn't do that! They are rare and expensive and if the Roman who ordered this and loaned us the secret plans were to find out we would all be in trouble." James was putting out quite a performance. Joseph by now had to sit down, appalled and amused.

"P-please! I h-have to have one! I p-promise I will not tell anyone w-where I got it! I'll pay you anything for it!"

"Well … if you promise to hide it and not let anyone else see it for a year or more … maybe it would be safe. But you have to promise or we all could get into a lot of trouble." James stroked his beard and slipped his hand over his mouth to avoid giving his smile away.

" I p-promise I will not t-tell f-for *t-two* years, you have m-my w-w-word."

"Well, in that case ... for you ... but it will cost you. Hmmm how about half what the Roman is paying for it, two hundred drachmae?" James was deeply into merchant mode and pushing the sale as far as he could.

"T-that's a l-lot of m-money."

"You're right, this isn't something for you, it is pretty special."

"N-no! I'll t-take it – just g-give me a d-day to get the m-mon-money!"

Joseph was laughing out loud by now. But he couldn't stand to see Agabus being taken advantage of so badly. But he enjoyed the laugh James brought him. Joseph rose and walked to pick up the piece of wood. "Agabus, my dear friend, you mean a lot to me, and I would be honored if you took this as personal gift from me with no charge."

Agabus was shocked and speechless at the valuable gift. His eyes were as big as banquet plates.

James was fuming, "Joseph, do you know what you just did? That is a priceless – uh – *fragliss* and you and Mary could have used that money! That is an extravagant gift from someone who needs money!"

"I guess I never will be a businessman like you, James. But look at the joy I brought to my friend. I can make another to sell, but it would be hard to do anything else to bring him such happiness. It was worth it."

James shook his finger at Agabus and said with frustrated anger, "Just make sure you don't show it to any Romans, or we could be in a lot of trouble. I hope you know what you have there."

"I k-know. Thank you Joseph, I p-promise I w-will lock it up and not show anyone for t-two y-years." He wrapped the secret piece of wood under his cloak and rushed out the door.

James and Joseph shared some wine and laughed, sure that within the hour some confused Roman would be shown the priceless frangulus by a bragging Agabus.

Curls of paper-thin wood wound tightly above the plane as Jesus smoothed the board they had cut that morning. Joseph sharpened tools and enjoyed the quiet music of the plane. It was a whisper of the wood. A little like the noise a serpent makes as he tests the air with his tongue. A long slow softness of a sound. It was gentle work with calm control. The fact that Jesus had already mastered this fine touch showed his father he had become a craftsman worthy of his tools.

"The grain is beautiful in this oak, Abba. I can hardly wait to see it when we put the finish on. Look where a branch was broken, then grown over. It looks like clouds in the winter, all streaming and turning in a flow."

Joseph rose and stood across the board from his son, to see the grain, and watch the work. But mostly to look at his face and the joy the work gave him as he became a man. "You're right, son. It will be a wonderful thing to look at in the table, a frozen sunset to the eye at every meal."

"Something is bothering me, Abba. As much as you and I love trees, why are there places in the holy writings that say some are bad and should be cut down? What do they mean about the sacred groves? What could be bad about a sacred tree? Why were we commanded to cut down those trees? And wasn't Abraham led to the terebinth tree of Moreh at Shechem to be given God's promise of this land for his children forever? You've shown me the descendants of that very tree on our way to Jerusalem. So why were other sacred trees destroyed? What was different about them? And you have taught me to listen to the language trees whisper. I can hear it now, too. Are we doing something bad?"

Joseph felt the smoothness of the wood where Jesus had run the plane. He ran his palm across it to test the flatness, but more to feel the holiness inside the wood. "Feel this, Jesus. Feel the smoothness of your work, and feel the grain that comes through. Then feel deeper. Feel the spirit of the wood. Feel this bit of God in his creation, the spirit of life and beauty. Feel it and listen to it."

Jesus closed his eyes and ran his fingertips across the newly exposed wood. Then he flattened his palm and spread his fingers to know it more. He spread both hands and lowered his head as if listening with one ear, but it was not sound he was listening to. He listened beyond sound into the soul of the wood and his own soul as they met in some new chord he had never felt before. A deeper chord than what he usually felt. It was a harmony as they touched. The Creator and the created both here in this tiny place and time. Everything else disappeared into this moment when they merged ... again. Jesus heard the wood, and it was good. Jesus thought of a word, the letters appeared in his mind. A *bet*, and a *resh*, and an *aleph*, and a *shin*, and a *yod*, and a *tav*. The word that came from nothing into the creation of the world. He felt how this tree under his hands had come from that word. And his body, and Joseph, and the donkey, and his mother's love, and clouds and rain and the colors of the rainbow. The wood remembered and so did he. It was the whisper of light remembered.

Joseph felt the hair on his arm stand up. He knew he was in the presence of something holy. Jesus didn't speak a word, but his father could feel it. They were as close as a father and son had ever been. He could feel what Jesus was feeling, although he could never understand, even though he was the one who had led him to this place he couldn't follow. He waited for a long moment, then his love could not be held back any longer and he reached across the wood and held his son and kissed his forehead. Jesus spoke with his eyes still closed.

"You're right. They know. They live longer than us and listen patiently. They are not bothered with traveling. They know what light means when it flows into them and forms the tree from water and air and soil. They know what it means to watch men be born and die and sons be born and die and still they watch. They know what it is to breathe the seasons and the years and write them in their rings. They know what it is to be. Just be. It is easier for them to know what God meant when He said His name is *I am*."

Jesus opened his eyes and looked into his father's as he continued, "They know they are not God, they are just a part of him. Each a story written from the words he spoke in the breath of life. All of us are. They just see more slowly and more clearly than our distracted view. I see that now. You taught me how to listen, Abba. You showed me how to hear the whispers."

Joseph felt the wood again himself, felt the smoothness, felt the deeper peace from inside the wood, inside himself. But he knew his son had felt much more. He was not jealous, he was glad. He remembered the angels and the Magi and knew it was all coming to be as Jesus grew into a man.

"But, Abba, I don't understand what could have been wrong so that God told us to cut the sacred groves down."

Joseph answered, "There is nothing wrong with the wood. Every sacrifice is laid upon wood. Without the wood there would be no sacrifice. The offering would just rot instead of being burned and raised to the heavens. It is the fuel that makes the fire that carries the prayer." Both men caressed the wood under their hands with reverence. Joseph continued, "Anything can be used wrongly, and in a way that takes us away from God in arrogance. Just counting the people with a census was enough of a sin for David that thousands had to die. Compared to adultery and murder it seems like no sin to us. But there is something deeper we need to understand. It was a way David was trying to measure his strength, when he had just been shown that he had none. He forgot, and thousands died. Then he remembered. Remembered like a tree hit by lightning."

Jesus stood upright and stretched. "Will you walk with me so we can see some standing trees? I want to see them with their green leaves in the wind. I want to see them with these new eyes and ... well, I don't know. I guess I'll know when I listen to them. But I want to leave this building and be in their world now. And I still don't know what was so bad about the groves."

"Men worshipped there. Not our God, but others. They worshipped the trees. Not the God of the trees. They got lost in the things they could see, and they carved wood into idols that looked like little men that they called their gods. And sometimes they did evil things in those groves with the excuse that it was for their gods. They hurt each other and sometimes killed men in those places. Sometimes they just forgot their wives and had drunken passion passing one woman to another. They forgot all about love. That is always the biggest sin. Forgetting love." Joseph wrapped his cloak around himself as they went through the door.

Walking through the streets of Nazareth, Joseph continued his explanation. "But some I'm sure sensed God in the trees, and reached to him with pure hearts. They could hear his whisper just like us. That is where Abraham was when he first heard God tell him he was home. Under a terebinth tree just south of here. Under those wide spreading branches that gave welcome shelter from the sun. He heard God's voice there, and I am sure many others have."

They walked in silence until they found a lonely tree that had stood mute witness through a century, waiting. They stood with eyes closed and listened to the wind in the green words that whispered God's name above them.

W e need to tell him, Mary. He is eleven, and he needs to know." Joseph and Mary watched Jesus sleeping early this evening.

"And how do we tell him … what, exactly, Joseph? What do we know for sure that we can tell him? I thought things would be different, that somehow this would never have come up, that he would know himself without us having to say anything."

"Mary, I don't know. I don't know anything for sure. He seems so … normal. I don't know what I expected, but not for him to seem so much a normal human child. He gets sick, he cuts himself and bleeds… he makes mistakes. He makes *mistakes*, Mary, not maliciously, but he is a kid. That is the thing that is different, though. He is so good. He never tries to hurt anyone, and that is not normal for a child. He gets frustrated and mutters, but he always still loves people, even the kids that make fun of him and taunt him. And they have been cruel sometimes."

"I hate it when they call him a bastard, and taunt him about angels. We never have explained this to him. How could we? I know it hurts him and he wonders why he is singled out." Mary shook her head.

Joseph waited a moment. "We have to. We have to explain it all to him as best we can. We have waited far too long. His questions demand a real answer. Whatever way we can."

"What do we tell the other children? How do we explain this to them? Family life is difficult enough now. Will they understand? Or are we just crazy?"

"James has an idea already, I think. They are best friends and he knows Jesus better than anyone. They are inseparable. He has asked me why Jesus is always so good. It makes him feel inadequate. James is a good boy, but Jesus is a hard comparison."

They had recently returned from the Passover in Jerusalem, and Jesus was asking questions. They didn't know how to tell him; up until now they wanted him live as normal a life as possible. People could be cruel, and they wanted to save him from as much of that as they could. They had raised him just like his brothers James and Joseph and Judas, and his sister. As far as Jesus knew, Joseph was his father. Joseph *was* his father in almost every sense.

"If he is to fulfill his destiny, he needs to know the truth. I don't know how he will become King, but he is supposed lead his people into freedom. The Romans won't like that. But, I guess God will be able to work things out. Look at the way our people were be freed from the Egyptians. Or a the way little boy took down a giant with a slingshot. It is impossible to see the way God will make his plans work. We just have to have faith and do our best to help prepare him, Mary. We need to teach him all a leader needs to know - compassion, patience, fairness and strength."

"And love, Joseph. Don't forget love."

Joseph hugged his wife, "I think he has learned from watching us all he needs to know of love." Then he pulled back and looked into Mary's eyes as he held her hands. "But I don't want him to think his mother had done anything wrong, and that is what some children say to him. And they tell him his father is a fool."

"He knows us, Joseph. All he wonders is why they pick on him to say these things."

...

Two nights later they sent the younger children to spend the night with their grandparents so they could be alone with Jesus. He was afraid he had done something wrong. Joseph calmed his mind and then started with the only opening he could imagine. "You know, son, you are different, better behaved than other children, have you ever wondered why?" Jesus replied he hadn't, and so left nothing for his father to build upon. He started again.

"There were some strange things connected with your birth, son. There was a miraculous star, and strangers who traveled far to see the coming baby it heralded. There were angels who appeared and told both of us you were coming. Your mother and I were each individually visited by angels who told us you would be God's son, not mine." Jesus looked confused. "What do you mean, Abba? Aren't we all God's children? Joseph smiled, "Not like you, you were born sinless, not of me but by God. You are the Messiah who will save Israel from the Romans and all evil."

Jesus looked at them. He looked disturbed, confused. Then he smiled, and started to laugh. "That's great, Abba, you always come up with great ones!" He laughed until he realized they weren't laughing with him. He stopped. "You're serious? Amma, you are serious about this, too?" Mary nodded her head. Then they told him the story, all of it they knew. They told him about the angels and the wise men, and the dreams, and the slaughter of the innocents.

Afterwards, Jesus said he wanted to walk outside alone to try to make sense of everything. This was a lot for an eleven-year-old boy to take in. *Could this be true? What does it mean? What am I supposed to do? Or are they all crazy? Wouldn't I know, if I were God? How could God not know who he was? God forgot?*

He walked under the stars, finally he came to a place inside himself where there was no thought. *Why don't I remember anything about this? How can I be God? That is blasphemy! I'm just Jesus, a boy from this little village, far from Jerusalem. If God was going to be born, wouldn't he live in Jerusalem, and not out here in the middle of nowhere? Why would my parents make all this up?* He couldn't think of it any more, so he came inside and held his Amma and his Abba, held onto the one thing he knew was true, their love.

L ife was never the same for the boy. He looked at everything differently now. He tried to imagine what he should do, and what his destiny was. He had no idea how he was to save his people. He was a boy of eleven. He asked his parents a hundred questions. He prayed more. He spent as much time in the synagogue as he could, learning the Law and the Prophets.

He asked questions of the Rabbis, he listened everywhere he was allowed. The old men argued among themselves constantly, he listened to hear every side of each argument. Something inside him was awakening. Something inside told him what was the truth. He asked his mother and grandmothers for their opinions, to get the woman's point of view. He talked with Roman soldiers guarding the town who were lonely men glad to talk about their homes, their gods.

He listened to the wisest men, he listened to the fools, he even listened to the rantings of madmen for a touch of truth. He was beginning to understand. Each section of the Law and Prophets added one thing more, as it became a part of him he was remembering.

Joseph took him to the synagogue as often as he could, and to Jerusalem for Passover each year. But the greatest school for Jesus was still the carpentry shop where he talked about these things with his father and brothers every day. But this year Jesus kept looking forward to Passover and seeing the Temple in Jerusalem again. This time would be different.

Spitting Song

ne beautiful fall day, James and Jesus sat in front of the house eating olives. Clouds floated by, dappling the bowl of Nazareth with shadows that climbed the hills to disappear. Jesus was always the good big brother, so he wanted to teach James a new skill he had learned from Abba one day they worked alone cutting a tree.

"James, watch this." Jesus sucked in a deep breath of air and pulled back his head, then spit an olive pit into the street. "Make sure you line it up on your tongue so it points forward."

James grinned, then squinted as he concentrated on the smooth pit on his tongue. "Here goes." He sprayed spit in an explosion of air but the pit landed just a few feet in front of him. "Dog poop! I'm no good at this."

"That's a good start, James, you just need practice. I've been doing this a long time, and you are just starting. You'll get the hang of it. Try again and just relax and let the wind take it."

James sent the next one twice as far. "Yeah, you're right! Let me do another one and let it fly like a bird." The third one almost hit the pit Jesus had spit. "Did you see that? It went as far as yours! Wow! I like this."

Jesus slapped him on the back. "I knew you'd be good at this – you'll be beating me soon." Here, now let's try to hit this rock as a target." He threw a small stone closer than the last shot.

Twenty shots later, James was the one who finally hit the rock with a satisfying click. He jumped up and danced until he noticed his mother standing behind them with her arms crossed in front of her.

"You two think you are pretty smart, huh?" Mary was pretending to scowl. She leaned down to pick up an olive. A moment later she missed the rock by a mile and her boys teased her unmercifully

"I guess this is the sort of thing that men are good for." Mary chewed a second olive for another try.

Spring flowers meant Passover was coming, so Joseph's family headed to Jerusalem, the way they did every year. Caleb knew when they packed up their cart this way they would be gone for quite a while. He stayed with the neighbors, whose children loved him, but it was not the same without his family. Caleb hated Passover time.

Many of their relatives and others from Nazareth traveled together in a caravan. It was a party for the children who ran from cart to cart to play with friends, even though it was the holiest time of the year. Every time they journeyed, Joseph always remembered the Egypt he came to know when they hid from Herod. He would never forget the Pyramids, the statues and the lush fields around the Nile. When they read about their ancestors' flight, he knew what home they were fleeing. He also knew what it was to flee for your life, like them. And he knew what the slaughter of the innocents in Egypt really meant, like all of Bethlehem now knew.

David's royal city was full of his family grown huge with time. Abraham's children gathered in small groups to hope for a time of peace when a new Moses would lead them to freedom.

After the noise of the crowd at the Temple, the slow trip home was a time of quiet introspection for Joseph and Mary. The caravan had been on the road returning home to Nazareth all day, and was stopped to set camp for the night when they realized that one of their sons was missing. They had assumed he was with someone else in the caravan. Their other boys hadn't seen him since Jerusalem.

They asked every family, but he was not with anyone. Jesus was *missing*. His frantic parents searched with torches calling for him after it became dark to see if he had wandered off the trail. A whole day's journey away from Jerusalem, they hoped he had stayed safely with some friends in the city. There would be no sleep for Mary and Joseph that night, so they left in the darkness and started back to find their son.

They traveled the rest of the night and much of that next day. Then searched with no success. He had been missing for two days already. The whole next day they searched the city, going to the homes of everyone they knew. No one had seen him.

169

The third day they were frantic, they were sure he was dead. Near the end of the day they finally found him. He was in the Temple, sitting with the wisest teachers, asking them serious questions, trying to learn. These learned men were astonished at his intelligence and his perceptive replies. They enjoyed the discussion with this twelve-year-old boy so much that they lost track of time and it never occurred to them to wonder where this child should be. They were embarrassed when two upset parents called for him.

Mary grabbed Jesus and hugged him to herself - hard. Then she held him at arm's length and demanded, "Don't you know how much you have upset and frightened your father and me?

Jesus innocently replied, "Why were you looking everywhere for me? Don't you know I must be in my Father's house?" Mary broke down in tears.

Jesus didn't understand why his parents were so disturbed with him. His mother still cried when she told him how much he had upset his father. James, Joseph, and Judas kept quiet. They had been afraid something had happened to him, too. They were glad he was well, but secretly, they were glad to hear him being upbraided. They had never heard their parents complain about *anything* he had done wrong before. Ever. They were normal kids, and they were tired of constantly being compared to their perfect brother. They thought it was well past his turn.

Mary quoted the commandment about honoring your mother and father to him. Jesus kept silent. Joseph took her hand, and said, "I think I understand what he meant, love." They rode in silence. They would never catch up with the caravan now, so they were traveling alone on a dangerous road.

Joseph started a song to break the tension, and soon they all joined in. They sang about all the fathers in their history, and made up a verse for each. Adam and Noah, and Abraham and Isaac and Jacob and later David and on and on, until Jesus made up a verse about their father Joseph and Joseph made up a final verse of the father of them all, God.

Mary waited a moment, and then asked why they didn't sing about the mothers. It was a long journey, so they started with Eve.

O nce a week, when the weather was good, Joseph took his family to the hills or the river or anywhere they could enjoy nature outside of Nazareth.

This day in the hottest part of the summer, they left early to fish in the river and swim. Joseph kept an eye on all his boys as they laughed and splashed in the water on this stifling day. Mary watched them from shore, with only her feet in the water. Joseph tried to fish, but all the splashing had frightened them away. Mary had bread and cheese, just in case.

The water was high and flowing swiftly tracing spirals near the bank. Leaves circled, trapped in eddies. Joseph waited for a fish to tug his line.

The older boys were in deeper water now, but the youngest boy was next to his mother with the little Miriam. Joseph thought he saw something moving in the water near the older boys, something that looked like a clump of sodden weeds slowly flowing with the current. As it passed near Jesus, he was suddenly pulled under water. He struggled to get to the surface, held under by an unseen force. Caleb started barking wildly and jumped into the water.

Joseph was in the water in an instant, swimming as hard as he could. James was confused, looking around for his brother. Joseph saw Jesus break the surface long enough to gasp a breath of air, then be pulled back down by the madman. Joseph grabbed the man's hair and pulled him back to break his grip on his son, but he held him under water anyway. Joseph released his hair and grabbed both his wrists to pull his son free. Jesus rose and coughed.

Joseph directed his boys to swim to shore. James and Jesus pulled Caleb along with them, calming him. Then the madman broke free and headed for Jesus again. Joseph caught up with him and locked his arm around his neck to hold his head under water to try to stop him. They struggled until the madman went limp. Joseph could have held him there until it was too late. Then he could have merely let go of him to drift down the river. He didn't. He dragged him back to the bank and forced the water out of him, and brought him back to life. He had tried to kill his son again. Caleb stood guard over the man, confused, waiting for Joseph to tell him what to do.

When the man stopped coughing and had regained his strength, he screamed an inhuman scream and jumped back into the river to swim away. Joseph held Caleb back. They all sat in silence for a time. James finally spoke. "Why did you revive him, Abba? He tried to kill my brother, he may try again."

Joseph replied, "If we don't show mercy, we're animals just like him, and he wins. There is a better way. If somebody doesn't show love and mercy, our world is doomed. God wants us to be merciful. I want this to be a better world for my sons and daughters. I think this is the way."

A few days later when Jesus was alone with his father in the workshop, he poured out his questions that had been festering. "Why did that man want to kill me?"

Joseph put down his plane and sat next to his son and said, "He is crazy. He believes he is the true son of God, and you are a pretender who is in his way. He has tried to kill you before, when you were still in your mother's womb. I stopped him then, too. And Caleb stopped him one night when we were asleep."

"Oh, I remember that. I was real little then." Jesus was quiet for a moment. "Will he try again?"

His father leaned back and looked down at the ground for a moment before answering, " I hope not, but I don't know. But I can't kill him for what he *might* do, only if that is the only way I can stop him if he was actually trying to kill one of you. Only if that was the *only* way. Do you understand the difference? Even then it would be a horrible thing to do. Once I knew you were safe, and he was unconscious and no longer threat to me ... well, then I couldn't let him die. There is much too much killing in our land already. Life is very precious, even his. There is even hope for him. Maybe God will choose to heal him someday. You never know. God can do anything,"

" I love you, Abba, thanks for saving me - again."

Joseph put his hand in his son's hair and messed it up, not saying a word, then pulled him to his chest and hugged him tightly.

Joseph spoke over Jesus' shoulder as he continued hugging him. "There ae no quick solutions that are right, son. Difficult problems take time to solve. And a wider perspective."

Jesus was crying. "There is so much I don't understand, why is life on earth like this, why is there so much evil?"

Joseph rocked his boy in his arms and said, "That's a question for your *other* father, I don't know, it makes no sense to me. This could be such a wonderful place."

Years passed. Jesus grew and learned. He learned everything his father and mother could teach him and everything the teachers could share. He learned from his friends and relatives. He learned from reading God's word. He learned from prayer and from listening.

He learned from work, and he learned from his heart that spoke the truth quietly. He pondered the paradoxes of human life and began to see the deeper truths that lay beneath, connecting everything.

He wondered what this destiny was that was waiting for him. He wondered what great things God had in mind. He hoped God had a love waiting for him that was like the one he had seen with his parents. He thought that would be a wonderful life, to love someone and be loved back that way. He wanted to be like his parents. He looked forward to a long life and grandchildren.

If what his parents told him was true, he was to be a king who would lead his country into a peaceful time, free of the Romans. He wondered how that could be. But his father sang to him from David's Psalms and from the Prophets, especially Isaiah. There were puzzling things in the Prophets that bothered Jesus as he tried to understand. There was so much evil in the world, so much pain.

He hoped he could find a way to make life better for his people. He had seen what some had tried that didn't work. He knew of the zealots and the folly of their skirmishes that only made things worse. He saw the Temple full of Pharisees and Sadducees fighting over their different views of truth. He knew the neighboring Samaritans and the descendants of the Philistines, and he saw the way they searched for God and truth in their own ways. His people hated them even more than they hated the Romans, if that was possible. It was an older feud. Jesus wondered what could finally bring peace and love to all of them some day. *If I were King, what could I do? How could I change this hatred? You can't order people to love each other.*

J oseph was already working when Jesus awoke, so he went to help his mother. He loved this sort of time alone with her. This morning he helped her with her cooking. "Amma, how did you meet Abba, and how did you fall in love?"

Mary looked away to relive a pleasant memory. "I remember it like it was yesterday. My little sister was late coming home. She was playing at your father's workshop, as usual, and I was sent to bring her home. She was having so much fun she had lost track of time. I had seen him on the streets before, and I had heard stories from children and their songs he made up for them - but that afternoon when I stood outside the door and watched him with the children, I knew. I knew he was the one. I knew he would make a wonderful father. I wanted him to be father for my children. I was right. Things just got a little more complicated than I imagined."

"Complicated? What do you mean, Amma?"

"It is a long story and I will have to tell you later when you are older so you can understand. But just let me say it was very difficult for him. But he loved me, he loved me like no man before has ever loved a woman. Love is a very powerful thing, son. It is stronger than anything else there is, stronger than hate and even stronger than fear."

"I love him, too, Amma."

"And he loves you, son, but you know that. You know he would do anything for you. He has spent his life protecting you, and giving you everything you need. He's enjoyed that, watching you grow, to become the great man you are. He's very proud of you. You've given him a lot of joy. No man could ever have had a better son. He always enjoys having you in his carpentry shop, ever since you were a baby. He thinks you are more like him than his other children, did you know that? He would never say that to you, he would be afraid to hurt the others. He thinks you have his sense of humor as well as his sense of the wood. He thinks sometimes you can even feel the sprit in the wood you work better than he can. When you were only eleven and scrambled up the cliff to get the twisted tree for him, that was a very significant gift to him. He knew then that you understood."

"That's why I did it - for him. I never told him, but I was very scared. But I wanted him to think I could do grown up work."

"He is a great father, isn't he? He is a wonderful husband. He has always been kind and gentle and shown me the kind of love I had dreamed of when I was a girl. And he is very handsome, too, like you".

Mary took Jesus by the hand, "Here, come with me, I want to show you something." She handed him a thick pile of parchment in the box Joseph had made for her as his first gift. She remembered the moonlight reflecting off the polished wood that night. Jesus saw her smile again. He loved her smile. Each piece of parchment had a song Joseph had written. Just words, like poetry, but as Jesus read them he remembered the melodies he had heard his entire life. The songs came rushing back to him. He remembered the place he first heard each song. His life had always been full of song. Mary hummed some of them, warm in her rememberings. She pulled one from the bottom, and rubbed it gently with her fingertips, like Joseph caressed the smooth wood in final test. She looked as if she were caressing her love's face as she stroked his words upon the page.

gabus came to see Joseph when he was alone in his workshop. He had never talked to Joseph without James around before, but since James was traveling, he used this opportunity to have a private talk with Joseph. "J-Joseph, y-you have t-talked about d-dreams about the future before. How d-do you know when they are r-real?" He was filing his fingernails violently, filing them down to the quick.

Caleb had been asleep when Agabus came in, but when he accidentally stepped on his tail, he stood up slowly, gave one short growl, and found a new corner where he could sleep.

Joseph walked across the workshop to set down his saw, and pulled over two chairs for them to sit. "Why do you ask?" He knew why, he knew that was the only reason anyone ever asked, because they were having the same sort of dreams.

"B-because I've b-been having those kind of dreams m-myself. I've b-been h-having them m-my whole li-li-li-li-li ..."

Joseph couldn't stand to hear him struggle so hard, so he broke in. "You've been having them your whole life?"

"Yes. Since I was a c-child. I j-just don't tell any one a-about it b-b-because I g-get made fun of too m-much already."

"I know what you mean," said Joseph. "It can be a lonely and frustrating thing seeing visions and getting warnings in your dreams. Look at how difficult it made life for the original Joseph. Of course using a little sense when telling your brothers you see them all kneeling down to you when you are the youngest might be in order. That wasn't very wise of him. Tell me about your dream."

"I saw t-terrible t-trouble for James. I saw Roman s-soldiers talking t-to him at his door. That was all I saw. B-but it was s-scary. Somehow I knew that it was very b-bad."

Joseph pulled his chair closer. "What else did you see? When was it?"

"I d-don't know. That's what is d-driving me crazy. I want to help, but I don't know what to do. It's always easy to see what it m-means afterwards, b-but I w-want to help him now, h-he's m-my friend, and I d-don't have many f-friends. I used to t-try to t-tell people about what I saw, but they either thought I w-was crazy or if they noticed that it happened la-la-laaaa-later, they g-got afraid of me. I think that is w-why I t-talk like this."

Joseph poured some wine for both of them. He wanted to let a moment pass. "I know what you mean. I learned early who I could share these things with. I have had my problems with dreams, too. Sometimes I wish I wouldn't see these things, they can be so frustrating and confusing. I mean, you never get enough information to know what to do. You still have to guess and just go by what you feel. There are never enough facts. You are never sure. It is not like carpentry where you can just lay the square up against the piece and know. It is maddening. But I can't imagine living without it. I like the warnings, they let me watch and be ready. Sometimes they have saved our lives."

"W-what should I s-say to James?"

Joseph answered, "I'll talk to him. I'll tell him to stop taking so many chances. I've been worried about him, too. He'll listen to me. I'll just tell him it was my dream, and you can relax, knowing you've done your job by telling me so I can warn him."

"B-but most p-people don't l-listen."

"I know." Joseph said. "That is the other maddening thing. It is so frustrating and … lonely sometimes. Thanks for sharing this with me. It is always good to have someone to talk to who understands what this is like."

Agabus relaxed for the first time and stopped filing down his nails. He put his sanding stones back in his pouch. "Y-you're welcome, it is good for m-me, too. I don't w-want to stop seeing things, I think G-God w-wants me t-to. It feels like it is God's gift. I m-mean he has spoken to p-plain p-people before. Sometimes they have f-felt inadequate to t-tell the world what he has said to them. I've heard a l-lot of things I want to tell, but I have a h-hard time saying anything – even Sh-shalom."

Joseph's mother, Ruth, was as spirited as Mary, but she was growing old. She often claimed she was still a girl inside, it was just her body that was old. The little girl still looked out of her eyes. She always loved games, just like any younger child. Joseph's sense of humor came from her, and his great capacity to love.

She had lived through many changes in her world and survived countless sorrows with grace and her sense of humor. She was often not easy to live with because she always found ways to get her way. She had learned the subtle art of losing arguments while getting what she wanted anyway. She was cute, and she used it. When she was young and good-looking, it was easy. But as she grew older, she still found a way to maintain the charm of her youth beneath her wrinkles and gray hair. Somehow she still utilized the cuteness of her youth inside the cleverness of her age. She was gently formidable. Most never even knew how she had outmaneuvered them. Only after she had walked away did they ponder how they had come to agree with her. And they wondered why they were smiling about it. *She* certainly grinned as she walked away, hiding her face. She was a child-like matriarch who loved to play and laugh. Her children and grandchildren loved her. Jesus was her first grandchild.

Joseph remembered when she sang to baby Jesus in her lap those two nights she could before they went to Egypt. It broke her heart when they had to leave. She didn't know if they would ever see each other again.

His parents' long-shared song lived and grew in him. It grew in Jesus, too. Ruth loved Mary and felt they were sisters of the soul. Both strong women loving life, they were fueled by the play of childhood that had never faded with the pain of life. Their world was wonderful and new with each sunrise. It was a magic childhood that would never die. It was the spark of life. It was the newness of spring. It was sheer joy at the wonder of the world. It was humor that lived through the darkest hours. It was faith that everything was going to be all right no matter how things looked. It was joy that knew it would return again after the night of sorrow, sure as a confirming sunrise. Sure as spring flowers after winter's long night.

Joseph replayed a lifetime of comforting memories of life with his mother. Memories of her healing songs in his ears as she rocked him out of fever's fears. Memories of her smile when he brought his gift of wildflowers to her. Memories of fights that were gentle exasperating disagreements he could never win. Memories of fresh-baked treats. Memories of play in springtime green. Memories of prayer and faith. Memories of the strength he gave her when his father died and she lived on without the man with whom she had shared her life. Joseph had held her and felt her fragile body drained of strength, moving almost lifeless through her first days alone. They grew closer then, and in the years that followed. He had a real gift to repay her with at last. He filled her life, he and Mary and their children. She slowly learned to live again; the child in her would not die.

Not until the end. She knew it was time for her to leave. Her body was worn out. Her spirit needed something freer to live in. Something bigger and beyond. This full moon night she was so weak she couldn't speak. Joseph whispered in her ear as she left this world. His were the final words before she let go. He had less than a minute to say everything he needed to say that he might regret not saying.

He was good with words. He was used to making up songs on the spot. This was the most important thing he had ever said. There would not be another chance. No one else would ever hear it. He whispered in her ear. It flowed from the heart, unplanned. It started with, "I love you, Amma." It grew from there. Seven sentences. No more, no less. Enough for both of them. Afterwards, he couldn't remember what he had said. It didn't matter. A mother and her son had said goodbye, to never see each other on earth again. The words for once didn't matter.

Afterwards, when she was gone, he walked outside and stared at the full moon almost directly overhead. He couldn't imagine not ever hearing her voice again. She had always been there. His child's mind that still lived in him thought she always would. Her voice had greeted him into this world, with her offbeat humor. His voice had comforted her as she left this world. Strange symmetry that made him sigh. A comforting sigh. An emptying sigh. A sigh that was a song without time. It seemed to him that all the air from his lungs was flowing out in sighs; he never noticed taking breath in. It was a great emptying waiting to be filled some day. It wouldn't be soon. He spoke to her in the great darkness of that night. He cried, he sobbed, he felt at peace. But he had never felt so alone. Mary comforted him. Jesus stood by watching, trying to understand his father's grief and his own. The moon seemed to make a cold sound with its light. A sound like a sigh.

It was the longest night, mercifully lit with the moon that would always remind him of the cycles of life. Death is just the other end of birth. The moon grows and shrinks and grows again. Children are born and take over for those who move on. Under the comforting moon, Joseph saw his mother's legacy. *Jesus will live on, and remember my mother after I am gone.* The closest thing to a smile for now came to him with that thought.

Jesus didn't know what to say. He just held his father and sobbed. They sobbed together as Mary laid a loving hand on each of their shoulders. She cried silent tears of sorrow and gratitude for what had been and was. She missed her friend, the woman who had prepared her son so well for her.

Joseph sat with his mother through the night. Mary came to the door at dawn with his friend James to take his place. James comforted him, then Mary touched his shoulder and said, "Come outside with me. I have something for you, for her." She pressed a small bag into his hand. She closed his fingers around it, then kissed his hand with one of her kisses that held for long enough to warm his flesh. He liked the feel of life again. He needed it. He felt it warming him inside where it had gotten cold. Joseph saw the small shovel in her other hand.

"These are seeds of the flowers your mother loves so much. We can plant a flower garden by our front door for her. And for you and me. I miss her, too." Mary looked at him with eyes as full of pure love for him as his mother's had always been. "We can see it every day and remember her and the way she loved these flowers. I think she can see them through our eyes."

It was a sacred time. They turned the earth and spread the seed lovingly. Joseph could not help but think of the earth that would soon cover his mother as they spread the dirt over the seeds. It was a thought that made him shiver with sweet reconciliation of deeper understanding. They watered the promises of future flowers; taking turns soaking the earth. Then stood silent at this grave of seeds where life would soon resurrect in a colorful song. Where soon, as the sun coaxed life out of these seeds, butterflies and bees would visit. Sweetness would come from these colors. A song for the eye and the nose. He knew his mother would see it, and he would share the beauty with her as he had shared bruised fistfuls of wildflowers with her since he had learned to walk alone.

Jesus watched them from the window, not wanting to intrude on this sacred act of love. It was a trinity with an invisible member. Jesus learned something new about love this day; about all kinds of love. He knew he would bring his mother flowers of his own that night. He dreaded the day he would have to say goodbye to her this way. He would plant a fine garden for Mary, he knew.

She would have loved it. It was everything she would have wanted it to be. People who loved her were gathered around. She was surrounded by flowers and her grandchildren and an ocean of tears. Joseph spoke with all his friends and neighbors who had loved his mother for the good woman she was. She was remembered in the best way. Only one man tried to spoil the moment, a Pharisee whose name meant, "Field the color of blood." His name carried on the memory of a battle long forgotten where many lives were lost in a meaningless battle. It lived only in his name and attitude. He took this sacred moment to tell Joseph how wrong he was to claim that Jesus was born of a virgin, and was the Son of God. He told him it was blasphemy and that the whole village laughed at him. This man was always sure he was right about everything. In this exhausted morning when his heart was broken, and tears filled his red eyes, Joseph looked at him kindly, and called him by name.

"You don't understand God's love at all, or you could not take this time to confront me. My mother is going to be buried now. My mother. How can you do this now?"

Then Joseph looked at this man's wife, who stood by his side. She was wide-eyed and afraid of what Joseph might do. Joseph the muscular carpenter towered over this little man. Joseph held her arm gently and looked in her eyes. He whispered. "Please explain this to him, he doesn't understand, but I think you do. God's love is not like this, it cares about people. Your husband makes a show of his religion, he prays loudly and gives money in an obvious way so everyone can see. My mother taught me how to worship God another way. I think you understand."

Jesus stood behind his father, listening. He saw the troubled look on the woman's face. There was nothing she could do. She knew her husband was much too secure in his world. He was deaf to any suggestion that he was not a totally righteous man. He believed he had a duty to make everyone believe exactly the way he did. He was in control of everything in his life. He was comfortable and blind.

Jesus watched his father turn away from the Pharisee and return to honoring his mother. Jesus thought that what he had done honored her more than anything else that day. Joseph looked into his son's eyes, and put his hand on his shoulder. His other arm wrapped around James and they walked together to the front.

Joseph sang a song as his mother was lowered into the ground. Before the first shovel of dirt could cover her, he dropped a single tiny yellow flower on top of her. It floated down as if drawn by her heart, where it rested forever. He had earlier picked it from the place where he had picked his first flowers for her in his tiny toddler's fist. It meant the same thing today it had meant decades before. It was a gift of love and beauty from a son to his mother. Jesus watched, and knew.

Empty Song

Home for James and Miriam was very different from Mary and Joseph's house. It was comfortable and quiet. It was full of exquisite things and full of love, but there was no sound of laughing children. Sometimes, when James was gone, the sound of soft sobbing filled their bedroom.

Miriam was afraid they would never have a child. Each month she hoped she would not start her period. Each day her hope grew until she felt disappointing wetness again. She busied herself with making their home spectacular. She cooked wonderful meals for her husband when he was home. But he was often traveling for his business. She spent too much time alone. Mary tried to persuade her to spend more time with her large family, to be involved with her children as much as she could. But the sorrow of her empty womb was pulling her away.

James loved her with a passionate love. And she loved him. They brought each other comfort and pleasure, except the pleasure of children that seemed to be denied to them. James showered her with gifts. He made her feel loved in every way. She was young, and had a lot of time to try to have children, but she was afraid she never would. Children loved her, and she was very good with them.

The hours alone began to eat at her, and she cried more in the long dark hours alone. James and Mary were worried about her, so Mary spent as much time with her as she could. Her children loved her - she was like an aunt to them. When James was home, life was fun and full. They often visited at Joseph and Mary's house for meals that were full of children's laughter. James was like a second father to Jesus and little James. He brought all the children gifts, but he enjoyed talking with these two older children most of all. They played their word games with him; they reveled in the stories of his travels. Sometimes James looked fondly at his namesake, thinking that this one at least would in some way make his name live on after him.

Alone in the night, James and Miriam drew close in undistracted love. Their passion was always pure and free, tinted only by shared comfort for each other's patient sorrow. They lived in hope, and in their lovemaking was always the possibility of a child. A wonderful child could come of all this loving, wanted so badly to be.

In the unspoken sadness flourished passion's intensity. They lavished pleasure on their beloved. They were full of each other's love; each hoped-for child in each coupling brought them closer. Soon James began to travel less. He couldn't stand to see her suffer, and he suffered, too when they were apart.

This night, some unnamed fear pulled them to each other. They made love three times in the night, melting into sleep to wake and merge again. They couldn't imagine life without the other. They thanked God for their love. It filled them, healed them, set them free.

They were lost in the cool warmth of naked skin that is more familiar than your own, and desired with a pleasant ache that fills. Wrapped in random angles of arms and backs and legs, they swam in dreams of comfort. A night washed on the shore between waking and sleeping, they feasted on quiet love.

T he morning sun had barely lost its gold to burn the white of day. Miriam and James lay in bed, softly touching, not wanting the closeness of last night to end. They heard the song of doves; then the stamp of marching and the clink of sword and spear stop just outside their door. Two heavy thuds shook the door as a Roman voice ordered them to open up in the name of the Empire. James called out and dressed quickly before they went to the door. He was dwarfed by the soldiers. One of them read from the paper in his hand, as the other two held James by his arms.

His ears were ringing as he heard the words of accusation for stealing tax money owed to the Empire. There would be no trial, no small punishment - he was condemned as an example. The word hit him like a fist. *Crucifixion.* Miriam screamed and tried to push them away from him, begging for his life. The one who had read the order pulled her back and said there was nothing he could do, he had his orders. There were no appeals. It was law. This soldier had been in Bethlehem fourteen years before, and had lived the horror of the slaughter of the innocents. Cruel punishment without mercy was his job when he was ordered. If he disobeyed he knew what fate would be his; and the punishment to his wife and children back in Rome would be assured. Roman discipline was harsh and sure. He knew by law a Roman citizen could not be crucified, but soldiers who disobeyed were made examples of in other effective ways. The power of the Empire rested in fear. Sure fear.

The soldier hated this. He was grateful he wasn't called upon to do it more often. He had become a soldier to fight other soldiers, armed and with a chance. The only armed ones he ever fought now were the silent ones who moved like a shadow behind a lone soldier to slip a knife between his ribs. These zealots fought the only way that made sense against such an overwhelming force. Retaliation came quickly, and innocent civilians were killed ten to one for each soldier lost. Anyone who thought he was helping his people this way was hated for the results

Miriam pleaded, she cried. Finally the soldier drew his sword and faced her. James shouted at her to move back, or else they would kill her, too. "Please don't let me be responsible for your death, that would be the worst thing for me," James voice became softer as the words continued, "That would be the worst of all for me, Miriam, please." Miriam sobbed and collapsed to her knees. She had feared this day would come. She had pleaded with James to not take so many chances. As they dragged James away, she told him she would get Joseph to help, and ran.

Joseph was in his shop, working on a small table to surprise Mary. It was half-round and unusual. She had mentioned that she wished she had a piece of furniture to fit by the door to be the first thing anyone would see when they entered their home. It would help convey a feeling of grace and peace. He was just finishing it as he heard Miriam screaming his name as she ran down the street. Joseph ran outside as she grabbed his arm and pulled him, dragging him in the direction from which she had just run. She was panting and crying and it made it hard for him to understand what she was saying. "They've taken him, Joseph, they are taking him to kill him. The Roman soldiers ... there is no trial, they are taking him to that place... that ... place. Help him, Joseph, help him!" Joseph told her to run to tell Mary, she would gather other people who could help, but he would go immediately to try to stop them or at least slow them down until maybe something could be done.

Joseph ran as fast as his strong lungs would let him. He caught up with them on the road. He pleaded with the soldiers. He looked at James' helpless eyes. He begged the soldiers to wait, that this was an important merchant, that he could get a lot of money for them if they would only wait. He told them James had a lot of connections, a lot of Roman politicians that would be angry when they heard of this. "Please wait a few hours, until this can be worked out!" Joseph stood in front of them to block their way; he was strong as a soldier from his work, and almost as large. But they had swords, and all three drew them together as they took a step in a well-practiced move. Joseph jumped back. He put his arms down at his sides and bowed his head. He pleaded softly, "Please, just hold him for an hour until the politicians he knows can be contacted. He gets many fine things for them, and they will not be happy to lose the supply."

They didn't even reply. They raised their swords and stepped forward together toward him. Joseph ran back and stood meekly off the road, out of their way. James told him, "There is nothing you can do. I've sealed my fate already. They are looking for an example for everyone who dares to think of holding back the money Rome needs. They are in trouble at home, and all the distant provinces need to be bled if the Empire is to survive. Too many people know what I have done, and I have enemies. A tax collector wants to make them happy with him for turning me in. He is under pressure not to let this sort of thing go on. He has as much to lose as I do. I should have known this would happen. Just stay with me, Joseph, don't let me die alone, stay with me until the end and protect Miriam for me. Keep her from doing something that will get her hurt."

The soldiers took another step toward Joseph, and he backed farther off until they replaced their swords and pushed James along the road. Joseph followed silently at a safe distance; he knew he dared not try to slow them any more. In a few minutes they were at the place. It was at the intersection of two busy roads. Crucifixion sites were always chosen to be very visible. This was not a secret torture carried out in a dungeon; it was intended to frighten those who might think of defying the rules. There was a cross on the ground waiting for him. One already stood in place with a different merchant moaning on it guarded by a fourth soldier. The soldiers told James to take his fine garments off, and they split them between themselves. He wouldn't be putting them back on. A crowd was gathering. The merchant already on the other cross had often cheated his own people, and he was hated. Some hated James, too, out of envy for his wealth, but most knew him as an honest and kind man who tried to help those in need whenever he could. No one he had befriended came to help as he stood naked between the armored soldiers. Miriam ran to get to him, but was pushed back by the soldiers. She stretched out her arm to touch him one last time and she told him that she loved him, before they pushed her to the dirt.

James yelled, "Miriam, don't ... stay back or they will kill you too." Then softly, "It is too late for me." Joseph held her back while she sobbed. One soldier stood between them and James as the other two pulled him to the ground and spread his arms out over the cross. Miriam screamed and struggled with Joseph, who held her back. "He's your friend, Joseph, he loves you, how can you let them do this to him! Do something, stop them!" Her screams and sobs broke his heart. One soldier raised his sword and took another step toward them. Joseph pulled her farther back. She pounded her fists on Joseph as she cursed him. She called him a coward. The pounding of her fists was matched by the pounding of the nails through his hands into the wood. Joseph had always loved the deep sound of nails into a large piece of wood, the deep hollow sound that made his chest vibrate like it did now with Miriam's fists pounding on his chest. He would never like that sound again.

Miriam stopped screaming, and only sobbed now as they nailed his feet. A smaller nail held a piece of paper above his head. It had a single word. *"Thief."* The soldier holding the sword told them to move back. He raised it into the air, and Joseph pulled Miriam back farther until he was satisfied and lowered his sword. Joseph never doubted he would use it. He returned his sword into its sheath so he could help the others lift the cross and drop it into place. When it fell with a thud, James screamed as his hands and feet were torn by the shock. Then he looked at Miriam and Joseph. It was a look they had never seen from a loved one before. Tears fell from his eyes from the physical pain and from the deeper pain of knowing he was saying goodbye. No one ever came down from a cross alive. Mary and Jesus and his brother James came running first. Soon everyone who loved James was there. It was too late. The four Romans stood with swords out and pushed them back again.

Mary pulled Miriam from Joseph's arms. She cried with her. Jesus and his brother stood numbly next to Joseph until he put his arms around them. "There was nothing I could do. They would have killed Miriam and me. They wouldn't wait an hour for us to get one of his Roman friends." Mary told Joseph that her father had gone to try to bring them, maybe there was still time. His wounds could heal. When Miriam heard that, she asked Mary if she would go with her to plead with the ones who were his friends. Miriam screamed up at James that she was going to see them - they would use their power to help him. "There is still time! Hold on, my love!" Then they ran.

After they had gone, James called to Joseph. "Please don't leave me alone to die like this, promise me you won't let me die alone. And Miriam, promise me you will take care of her." Joseph gave his word again. It was Sunday morning. The real horror of the torture began. Joseph watched his friend struggle to breathe by pushing up against his nailed feet. It looked like his arms were being pulled out of their sockets by the weight and strange angle of the force. He watched his friend struggle for breath; he watched the blood flow from the deep wounds that went all the way through both hands and feet. Joseph knew that even if some miracle occurred and what had never happened did, James would be a cripple for the rest of his life with his mangled hands and feet. But he prayed he would survive somehow, anyway.

Jesus and his brother James stared at their father and the helpless look on his face. "Can't we help him, Abba?" Jesus said. "Why would God let this happen to him?" Joseph didn't know what to say at first, he pulled his sons close to him. He cried. He sobbed as he held his children in his arms as he helplessly watched his closest friend suffer in the air above them. He wiped his eyes on his sleeve, and then he said, "I don't know, Jesus. I have seen God let some horrible things happen that seem to make no sense to me. Why should a good man like this die for such a small thing? Just an offense against an unfair tax from these invaders who have stolen our land. Does God think that is a reason James should die like this? I don't know Jesus; I don't know why He is letting this happen to my friend. I don't know why He has let the Romans do all that they do to us. Are we being punished? I know He has the power to do anything, I have seen miracles with my own eyes. I have been praying for one since Miriam came for me this morning, but it doesn't seem God will stop this. I don't know why."

The sun was higher and shining in James' eyes. There was no way to shade them with his hands nailed above him. The heat of the day was drying him and he cried for a drink of water. Joseph asked a soldier and if he could give him water. The soldier replied, "You'd be doing your friend no favor, you would only be prolonging his suffering. It is better for him to die more quickly then to try to have some false comfort, his thirst will speed his release along." Now Joseph felt like he was going mad, here his helpless friend was begging him for a sponge of water to ease his thirst, but if he gave it to him, he would make things worse for him. If the Romans would even allow it. How could he say no ... how could he say yes? He had never felt so helpless in his life. The moans of the two hanging above them were increasing. The hot sun was adding to their torture. Joseph could hear the ragged coughs, as fluid began to settle in their lungs. They were both struggling for breath and trying to raise their bodies up on their bleeding feet. Every time they pushed hard, the clotted blood broke through again and new red blood painted the wood below their feet. The old brown blood was reddened again with a new layer. More of his life leaked out.

Mary and Miriam had not returned. No one would agree to help him. Jesus and James kept asking Joseph when they would return. He was losing his last vapor of hope. "Do something!" Jesus said, "Can't you do something to help him? Don't let him die like that." James could hear quite clearly up above. Like a man on a roof who could hear whispers on the street below when the ground reflected the sound up with no obstructions. He could hear every word. Even in his position, he felt pity for them. He knew he was dead already, it was only a matter of time. He knew he would be freed from this pain eventually, but they would remember this horror for the rest of their lives. He looked at little James, and wished he could make this easier for him. He had wished he could watch him grow up to be a man. He knew he would be a fine man; he had a lot of strength and compassion already. Joseph and his big brother would help him, he knew. James wished they wouldn't remember him this way, but there was nothing he could do. He could hardly muster a whisper now, slowly suffocating on that cross. His eyes brightened as he saw Miriam and Mary return. But they had no hope on their faces. He knew there would be no rescue.

Joseph knew, too. They told him that even those who wanted to help were told it was too late. The Romans could not weaken the horror of their punishment by ever letting anyone survive. It had to be a certain death with no hope. That made the horror worse. This was a punishment with a purpose; they needed this to keep the provinces in line. Rome was fighting invaders, and had spread itself too thinly, and if it looked like they were weakening, they would end up fighting a battle on a hundred fronts at once. Even their empire couldn't manage that.

Now that the end of the punishment was certain, the soldiers had moved back to rest and pass the time. Miriam went to the foot of the cross below her love. She wished she could reach high enough to just touch his foot one more time. All she could touch was his blood. She told him things that were too private for anyone to dare to remember. Nothing that wasn't ordinary words, but this was no ordinary day. She didn't want him to die, but she didn't want him to suffer like this much longer. He told her that he loved her, and he gave her some instructions on things to do when he was gone. Mary came behind her and held her as Miriam rested her head against the cross. Slowly, she slumped down on the ground, with her arms around the wood like they were holding him.

Joseph watched the sun growing low in the west. He shuddered to think of the night. When the heat of the desert day was gone, he knew James would be unprotected by the sudden cold of the desert night in the darkness. To Jews, the setting sun started a new day. It was Monday.

What would have been a beautiful sunset on another day was a sea of blood in the sky. It was as if he was filling it from himself for those few minutes, pouring his blood into the clouds. Then the blues of twilight started this moonless night. Torchlight cast the only movement on the crosses except for shivering. James didn't want to leave her. He felt he was deserting her, somehow. She would be a lonely widow. He was sure she would never remarry, though he wished she would. He hoped it wouldn't be long until she laughed again. He knew it would surprise her and she would feel guilty. She would live on; he wanted that. She would see a sunset that was magnificent that would not remind her of this one. She would eat a meal and feel pleasure. She would remember a happy day with him and smile. She would live.

His shivering grew worse, then slowed as his remaining strength was exhausted. He didn't think he could keep pushing up to breathe much longer, but every time he slumped down too long, he choked and struggled for breath until he had to push against the pain once more. He held on to life in pain, impossible as rescue seemed. He wasn't ready to leave yet. He wanted to see Miriam's face in the morning light. And his love was strong.

Joseph asked Mary to take the children to her parents where the others were waiting. He wanted her to take Miriam with her, too. He said he would keep this night watch. He knew he could never leave his friend alone. He had promised. Miriam wouldn't leave her husband. She stayed at the bottom of the cross and spoke to him often, telling him how much she loved him. There was nothing else to say. There was no future, no hope. James had said everything he needed to say to her while he still had a voice. He remembered how warm he felt last night sleeping with her in their bed. He knew he would never feel her touch again. But he could still see her, hear her soft voice. He watched her sleep below him in the light of the shrinking torches this moonless night. He loved her face; he drew peace from only looking at it. The terrible resignation of saying goodbye forever tore at him, but eased with time as he came to peace with it. Hanging in between the living and the dead, he slowly let go of all that he had hoped. Even her. It would take her longer, much longer.

Miriam finally fell asleep, drained of everything. Joseph was alone with his friend, this shift of Romans had moved off to sit around their fire. At best, James slept for a moment until his choking woke him. Joseph moved close and spoke softly to him, standing above sleeping Miriam.

James cleared his throat so he could speak in a hoarse whisper. "I guess invisible hares won't get me out of this one, old friend." He struggled for breath until he could speak again. "Please sing for me, sing that song you wrote about Miriam and me."

So Joseph sang softly in that terrible night; it was the only thing he could do to bring comfort to his friend and Miriam. Soon Mary returned to find him singing. She had brought blankets and food and wine. Joseph sang as much as he could throughout the night, until he had no voice, no words.

The Song of Saint Joseph

The second morning came with golds and blues that lit Miriam's face for James. He could still see beauty; he could still feel love. They couldn't take that away from him. Joseph's voice had returned enough for a whispered morning song. It was one of the Psalms. The sunlight showed James body terribly changed. His ribs were protruding like a skeleton, his face was gaunt; his bowels and bladder had released and fouled the cross below him, mixing with his blood. He was pale as the sand. His head hung down as if he didn't have the strength to ever raise it again. Joseph wondered how long this could go on. The other merchant was moaning. He was alone, his family was afraid to come.

Miriam stared at her love, torn between wanting him to be at peace and out of pain, and hoping for some miracle. *If only she could ask God face to face, how would he be able to say no to her for this good man?* Mary returned with Jesus. She comforted Miriam and Joseph. Jesus stood alone and stared at his suffering friend. He looked at his helpless father and the unconcerned Romans by their fire. *How can people do things like this?* Jesus scowled. But Miriam moved Jesus most of all. He saw how much she loved James, as he was being taken from her bit by bit. Here she was, healthy and safe while above her head, just out of her reach, the man she loved was being slowly tortured to death. Mary held her and stroked her hair. Joseph comforted his son James, named after the man on the cross, the man who had been so kind to Jesus and James as they grew up. Jesus couldn't imagine life without him. He couldn't imagine what this must be doing to his father who somehow was managing to sing comforting songs through this hell. Jesus felt pride for his father and his great strength he shared with everyone who needed it. Who did he get his strength from? He knew it was from his faith in God. And from the Psalms of David, and his own songs that flowed from his heart. Jesus had learned much from his father, but never more than from these last two days.

A loud moan from the cross drew everyone's attention. What could they do? There was nothing except being there, and praying. A fresh change of guards marched up to relieve the soldiers. One yelled up at the men after reading the signs, "Hey, thieves! Are my things safe down here if I want to go to take a leak? You look like pretty tricky ones to me!" They laughed at the helpless men. "Your women will be needing men soon, maybe we should help break them in right now." The leader of the group yelled at that soldier to stop. He said that would not happen on his watch, unless he wanted to join them on a third cross.

Joseph knew there would be no singing during this watch. These men were cruel. These men were dangerous to the rest of them. Jesus asked his father what they could do now for James. "Just wait, son." He knew James was hungry and thirsty and exhausted. He knew he had lost a lot of blood and was weak. He knew he was struggling to breathe. *How long can this go on?* Joseph knew sometimes it took many days for a man to finally die. He hoped it would be soon. James didn't speak any more. He moaned occasionally. Sometimes he struggled for breath and coughed so much they were all sure this would be his last. But he lived on. Joseph prayed for his friend to die right now, and hated himself for his prayer.

The day burned like an oven, there was no shade for the men on the crosses. Every time Joseph took a drink of water he felt guilty. As the day went on, James' wounds opened with his struggle to breathe and new blood painted the cross. He was covered with flies. They fed on his blood, they ate from his wounds; they crawled in his eyes and his nose and mouth. They knew he couldn't defend himself, and there was nothing the people on the ground could do to keep them away from him. He was a safe meal they could feast on leisurely.

Jesus had to leave. He couldn't stand watching helplessly, and he had to take his little brother away from this. He took him to walk by a peaceful stream. They walked in silence, trying to forget. They skipped stones trying to clear what still filled their eyes. Jesus hoped he would be dead by the time they returned. He felt guilty for the thought, but it was true. He didn't want to watch him die. He was afraid it might be worse.

Near sundown they returned to find him still alive, moaning. They stood in silence watching the strong man who had often carried them turn into a thing that didn't even look human anymore. The sky reddened into Tuesday. A colder night was coming. They couldn't imagine how he could continue to survive. A kinder watch had returned. Joseph sang to his friend again, and Miriam. Joseph could tell by the torchlight that his friend was still breathing. He prayed to see him stop. *Enough already, God, stop torturing him and all of us.* Eventually Joseph fell asleep. He hadn't slept since this had started Sunday morning. He didn't want to leave his friend alone, but his body just gave out.

Jesus took his brother home for the night. After his brother James was asleep he prayed and God, *Why?* No answer came. Jesus struggled with all he had seen until he finally fell asleep.

Joseph awoke confused. He remembered where he was. It was still dark and he didn't know if he had slept minutes or hours. Before he looked up, he prayed that James had died in the night, but was guilty at the thought that he might have let him die alone. Miriam was still asleep. And Mary. He looked up to see James struggling to raise himself to breathe.

James struggled and managed a hoarse whisper to Joseph. "It doesn't hurt anymore. I think I am ready to go."

Joseph stood and began to sing. He sang a song about their friendship, he sang about the good times they had shared, he sang about Miriam and saw his friend smile before he slumped down the last time. Mary and Miriam had seen it. His singing had awakened them. They saw his last smile. Miriam told him to go in peace, that she would join him soon. She hoped he could hear her tell him she loved him, so she repeated it many times. She wanted her love to be the last thing he heard on earth.

Joseph slumped down to the earth. Miriam and Mary sobbed. Joseph couldn't believe he had let his friend die like this. As long as he was alive, he thought there might be some tiny hope of a miracle. But he was gone. When he asked the soldiers for his body he was told he would have to wait until the other merchant died. They had to watch his dead body hang up there for eleven more hours as flies covered him, feeding and laying their eggs. They were powerless to even save his body from that humiliation. They prayed they could prepare and bury him before the corruption went even farther. He would start bloating soon in this heat. Miriam sat and stared. She was losing her mind. *What more could they do to him?*

Jesus and his brother James found their parents and Miriam sitting in dumb grief. They joined their silence. Finally Jesus spoke. "Abba, Why?" Joseph held out his arm to his sons, who were glad to be cradled in his arms. Joseph had never left his friend for these three days except to relieve himself nearby. His hair was matted, his eyes looked like he had not slept at all. He hardly had. He was almost mad from exhaustion and grief. His voice was so hoarse he could barely talk, but he knew he had to help them understand, even if he couldn't. He had to try to help them through this nightmare that had no waking.

"I don't know why. We never know. We only can believe that God..." Joseph stopped before he could finish his sentence. He looked up at James. He knew he couldn't tell them there was anything good about this. He just pulled them tighter to him, embracing their vital life, and feeling that hope of youth like warmth flow into him. He wanted desperately to give them strength and peace, but he was having a hard time himself. He started crying, he sobbed. They all cried. Jesus struggled and finally from his lips, one of his father's songs broke timidly into the still air. It was a song of James and love and hope. His father joined him, then the one who carried on his name and memory. It brought comfort to Miriam, and sad pride to Mary.

Finally the other died, and they lowered the crosses. The guards ripped James' body free from the nails, leaving bits of his flesh behind. Joseph cleaned the nails with a clean cloth, gathering all of his friend. He folded the cloth and placed it in the shroud with the rest of his body. He knelt before the body and sang a tearful Kaddish before they carried him home for preparation.

Yit'gadal v'yit'kadash sh'mei raba ...

Then Jesus and his brother James led the way, carrying James' legs while Joseph carried the weight of his body. Mary and Miriam held each other up as they walked behind. Joseph had time to remember places they passed along the way that they had shared in a lifetime of friendship.

It was a silent journey. They passed trees they had played under when they were children; he remembered the way James had stuttered as a child. Joseph had forgotten that. He remembered the races they had run down this street. He remembered fifteen-year-old James stumbling over words as he tried to talk with Esther without staring at her chest. Joseph felt the first small smile form itself against his will on his grieving face. The first hope of healing time had begun. He pondered what his answer would be to the question his son had asked. He wanted to answer Jesus, but he wasn't sure how to yet. Slowly his own answers came to him as they walked carrying a lifeless James between them. His sons on one end, he on the other, and remembering in between.

They would bury him and mourn and sleep at last. When they had rested he would talk with Jesus and his brothers that were old enough to understand. He would have to answer his question. He prayed for wisdom. He prayed for grace. He prayed for words. He prayed someday there would be another song.

Three more sunsets had changed the days and it was the Sabbath now. Mary lit the candles and sang the ancient prayer. The children and Joseph and Miriam held hands in a circle around the table. Miriam stared at the candles and saw the horrible flickering torch light in her memory. She had always loved candlelight before. Her eyes could hardly see this world for the awful pictures that had been burned into her mind. She saw the fading red outside the window and remembered the light around him on the cross. She would see him in the darkness and the blinding light of noon. It would be a long time before she would push away those memories and replace them with comforting memories of earlier times. They came slowly. Tender moments came first, then memories of laughter. Eventually memories of passion and even memories of quarrels would sweeten her days and her lonely nights. She stayed on her side of the bed and held some of his clothing for comfort. She inhaled deeply of his fading smell that still lived in them. She wet them with her tears. But this sunset she stared at the candle flame until one good memory comforted her. The years together were short. The years alone would be long.

Mary saw Miriam staring at the candle flame and knew her thoughts. She squeezed her hand. Mary was reluctant to let go; it was something in this silence that could hold them together more than symbolically. This circle of broken people needed something. The laughter that usually filled the room around this table seemed an impossible memory. Hands held on in an awkward silence until Miriam finally loosened her grip. The circle disconnected and everyone sat in silence.

Joseph rubbed his fingers on the smooth wood of the table he had made long ago. He let his eye be lost in the beauty of the grain. The curves and spirals of light and dark let him journey to a calmer place inside his mind. He felt his held breath release. Comforting wood crafted into a place where meals were shared and dreams grew into reality. He touched the wood like he would touch a friend. He remembered the many times James shared a meal with his family here.

Jesus and the younger children looked to the adults for their cues. Everyone was in pain. Each had their own James they knew and missed. Jesus kept his questions inside, anxious for the time when his father would make all this clear to him. He looked at Joseph, who reached across the table to squeeze his hand and nod his head at him.

Silence. Mary broke the silence when she passed the food around. Her words were eaten by the silence - it came from a place too big to fill with words. It was filled with the simple things of living like bread, wine, figs and grapes. And touches that were slightly more than what was necessary to pass the food. Touches that fed the soul, like the food the body.

Fragile words survived the silence and were joined by more. Soon small conversations filled some moments, more as time went by. Healing tiny normal things as life went on. Then the first laughter that came from the desperate need in response to words that weren't nearly as funny as the response would indicate. From Miriam's first laughter, her face changed, and turned into a tremble. Tears filled her eyes and then she sobbed. "I miss him! I miss James so much. I want him here with us. I feel like it is only a bad dream and he will walk through that door laughing as he always does when he returns from a trip."

Mouths were frozen in mid-bite around the table. Mary wrapped her arm around Miriam. Jesus couldn't stop himself; he asked his father the question that had been consuming him. "Why does God let things like this happen to a good man like James? He didn't do anything to deserve something like this. Why would he let this happen? If he is all-powerful, and can do anything, and loves us, how can he let this happen? If we are created in God's image and our love is like an imperfect version of God's and if we would do anything to save him we would have... why didn't he?"

No one looked at Jesus. Everyone stared at Joseph, wondering what he would say. He looked at his son with what would have been a smile on an ordinary day. "Son, I had hoped to talk with you about this later when I had time to think it through myself. It is an important question that is on all our hearts today. I wanted to prepare my thoughts, to slowly understand. But life doesn't work like that; we have to come up with answers earlier than we are ready to. Imperfect answers, incomplete. Patches to hold our hearts and minds together until we can know. We answer in whatever way we can until faith takes us through this time. Time heals. Love heals. It hurts a little less each morning, after the heart remembers, and twists itself to fit inside the new world the loss has left. But that doesn't answer the why; it only answers the how we go on anyway. *Why?* Why does God allow this, or does God *make* this happen, and if so, how could a God who loves us let this be?"

No one moved at the table. Silence waited for his answer. The moment grew longer; then he pushed away from the table and rose. Joseph closed his eyes, then opened them to heaven and began to sing.

Then the Lord answered Job out of the whirlwind and said,

Who is this that darkens counsel by words without knowledge?

Gird up your loins like a man; for I will demand that you answer me.

Where were you when I laid the foundations of the earth?

Declare, if you have understanding.

Who laid the measures thereof, if you know?

Or, who has stretched the line upon it?

Whereupon are the foundations thereof fastened?

Or who laid the cornerstone?

When the morning stars sang together,

And all the sons of God shouted for joy?

Or who shut up the sea with doors,

When it broke forth, as if it had issued from the womb?

Jesus looked around the table. Everyone was watching his father. Mary was nodding her head. Miriam was crying softly. He saw his father's eyes were wet, too. Joseph continued with God's questions for man's questions. Soon Joseph's voice took on a slightly higher pitch. It was an incomparable song. It didn't sound at all like what Jesus had heard in the Temple. It wasn't even like the way his father had sung it before. This was a new song that came from a place of knowing. It was his song now, as well as the song written by the author of Job. Jesus wondered if the book had indeed been written by Job, since he was the only one who could know it all so intimately. Or maybe by his wife. Job would have had the kind of humility that would not have wanted credit for the story. It had an autobiographical quality to it, Jesus thought. Writing in the third person gave Job freedom, if indeed it was him who wrote the record. Jesus could feel the power in his father's voice, it made him shiver.

Can you bind the sweet influences of the Pleiades?
Or loose the bands of Orion?
Can you bring forth Mazzaroth in his season?
Or can you guide Arcturas with his sons?

Jesus remembered all the nights his father had shown him the stars and named the constellations for him. Joseph sang on for minutes by memory. A hundred astonishing images of God's grandeur and man's insignificance. Then he paused, and continued from the Psalms.

When I consider your heavens,
The work of your fingers,
The moon and the stars, which you have ordained,
What is man that you care about him?
What is man, that you are mindful of him?
Or the son of man, that you visit him?

Then silence, as he searched his heart for what else to say. Joseph looked at the hungry faces at the table, desperate to be filled with solid answers. He looked at his children, his wife, and Miriam. He had emptied his soul in song. It wasn't enough. These answers were all still questions. These answers weren't enough to ease the pain. Not enough to stop Miriam's tears. Not enough to answer the question in his son's eyes. Not enough to bring peace and comfort to his own soul as he sang the words he had memorized. He looked at the candlelight reflected from Miriam's wet cheeks. Then a fragment, a phrase, came to his mind from the prophet Isaiah.

He will swallow up death in victory;
And the Lord God will wipe away tears from off all faces

He didn't know what else to sing. It would have to be enough, it was all they had. The silence wasn't broken for a time. God's voice whispered in the silence again. The meal continued. Life went on.

Simon's Song

Simon had been growing unnoticed in Mary's belly when James had been killed. He was Mary's sixth child. God had blessed her; none of her babies had died and all were healthy. She had not known the sorrow of other women who had carried a child in joyful hope only to have a stillbirth with no cry of life to announce itself to the world, but only a body slowly cooling without a move. She was never the struggling mother trying to wake empty flesh. Never the stunned mother who thought she was giving life. For them, no joy, just expectations and preparations ending with a quiet burial of a life that never was. Just a hope that died.

Mary had tried to comfort many women in their inconsolable grief. Now she was worried that this might be her turn. She realized she had carried this life to witness the death of her friend.

Yet she knew life conquers death with these babies - these first ones born after loss. They fill the empty place with their loud song announcing their arrival in this shocking world. From soft warm darkness to hard cold light; there is no going back to that comfortable world that was their home. They complain and then adapt.

Mary didn't know how she could tell Miriam that she was carrying yet another child while her friend still mourned not only the horrible death of her husband, but the end of all possibility of a child herself. But when she arrived at Miriam's home, she found her staggering, clutching her belly, laughing and crying at the same time. She was carrying a child, too. James' son, she hoped it was a son. Another James would live.

God brought life from death again.

...

Sometimes Mary lay awake at night worrying about her children. She didn't want Joseph to know how much she worried. None of them ever was the same since the death of James. Now they knew death was not something far away, it lived close, waiting patiently. Mary saw Miriam was changed forever. She still smiled and laughed occasionally, but the sadness had taken over her life. The terrible sadness of a young widow who had watched her husband slowly tortured before her eyes. Barely out of reach, intentionally. Miriam hated the Romans, the monsters who tortured the survivors as much as those they crucified. They condemned them all to days of helpless watching as life slowly leaked away. It was plenty of time to burn their helplessness into their souls forever. There was a point she knew when James gave up and relaxed. He didn't struggle anymore. He waited patiently for the death that came eventually to release him, and them.

Mary didn't know what else she could do for Miriam. She was afraid these thoughts would somehow affect their babies, all this sadness color the way they grew inside them. She didn't want a sad destiny for these children. She had five children who were started well; she hoped the same for these, too.

Mary could feel Joseph was awake next to her, thinking his own thoughts that kept away sleep. She touched his arm, and he turned to her. "You can't sleep, either, love?" He reached for her hand and their fingers slipped together as naturally as one person's fingers interwove in a gesture of prayer, or a moment of rest. It was a simple thing that brought calm comfort. They both looked up at the exposed beams of the ceiling. They remembered the night they sat on the ground below as they watched the stars through the spaces between those beams. They remembered their dreams of a home filled with children and love. It had been different than they had imagined. They hadn't guessed angels and glory and horror and death. They had imagined an ordinary life. An extraordinarily normal life.

They lay in silence. Mary shifted, rested her head on Joseph's shoulder. He slid his arm around her. Mary whispered, "It won't be long now. I pray this baby will grow up in a safer world. When will these Romans get tired of struggling with their bloated empire and go home? I want this child to grow up without all this death around him. I want him to live to a peaceful old age."

Joseph pulled his arm more tightly around his wife. He kissed her forehead. He caressed her belly with his left hand. "I pray the same for all our children. May peace come soon. I love our children and I love you." Mary settled in closer, and soon she was asleep. Joseph was awake for another hour, thinking, praying, wondering. *How would their Messiah bring them peace?*

Another week passed and Mary gave birth to healthy son. Simon. He was bright and alert, and a happy baby. Miriam was midwife, and when he let out a loud cry, then settled down to look around the world with curious eyes, the first person his eyes were drawn to was Miriam. She smiled at him and cradled him in her arms. He relaxed into her and smiled. She returned her first real smile at last.

Slowly, with this birth, life began to reassert itself. Laughter and love and the beauty of an innocent smile looking out on a world that was new to him. Like the first fragile spring green that timidly takes a chance that it will not freeze, but be fed by the warmth of the sun. This baby was that kind of hope for all of them, and when Miriam held him she first began to believe in life again. Her fears were fading, her nightmares eased. She had suffered many nightmares of her baby being stillborn or both of them dying in childbirth.

Miriam was huge now for such a tiny woman. She lumbered off-balance and everything was swollen. She still looked like a girl, but swollen now with life. James still lived in her from that last night before the memories she ran from in her mind. Every time they started she pushed them away, to think of some loving time with the man who still lived in her heart and in her womb. She wanted to forget his suffering, her suffering.

Miriam endured the nightmares, less now as the child's time was nearing. Mary feared what would happen to her friend if this child should die. And Miriam was not built for giving birth and this child was large. This child was more than a child. Mary feared what that would mean. This was her first childbirth.

Mary watched her friend hold Simon as she held her dreams. Miriam's eyes were closed as she pretended this was her own child already in her arms seeking her breast. James had loved her breasts. He had caressed them gently like they were tiny birds when he was in bed with her. She wished he were here with her to watch her feed their son. To watch her be a mother and use these breasts to give life to their son. She knew it was a boy, she could feel him - feel the sense of James in her. This big boy would carry James' name and memory. James' line would go on. She would see his face again, and tell him that she loved him in his son. Every time she spoke his name it would be for both of them. Her eyes still closed, Miriam hummed one of Joseph's lullabies to Simon as she cupped his fuzzy head in the palm of her hand.

At the lighting of the Sabbath candles, Miriam's water broke. She was puzzled by her twin emotions of relief and fear. Her time had come, and her baby had taken control of her body now. She struggled with life as long as James had on the cross. Three days of struggle at the edge of life for her and for her son. She knew it would be a son, she could feel it. She moaned and then there was silence, as she lay motionless. After the struggle she lost consciousness and lay still, with only the movement of the child twisting in her belly. It looked as if her womb was moving on its own. Her only other movement was the slow rise and fall of her chest.

Mary whispered something in her ear, and kissed her cheek. Joseph and his sons stood silently by, praying. Jesus came to his mother's side and asked what he could do.

"Just pray, like all of us, that God will protect them and bring them safely through." Mary held his hand. He saw the tears in his mother's eyes as he felt his own tears swelling, blurring the scene. Jesus felt his love for Miriam flow from his heart through his hands as he touched her forehead, then put both hands on her belly and prayed.

Miriam stirred, then slept for a few minutes. When she opened her eyes, she looked for Mary. She held out her hand. "I'm frightened, Mary. What should I do? I feel myself pushing. I have to do this. Even if it kills me, he must live! Promise me you will raise him as your own if I don't survive."

Mary knew Miriam was exhausted. But she knew how much she wanted this child, and how much she wanted to live to raise James' son. She knew love is the greatest power in the universe. Joseph put his hand on his wife's shoulder, then he bent and whispered in Miriam's ear. Without opening her eyes, she smiled. Jesus wondered what his parents had said to her in secret. He continued to pray to his father in heaven. Then he whispered something in Miriam's ear, and held her head in his hands. She opened her eyes and they looked into each other's eyes for a moment. Jesus held her belly between his hands. He closed his eyes and felt the love like prayer flow out of him and into her and all the life she carried. It was more than she thought, and Jesus understood, but he didn't tell her. He thought it would be too much for her to know at this point in her struggle. She had all she could stand for this moment. There would be time.

Joseph and Mary watched their son and felt the love in his eyes. They didn't know what he was doing, but they knew how he felt, and who he was. It was love, the healing power of love that can work miracles. They knew that love - they had lived it.

Miriam smiled. She nodded her head and asked for water. After she drank, she said, "We're ready." Then she began to push and strain. Joseph sang to her. Mary wiped her face. Mary's mother, Anne watched the progress and she and Mary told her what to do. Miriam rested for a moment, and felt the movement that comforted her. An inner force took over and pushed her child toward the bigger world.

The third night was over and the golden sunlight lit the room as his dark hair crowned. Miriam screamed and pushed and screamed again as his head was forced out of her. He cried at the first shock of light as he slid into Mary's arms. Miriam cried in relief. They cleaned him and put him in her arms. He was much smaller than she imagined. "You're handsome, James, just like your father" she said, as she straightened his fine hair that was plastered to his head. But something was wrong; her pain wasn't over. She was still pushing against her will. She wasn't done.

Mary looked concerned and whispered with her mother for a moment. Then kissed her friend on the forehead and kissed James. "He won't be alone, Miriam. You have another child."

The second birth was easier. She named him Joseph. James and Joseph were her two sons, and they were close as the two they were named after. They soon were feeding together as she rested, her two sons filling her chest.

Miriam's breasts were not enough to keep both her sons full. She was in a mother's torture. She couldn't make enough milk to feed them both. She had longed to be a mother, longed to have a child, but she never dreamed she would have twins. Her babies suckled on her desperately as she ran out of milk, and then they cried. Hungry. She had to feed her babies. Mary knew.

Mary stood next to her and her crying sons. "Here, Miriam, hold Simon for me, he is full. I've nursed six children now - one at a time - and always had more milk than I have needed. I have plenty to share. Two boys eat a lot." It is what a friend would do. James and Joseph filled themselves, and then Mary put them back in Miriam's arms.

Miriam was relieved that her sons were safe but embarrassed that she was not able to give them what she needed by herself. Four breasts, three babies, there would be plenty this way. Three healthy boys and two women who grew even closer than before with this bond. Sometimes Miriam fed Simon, too. And as time went on her milk increased.

Miriam moved in with them, of course. She was one of the family now. She was close to Jesus in a new way now; she would never forget what he had whispered in her ear. She thought he was very wise for his age. For any age.

Chorus

Joseph and Mary were overjoyed to keep their promise to James. James had been able to die in peace knowing that his wife would be protected and not be left alone. They couldn't save his life, but at least they could let him die in peace. Joseph was proud of the way his wife eased her pain. He loved to listen to Mary and Miriam talk and sing to their three babies as they fed them together. Miriam became even more like a sister to Mary as they shared a home.

The people of Nazareth had thought their family was a little strange before, but now that Miriam lived with them and Mary shared her breasts with her twins, people began to call her by her real name in a joking way. They laughed at Joseph in a good-natured way and said, "First a virgin birth and now he lives with Mary and *The Other Mary*. What do you expect from a singing carpenter in a house with three Joseph's and two James' as well as three Mary's? Sounds pretty confusing!"

They were right. Love sings complicated songs.

Stolen Songs

The seasons changed and the babies grew. What had started as a simple cold had overtaken Joseph. Although he was a strong man, this sickness was worse than anything else he had ever experienced. He was on fire with fever and his ears were in terrible pain. Mary bathed him with cool wet cloths, but it took days for his fever to break. He slept for days afterward, groaning in and out of sleep. Jesus and James stood helplessly by as their father suffered. He had always been a strong man but now he looked like a fragile bird.

Mary held his hand and read the map of scars that told the journey they had shared without a word. She wondered about the map of scars written upon his heart. She knew the journey with her had not been easy. It was not the life he had planned. Or she. Who could plan something like this? But it had written a map of love.

Mary called his name to wake him, but he didn't move. She called louder, then yelled. Still he lay motionless. Frightened, she shook him, and he opened his eyes, confused. She told him that she loved him and was glad he was finally awake. Joseph had a look of fear in his eyes, and he sat up to get closer to his wife. He said, "What did you say? I couldn't hear you, Mary, please speak louder." He did not know that he was shouting.

Mary spoke louder, and he looked more afraid. He couldn't hear a word. The man who lived for music and song was deaf.

Joseph spoke much too loudly. "Mary, I can't hear you at all. All I hear is a loud roaring and the thunder of my own voice inside my head."

Mary kissed his hand as she tended him the way she had when they first met. She stopped his fear like she had stopped his bleeding that day. She brought him nourishing soup and bread. He ate slowly and then fell back to sleep. Jesus and Mary talked alone into the night next to the bed where Joseph slept. They prayed for him, and he was getting stronger - but deafness would be an awful thing to him. Jesus prayed as hard as he ever had, he needed God to listen. His father had a lot of songs to sing that hurting people needed. If God wanted these good things to be, he had to make it possible. Jesus knew God could do anything. He was sure God would answer their prayers. He struggled in prayer for an hour. Then there was a loud noise at the door.

Agabus was desperate to warn Joseph about his dream, but it was impossible for him to get his message across. He stuttered worse than ever, frustrating everyone. Finally he turned to Mary.

"T-t-tell him t-t-to b-be c-c-ca-ca-careful o-outside."

Mary took his arm to walk him back to the door. "Thank you for caring, Agabus, but he needs to rest now. I'll make sure he knows." She closed the door and returned to tend Joseph until he returned to sleep.

She wiped her cheeks. And again. Then she let loose and sobbed. Jesus and James heard her, but they decided this time she needed to cry this out on her own.

Jesus was surprised in the morning when his father woke still deaf. He couldn't understand why God hadn't answered his prayers. He knew his father deserved to be healed if anyone did. Why would God let this happen to him? It wasn't fair.

Buried Song

Two weeks had passed. Joseph was strong enough to return to work in his shop. Jesus came in the door behind him and called, "Abba", then again more loudly. Still no response. Jesus stood silently. He watched his father go about his work as he always did, but songless and without a smile.

Joseph told his son that the only sound he heard was a loud rolling wind that tumbled inside his head with a high-pitched noise like bells that never fade. It was a pure bell tone that continued forever, pulsing louder and softer, but always at least as loud as someone yelling in your ear. They were chords that never stopped, made of high-pitched notes like a toddler's shrill scream or a summer insect's song. Jesus thought that noisy silence would drive him mad if he had to hear it every minute of every day. He didn't know how his father could stand to be robbed of real sound for this imaginary noise.

"Do you have the big axe my grandfather made?" Joseph asked, pointing by the door. "It's missing."

Jesus shook his head, and searched for it behind the pile of curing wood. It wasn't there. Jesus was afraid his father had misplaced it. He feared the sickness had affected his sharp mind as well as his ears. He asked his brothers later, but none had seen it. But the workshop had been different when his father was sick and wasn't there every day. There was no song, no children's laughter, no jokes.

The roaring wind in Joseph's ears grew softer as the weeks went by and opened a space for some real sound to sneak in. He began to hear voices. He couldn't understand what they were saying yet, but he could recognize people by their voice first. The cadence came through. It was like recognizing people by their walk in the distance before they were close enough to see clearly. Eventually he began to hear more. A birdcall from outside the window, the sound of a saw, and his Mary's words of love.

The ringing was still loud. It would never go away. Four notes that wavered like the scream of insects in summer's heat. It would be with him the rest of his life, but he would learn to ignore it and let the real sounds come through enough to enjoy the world again. He began to sing again - sing along with the notes that would never leave him - and Jesus realized his prayer had been answered enough.

Another Mary's Song

Simon was walking and talking when his little sister was born. Five boys and a girl filled their home. Jesus was a man now, as was James. They helped their father in his shop and they helped take care of their younger brothers and sisters. After six, Mary knew all about giving birth. Her seventh would come before morning, she knew.

Miriam was with her, holding her hand. Her sons James and Joseph considered all Mary's children as their own brothers and sisters. Simon was just a week older than the twins, and they were best friends. Miriam's sons had the older James and older Joseph and Jesus as bigger protective friends. They loved them as much as they had loved their father. They remembered all he had done to help them when they were young. And they couldn't forget the horrible way he died. They had listened to his plea for Joseph to protect Miriam after he was gone. James never thought he would have a son. He died without that hope. Hope sometimes lives for us when we have none of our own. Real hope is greater than our own. Hope lives in faith and love.

There never would be another man for Miriam. She was still a young woman, and beautiful, but she would never love like that again. She spent much of her time at the Temple, and in service to the sick and poor. Most of the joy in her life came from her sons, and from Mary's children, especially James and Jesus. She had watched them grow from babies into men. Jesus and James had been very close to her husband, and his death had bound them with Miriam in sorrow and loss. Watching helplessly while someone you love suffers such a slow horrible death scrapes the very corners of a person's soul. No one ever recovers. The horror has had too much time to burn itself into the memory. The Romans were very good at their work.

But life goes on in the babies born. Simon and James and Joseph and Miriam and this new one who would meet them this day. Miriam wondered where they came from, these souls that make their way to earth. From love to loving they come in mystery.

In the early hours a new endearing Mary joined them. Her first weak cry grew stronger in the night. She was passed from arms to arms of all her loving family. Her father held her, smiling as he held a memory of his own young Mary here again with them. He saw her in this baby's eyes. He saw the two of them together.

Mother Mary lullabied her little one, and was joined in whisper song.

Unclean Song

Three lepers lived outside Nazareth. Pitiful creatures who survived by begging and finding whatever food they could in the wild. Whenever anyone walked close to them, they were required by ancient law to cry out, "Unclean!" to warn away the uninfected.

Joseph and Mary often took them food and clothing. The winter in the hills of Nazareth could be very cold. Jesus wondered about these poor souls, outcasts suffering like Job as their flesh rotted away. One man had no fingers left at all, and no nose. One man seemed whole; he merely had whitish scaly patches on his skin, the early stages of the disease.

The healthiest man had a strong voice that carried well. "Unclean! For the love of God, please have mercy and give us alms!"

Mary had not only brought them bread, but had made cakes with raisins and dates for them. It brought a tiny spot of pleasure into their dreadful lives. They were slowly dying, bit by bit, outcasts feared and shunned. They were torn away from any family and even from any hope of comfort from the synagogue. They were alone and exposed to the elements in their weakened states. Mary and Joseph did what they could for these people touched by an unkind hand of God. Or at least, so it looked to Jesus. "Why would he let these people suffer like this?" He asked his father and mother to explain it to him. Joseph told him he would, as soon as they had left these men, but one of them had overheard and asked him to please tell him if he knew. In the lonely nights as he suffered there unable to sleep, that was the question that would never find an answer in his mind. He said he loved God, and trusted him, and prayed for healing, but it never came. He said he only had the horrible example of his future in the two men who had been slowly consumed by this disease in front of him. He saw his future every time he opened his eyes, it was moaning in front of him.

Mary looked at her husband, wondering what he would say. He put his arm around Jesus and they sat down near the lepers, as close as they dared. Joseph prayed silently for wisdom, to know what to say to help Jesus understand the things he didn't understand himself. He prayed for the words to bring some comfort to the hopeless men in front of him. Mary held his arm, and gave it a slight squeeze to let him know she had confidence in his ability to say the words that were needed. Words were the only power in this horrible situation.

Joseph closed his eyes a moment, then softly sang the song of a suffering David in his Psalm:

> *My God, why have you forsaken me?*
> *And are so far from my cry,*
> *And from the words of my distress?*
> *O my God, I cry in the daytime, but you do not answer;*
> *By night as well, but I find no rest.*

Jesus knew this mysterious song from the synagogue, the moving words that had always disturbed him. His father's eyes were closed as he sang, and tears leaked from behind his closed lids. His mother looked off in the distance to the little clouds moving quickly across the sky. The lepers leaned in to hear these words that they identified with, sung here by David's son.

> *Yet You are the Holy One*
> *Enthroned upon the praises of Israel.*
> *Our fathers put their trust in you:*
> *They trusted and you delivered them.*
> *They cried out to you and were delivered;*
> *They trusted in you and were not put to shame.*
> *But as for me, I am a worm and no man,*
> *Scorned by all and despised by the people.*

Joseph echoed the tears filling the lepers' eyes. He paused, took a breath, and looked at Jesus before he continued. Mary's fingers held his arm tightly. He was grateful for her touch; tears were filling his eyes, too.

All who see me laugh me to scorn;

They curl their lips and wag their heads, saying,

"He trusted in the Lord; let him deliver him;

Let him rescue him, if he delights in him."

Yet you are he who took me out of the womb,

And kept me safe upon my mother's breast.

I have been entrusted to you ever since I was born;

You were my God when I was still in my mother's womb.

Be not far from me, for trouble is near,

And there is none to help.

Joseph sang on through the rest of the Psalm, through the descriptions of great suffering and humiliation. Then he came to a verse of hope:

For he does not despise or abhor the poor in their poverty;

Neither does he hide his face from them;

But when they cry to him he hears them.

Peace began to settle upon all of them. The lepers had the first spark of life in their eyes, even in their wretched conditions. Jesus saw the power the words had on these men to give them hope and the knowledge that God had not forgotten them. Joseph sang on to the end of the Psalm. Then there was silence. Silence broken only by the sound of the wind and the distant call of a dove.

One of the lepers broke the silence. His words were hard to understand through his diseased mouth. "But I *have* been praying throughout the horrible years this has been eating my flesh away." He held up his hand missing most of three fingers. "When I lost my first finger, it was terrible; but as others have fallen off, I have become more used to it. I expect it now and it is no surprise. That is the real horror of it. I once was a man like you with a future. Now the only future I can see is a slow death as I become more crippled and there is less of me each day. You say God is listening and will answer my prayers? Do you think I will be healed? Do you think I have any real hope? Why would God torture me this way? It could happen to you, or that cute wife of yours. Or your boy. Would *you* still say God was listening as you watched the ones you love lose fingers and noses and legs? Tell me the truth, your son is listening to your words."

Joseph looked at his son, who was watching him, waiting for his answer. Mary stroked his arm she had been holding. He could feel her love. It gave him strength; it always did. He knew love was the most powerful force in the world.

He didn't know what to say, but he knew he had to say something. He prayed for wisdom for words that would comfort these people and touch truth. He didn't know anything except what he felt. He waited for a word from God, but the silence was becoming uncomfortable. He decided he would have to start talking, not knowing what he would say. The words would come to him - they always did if he spoke from that honest place within his heart.

"I'm just a man, I don't claim to know the mind of God, but here is what I feel. We are not gods or angels, we are mortal, and we all die. It is only a question of when and how, and what we have done before we do. But more than that, I think it is what we choose to be inside, that determines who we are. What we do, flows from who we are."

Mary slipped her hand down to his and their fingers twined automatically, as they always did.

"Some souls die before a breath. They come cold and blue from the womb. Some die as infants, with only months to leave their personality in our memories. Some die as children known for who they are, not for anything they have accomplished. And some live eighty years or more until the weight of time finally pulls their strength back to the earth. They are mourned by great-grandchildren and their works remain with their descendants. All of us have trials and testing. All have some challenges to face. None of us face our trials alone unless we choose to."

The most disfigured man made a wet noise of disgust.

"No man knows another's soul, and what he has to face in that time alone when we are face to face with our greatest fears. The angels watch us, waiting to see what we choose to do and how we choose to feel. God watches us too, and listens to our prayers."

Muffled sounds came from the man whose disease had ravaged him longest. He had no nose, his lips were partially gone, he had stubs of fingers on one hand, and none on the other. What was left of his legs was useless. Joseph couldn't hear what he was saying, but it was clear that he disagreed. He didn't know what to say to answer him. He looked at Mary, hoping she had something to say. She shook her head, and squeezed his hand. Joseph silently thanked God they had their fingers.

Not knowing what to say, he started anyway. "I'm sorry for your pain. I don't pretend to know what you are feeling. I don't know what I would do if I were you. I'm sorry. I wish I could do something, I wish I had the power to heal you, but I don't. All I can do is pray and hope God brings you comfort and peace at least. I wish I could do more. And I can be here. Be here and let you know I care."

Jesus wasn't satisfied. Neither were the lepers. Jesus pushed his father for answers to the deeper questions. Joseph pulled his hand free from Mary and stood up. He paced for a moment, then said, "I have no wisdom to explain these things. I only have faith, and stories of those who have struggled with these questions before. And I have David's songs. But we are here now. and there is real pain. Some people say we suffer in punishment for our sins, that sickness comes because we have done evil in our lives. But everyone knows good people who have been struck down while some truly evil men walk whole."

"Job struggled with these questions and his friends, demanding an answer from God. God spoke and never answered the questions, but Job, who had kept his faith despite his suffering, was rewarded with a glimpse of the mind of God. It embarrassed him, and he apologized."

"I know no other answer. I only know what I must do. Each man must decide for himself. All I can offer you are my prayers, some food, and friendship. I dare not touch you, I know you understand. One thing more. I am a carpenter, and I will build a shelter for you to keep you more comfortable than that ragged tent you have. I can make a place where the wind and rain won't torment you, and make your time a little easier. That is all that I can do, the rest is up to God and you."

Jesus told the men he would help his father build the shelter, too. They left for home and talked about the times men had heard God. Mary told Jesus about the prophet who waited for an answer from God. He waited on a mountain. A strong wind came and broke the boulders surrounding him. God was not in that wind. Then a great fire passed. God was not in the fire. Then a whirlwind. He wasn't in that either. Finally a deep silence. God was in the silence. In the silence he could be heard.

Caleb had lived a longer life than most dogs. But time had worn him down. His bright eyes were now dull blue with cataracts, and his keen ears were almost deaf. He slept most of the day; and when he limped outside, he stood still and wobbled as he remembered running in the wind. He sighed. He sighed again and just stood, sniffing with his nose -that was the one sense he could still rely on.

It was hard for him to get up after sleep. Arthritis had stiffened him. A few lumps had formed under his skin, and his once bright coat was dull and had spots where the scaly skin below showed through.

Joseph watched him from behind. He remembered the puppy that hid energetically under his cloak that first day he brought him home to his new family. He remembered the puppy that splashed in the mud below the first rainbow that Jesus saw. And he laughed out loud as he remembered Caleb holding the night threat on the floor. He would never forget the madman's face and screams. Caleb was the only one in the family who seemed to know how to reason with him. He never came close again while Caleb was around. "You have been our best angel. You have always been there, unlike the others with wings that seemed to be too busy to spend time here on the ground where our trouble was."

Joseph bent down behind him and put his hand on Caleb's head. He jumped, so blind and deaf he did not know Joseph was there. Then he sniffed to know him and rubbed his head against Joseph's hand. Joseph knew the time was near. He was so much a part of the family and so much a part of each child. Great playmate and better protector, now fading sadly. He had lived too long. It is a tragedy to die too early; it is worse to die too late.

Joseph turned and saw Jesus watching from behind. *I guess I'm an old dog, too. My ears are not what they used to be.*

Jesus said, "He is miserable, isn't he, Abba?"

"He's lived a long and happy life, but he is worn out. He has lived longer than most dogs ever do. He was a great friend to all of us. Dogs are full of the best love God ever created, maybe they drain themselves giving it to us and that is why they die so soon."

"He's always been there for me, and the other kids. It seems like he is slowly leaving, sleeping more each day until he just here less and less each day and more in the world of dreams. I'll miss him. Why do all the good ones in my life have to die so soon?"

Joseph took him in his arms. "We all die. One day we all die. Look at him, how miserable he is becoming. It is God's gift that we die instead of suffering like that forever. But we just die here to go on. We join God. And though some people think animals just end, I hope Caleb will be with us someday. I think God would love him, I can't believe someone as good as this faithful friend won't be with us. He has been better to us than the angels."

"I hope so, too." Jesus said, as he bent to rub Caleb's head.

The next morning when they woke, Caleb didn't.

J oseph rested on the grass as Mary and the children spread the meal on a cloth. This was the hillside he loved. The hills where he had walked with his young love in the moonlight. He closed his eyes and let the song of his family fill his soul. Jesus knew what his father was doing, so he sat down quietly next to him and began to sing a song. Soft as the wind at first, then loud enough for him to hear the words. Soon the other children heard him and joined in, and Mary and the other Mary - Miriam, too. The whole family was singing Joseph's song. Tears swelled out from behind his closed lids.

Little Miriam put little Mary on her father's chest. He cuddled his baby daughter and listened to the song he loved best, the giggle of a gleeful baby. Doves joined from the distance. Insects added texture to the song, insects that were like the sound he always carried with him now. The sound that was the scar the sickness left in his ears. The sound he had learned to ignore most of the time. He had to. Tiny fingers played with his face and pulled on his beard. The lips he knew so well rested on his forehead, then whispered in his ear. He left the world of song for the music that filled his eyes.

The little ones were playing. Jesus and James were sitting off to the side deep in conversation. Little Miriam was fussing with the arrangement of the food, trying to make it perfect, as she always did with everything.

Little Joseph and Judas and Simon and the other Mary's children were spinning around in circles with their arms outstretched until they fell to the ground.

His world was full of laughter again and full of song.

A month had passed. Tonight's sunset was building into what promised to be a gorgeous finale. Pinks eased to reds while soft peach tones hardened into deep orange. The shadow side of clouds began blue then darkened into deep violet. Jesus walked alone with Mary and Joseph into the hills to enjoy the beautiful show and the relief of cool air after a hot day. They laughed and shared their favorite memories of a wonderful life. Jesus loved his parents and they loved him. He had always been a good child, but that was to be expected. He had learned life from these two who loved him and did whatever they could to prepare him for his destiny. They had no idea what that might be, just that he was to be king of Israel. More than that, he was to bring the world peace at last somehow. He was Emmanuel, *God with us.* But to them, mostly he was their son.

Jesus had his father's sense of humor. He repeated an old joke Joseph had told him in the carpentry shop when he was a boy. They all laughed, and Mary shook her head. The two of them, these men, were always deep in wordplay. She tolerated their puns, but rolled her eyes heavenward to the One who set this all in motion. The One who chose this singing carpenter to mold a child's image of what a man should be. *Your ways are not our ways, Lord . . . or maybe they are.* Mary thought to the sky. Then Jesus said, "You know, mother, when that donkey of ours was first born it was small enough for me to pick it up..." They all laughed again. Mary released an exasperated squeal. "Enough!"

Mary looked at these men she loved, her husband and her son. She had other children she loved, too, but this was her firstborn, and the Son of God. *I am truly blessed above all women to know these men, this love.* She remembered the first night she walked those hills with Joseph, and the day he asked her to be his wife. Their world certainly changed since then. She wondered what else God had in mind for them. Twenty-three wonderful years. She couldn't imagine what her life would be like without them in it. Jesus had learned from his father how to cheer a woman's heart with flowers or a gift made from the heart. Whenever wildflowers bloomed, they both kept Mary supplied. She remembered the first bruised handful of weed-flowers that were offered to her in her son's tiny fist. He was so proud to give her a gift like he had seen his father do may times. And Joseph had helped him gather them for her. She smiled at both of them for that, remembering.

Joseph saw the shadow flicker out of the corner of his eye and turned to see the axe swinging toward his son's head. He only had time to push him away and step in front of them. Jesus and Mary fell, covered with blood. Joseph's blood. Mary screamed as Jesus pulled the axe from the surprised madman's arms, and pushed him to the ground.

Jesus turned and fell to his knees above his father. His head was split open and the ground was covered with his blood. There was no breath in him. His eyes were open, but sightless. He was gone. Jesus knelt over the man he loved and cried. He touched his face and closed his sightless eyes. His mother joined him on the ground.

The madman rose and stood over them and screamed, "You were the one! You were the one, why did he have to get in the way? You were supposed to be the one. You are the pretender who is in my way!"

Jesus looked through him, past him. He saw Mary slumped on the ground, too shocked to cry yet. She was trying to push Joseph's head back together and she was rocking him like a baby. She was covered in his blood. The first stars were appearing as the madman babbled on. Jesus touched Mary's shoulder. He watched his father's killer laugh. Then Jesus stood and held the ax high in the air above his father's killer's head.

"Kill me, kill me, or I'll kill you and your mother when I get the chance. There can only be one of us in this world. I'll never stop, you know, I'll win eventually. After I am rid of you I'll rule the world my way. I am the king. I am the king of everything in my world."

Jesus felt his father's sticky blood on the axe handle in his hand. He gripped the axe so tightly he was shaking. He realized it was the axe his great-grandfather had made that had been missing from its place by the door. That angered him more – he had killed his father with something they both loved. Jesus felt the familiar tool and felt the weight and balance of it that was so familiar. But it was dripping his father's blood down to his hands.

Jesus knew he could stop this man forever in this moment. He knew if he didn't, he might stand over his mother's bleeding body some day soon. It would be a terrible life of waiting, never able to relax. *Where were the angels who could have protected my father? Where was God?* If someone were to stop this man it was here and now. This man was evil. There was no question of that.

"Do it! Kill me now, or I'll drink your mother's blood and eat your eyes! You will never know when it will come. After you are gone, I'll kill your mother slowly and do everything to her you fear."

Jesus knew no one would blame him. They would thank him for ridding the town of this dangerous killer. He could kill an innocent child; he had tried to kill the baby in Mary's womb twenty-one years ago. Jesus heard his mother's brokenhearted sobbing. He looked down at the man he loved. He remembered. He pulled the family axe far back and closed his eyes. He remembered. Jesus opened his eyes and looked at this dangerous man who had just killed his father, this man who might kill his mother someday. Jesus let out a great cry and swung the axe as hard as he could and threw it far away. Then a single soft word. "*Go.*"

He remembered his father and what he had taught him. He remembered Joseph's words to this man years ago when he could have killed him then and saved them all this pain today. He could have. But he didn't. He had mercy and faith. Joseph understood that some things are more important than life. Jesus remembered his father's love. He remembered his other father's love, and he remembered who he was.

The madness calmed, the murderer walked away.

Jesus sang softly. *Yit'gadal v'yit'kadash sh'mei raba ...* A wolf howled in the distance as *Amein.*

Mary and Jesus stayed with Joseph until the sky filled with stars. Jesus carried him home to the house he had built, to the house that had been their sanctuary. When his brothers and sisters asked what had happened, Jesus told them, "He sacrificed himself for me."

Mary added, "And me. He took the blow of the madman's axe that was meant for us."

They never got to say goodbye.

Requiem

They sang over his body at the funeral. Many friends talked about his love. His family remembered how much he loved life and loved them. They repeated his silly jokes and praised his craftsmanship. They remembered his quiet faith and his patient grace. They remembered all he had read to them from the Law and Prophets. Jesus had learned much from his father, he had learned what it meant to be a man, and to be a man of faith. And Joseph and Mary had taught him how to love. But Joseph had brought music into his life and all that means.

They sang his songs, all that they could remember. His whole life was a song.

They kissed him before they put him into the earth. Mary took his hand and kissed the scar. She held the strong hands that had touched her with love. She kissed his cold lips one last time. She smoothed his hair and whispered her secret name for him no one else had ever heard. Then said, "Goodbye, my love."

Jesus touched his body one last time. He was shocked at how cold it was. His father was gone. This man Jesus loved was gone from them. Gone. Jesus knew what death was now, after this cold touch. Death that had a purpose. Death that was love. But death that was cold and close.

They returned to an empty home. They talked about this most human man who had taught the Son of God the one lesson he could never learn from his other father. He taught him what it meant to die for those you love.

Waking Song

Jesus woke to the sound of quiet crying. He heard his mother's ragged sobs; he heard his little sisters. He lay there thinking with his eyes closed until the wetness on his cheek told him he was crying, too. Every morning there was a moment before he had awakened fully when the world was still whole. Then the emptiness ate a space in it that couldn't be filled. It was a new world, a world without his father. Jesus fought it for a moment, tried to pretend it was only a bad dream, but the reality of the muffled sobs convinced him it was real. He couldn't imagine a world without this man. He didn't know how his mother would go on. He had never seen another love like theirs. This man had taught him everything.

Jesus kept his eyes closed, still not wanting to believe this day. He wondered what he should do. Things were difficult before, financially - now they would be worse. Ever since James had been killed, they had been much more cautious. Jesus had lived in fear of a crucifixion for his father ever since that day. He was glad he had been spared those days of torture for a quick death. A death of purpose to save those he loved. Jesus opened his eyes, not willing to let the horrible memory of the sight of his dead father fill his mind. He filled his eyes with morning light instead. Whatever this day held, it couldn't be as bad as that vision of his father on the ground.

What would Joseph do? Jesus knew. He would lead his family and protect them for his father. He would find a safe way to feed them all. His brother James would share the burden, and the others as best they could. His mother wove fabric that could bring in more money, too. If they could just pay the taxes and keep their home they would survive. Their garden helped feed them, and there was a lot of work available to build Sepphoris, the Roman city being built nearby. He would not take chances, though. He knew his mother couldn't stand to see him die. Certainly not the kind of death they had watched James suffer through for days.

Jesus closed his eyes, gathering strength. His family needed him to be strong. They depended on him. He pretended for one last moment that this was all a dream and he could hear his father's song coming from a nearby room. He curled up in bed like he had when he was a child - safe in the security of the world he lived in then - safe in his parents' love. Safe when he still had Joseph to rely on. He had always been there, but now he was gone. Jesus pulled his legs up to his chest, and wrapped his arms around them. Twenty-two years out of the womb; he wished he could return today. His father had always protected him, kept him safe from every kind of danger. He taught him how to disarm fear. He taught him how to take the threatening serpents of fear and break their fangs off. Jesus smiled as he remembered the image his father had told him of helpless serpents with their fangs gone, only annoying them as they gummed their legs helplessly. Toothless serpents, that's what Joseph called fears faced bravely. Toothless serpents. Jesus rose from bed with a weary smile.

Work Song

The shop was empty. No song came from the idle saw. Jesus sat alone in the morning light. Things were just as his father had left them. The table he had almost finished was in the middle of the room. The smoothness stopped halfway, unfinished. *My father was just taking a break to sleep, he would return. He never left anything unfinished.* Shadows moved; the sunlight lit a distorted rectangle on the wall and inched across his father's world. His plumb line and square were lit first. Soon they were dark as the light moved on to his ripping saws. Jesus realized he was standing above the table feeling the place where the smoothness on the table stopped, and only roughness lay beyond. His father had touched this spot a week ago; this would have been his next few inches of wood to smooth. Jesus looked up at the plane hanging on the wall, a tiny curl of wood left on the blade, the last wood his father worked.

He would not complete his father's work. Not this table, at least. He would keep it and often come alone to touch he spot where the rough became smooth and stopped. He would walk to his father's table for years, remembering him. Remembering all he had learned and his sacrifice. *Anamnesis,* Jesus thought to himself.... *remembering* in Greek. He had learned some Greek and Greek philosophy from the learned men he spoke with in the synagogue, and the rich Romans he worked for. *Anamnesis.* It was a word that meant more than just remembering something - it was being there with the one remembered in a mystical way. It was a feeling that the loved one was still with you in a place outside of time that was no less then than now. *Anamnesis* ... he came to this table each time remembering. He ate meals there alone, pretending his father was there with him. He ate meals with his brothers in the shop, sharing memories. It was sacred to him.

Jesus put a cloth over the table to protect it. He started a new table exactly like it to replace it for the customer. He chose a piece of wood. He measured it against the standing table. He started ripping the wood to size with his father's saw. The saw set the rhythm. Joseph's song came from Jesus' lips.

Dissonance

Jesus had no money to pay the taxes that would be due in a few weeks. He knew his mother and little sisters and brothers would all be homeless if he couldn't pay. There were some people who owed his father money, but he knew they were in the same kind of financial trouble that he was. The tax collectors were being pressured, and some of them enjoyed taking away property for the great profit they received. They were the ones becoming rich with the Roman army protecting them. They were helping to destroy their own people by intentionally overvaluing property to take advantage of the poor.

Jesus visited all his father's debtors. It broke his heart to see them struggle with the same dilemma. He realized if he took mercy on them, his own family would suffer. He knew he couldn't try to cheat on his taxes, no matter how unfair they were. He might end up like James. He couldn't do anything that would take a chance at breaking his mother's heart like that. He couldn't let her see her son get crucified. Joseph's death had been hard enough on her. He didn't know what he could do. He couldn't let his mother suffer, but how could he do the same things that he feared for his family to his neighbor's families? He couldn't force them to pay what they owed.

He went from home to home, down his list of debtors. The smiling faces greeting him fell to fear and shame. He was making them miserable, and himself. He dreaded each new house. They told him how sorry they were about Joseph, and how sorry they were that they couldn't pay. He knew some of them could pay at least a part, but they knew he wouldn't do anything to them. He realized his mercy was costing him and his mother. He didn't know what to do.

He collected a little money, but he was far from close to his tax debt. He was at war inside himself about what to do. He wished his father was here so he could ask him what to do. He prayed. He begged for a miracle, or at least wisdom and a chance to keep his family safe. He walked the Galilean hills his father loved, the hills they had searched for trees. He felt his father's presence there. He remembered conversations they had shared on long journeys to find suitable trees. He remembered his father's example, the mercy he showed, and the gifts he gave to people in need.

He remembered Joseph's words, "If we didn't forgive our debtors, how could we expect God to forgive us our great debt? Everything is a gift from God loaned us for the little while we are here."

Jesus remembered a song that came from his father's mouth on that same hill he walked tonight. It was the answer he needed. He remembered why his father had been so merciful and patient with people, and why he had forgiven so many debts. *It was because he knew God would provide.* He knew the secret. It wasn't angels or miracles, it was quite mundane and up to him. *He* was the miracle that would happen in the grace of God. God had given him a good mind and body, so he could make a plan and find new ways to keep them alive. He wasn't alone. He had friends and family, and God was watching everything. He just had to work and believe and not let the fear of failure win. His fears were *toothless serpents.*

Snake Charming Melody

Taxes were due today. The man who had reported James to the Romans was threatening Jesus now. He was a short man with a red face and a bulbous nose. He shook his finger and pointed as he yelled. He thought he could frighten Jesus like he had frightened everyone else. Jesus looked at his face and saw a snake with only stubs for fangs, and couldn't help smiling at him. The tax collector jumped back, disarmed by this unexpected smile. He had never seen that before on someone's face as he was threatening him. He was a little bully with no strength of his own, only the Roman Empire standing behind him like a strong big brother behind a nasty little child, sputtering for a fight.

Jesus saw the tax collector gumming his leg in his mind's eye and could barely restrain himself from laughing. Jesus offered him a deal. He would pay him twenty percent more than he asked at the end of the month. The little man agreed. When he was alone, Jesus sat at his father's table with parchment and quill and began to make a plan. He had barely over three weeks to make this work. He made a list of everything he could sell that was ready. He made a list of every way he could think to sell them. He thought of things the Romans might need, he made a list of all of them who had bought from his father before. He divided the days, and loaded the donkey cart with each day's opportunities.

He took his brother James with him, knowing that his name would remind some of these Romans of his father's friend who used to sell them exotic things they loved. They came home with an empty cart that evening. They had orders for more things their customers wanted them to build. In two weeks they had met their goal, but they kept on. They could relax a bit. Jesus brought his mother the tax money and handed it to her with the same pride he had felt as a child giving her his first handful of bruised flowers. He also gave her another handful of wildflowers this day along with the bag of coins.

Jesus had to be the one to take the payment to the tax collector since James couldn't stand to talk with him. He had never forgiven him for his part in his namesake's death. Jesus could feel the regret in this man. He knew he had seen the sorrow he had caused, it was a small village. Jesus could feel his troubled soul that bubbled out in angry threats. His snakes still had fangs that frightened *him*.

Sabbath Song

Shabbas came with the sunset. Mary lit the candles as she sang her prayer:

Barukh atah Adonai, Eloheinu, melekh ha'olam ...

The light of the candles echoed the color of the fading sunset on Mary's face. Jesus thought his mother looked beautiful. The chair next to her was empty. No one could think of removing Joseph's chair. As soon as Mary finished the blessing on the candles, Jesus started one of Joseph's songs. James added his voice first, then everyone else. Mary looked around the table at all Joseph's children. James who was strong and kind and good with wood and words. Joseph who had his father's voice and sense of humor. Judas who was the scholar with the lonely mind who liked to be alone. Miriam, the beauty with a kind heart and an artist's eye. Simon, the dreamer and absent minded. Mary, sweet Mary, her father's baby. And Jesus. What would life bring to all their children? Mary had hoped the Romans would be gone by now. Things were getting worse each year. Joseph's adorable children, she could see his face in all of them, even Jesus. Mary could feel Joseph with them this evening. They sang three more of his songs before they sat to eat.

Jesus talked about business. He shared his ideas with his family on how they could make more money. Mary thought he sounded like his father's friend James. Jesus and his brother James would spend the days working in Sepphoris, then in their shop each night. Joseph would stay and tend the shop with Judas. The younger children would help out as they could with the sanding and finishing.

Mary told all her children Joseph would be very proud of them. Bittersweet silence followed as they remembered him. This time would pass and the pain would ease

Jesus rose from the table and left the room. He returned to hand his mother a polished box of olive wood. Mary closed her eyes and felt the cool smoothness. In a few moments, she swung the lid of the box back. She took out several pieces of parchment and read them slowly. Then she passed one to Jesus, who started the song with his strong voice. Mary closed her eyes. She thought Jesus had Joseph's voice.

Whispered Melodies

Jesus woke in the middle of the night to flickering lamplight from his mother's room. The position of the moon in the window told him dawn was still hours away. He stood at her doorway without disturbing her. She sat reading Joseph's songs, and softly singing. The box was open. Parchment spread songs before her like the memories that filled her life. The birth of children, first steps, days of summer picnics, fears conquered, people who had gone on long before, and sunsets seen and felt, all pieces of the love of life.

Jesus watched her from the doorway as she touched her husband in her mind. She ran her caressing fingertips across the pages, then lifted them to her chest. She was touching him as he was touching her. Love lasts beyond life.

Jesus knew he had been blessed to know this kind of love, to watch the way his parents made a life together. The emptiness she felt with Joseph gone was fuller than what most people know when they are together. He was still with her in memories and words and the most enduring thing of all, melodies. The rise and fall of notes, the intervals of sound and silence, the patterns that form a whole. Simple melodies that are the center that time builds upon. Each repetition builds something stronger. Jesus listened as Mary hummed softly in the night, and they were with Joseph in his song.

Jesus passed through the doorway as if it were the entry to a holy shrine. He rested his hand on his mother's shoulder. She didn't turn to look at him, just held the hand that rested on her shoulder, the way she had each time Joseph put his comforting touch there. She closed her eyes and pretended he was back with her. She kept humming with her eyes closed, rocking slowly back and forth as she stroked the back of Jesus' hand, feeling for the familiar scar. It wasn't there.

Children's Song

Jesus and his brothers worked almost every day in the carpentry shop or at Sepphoris, except the Sabbath, of course. At first, after his father had been killed, only a few sad-faced children came to look around and remember. Jesus hadn't realized how many children missed his father. His family had been too involved with their own grief and the difficulties of making a living to notice all the songless children in the neighborhood. When he realized how much they shared his grief, he started singing with the saw the way his father had.

He didn't know each child's song like his father had; he needed to ask some of them to teach him while he worked. Soon the shop was filled with children and song again. Some days Mary came to listen; it made her feel like Joseph was back again and the world had righted itself.

Jesus had a remarkable voice like his father, but couldn't make up songs so quickly. Jesus didn't sing as well as Joseph, but he was a natural storyteller. Songs would fill the work time; but when work was done he would gather the children together and tell them stories. He told them about his father and mother, and about the heroes in the Bible. David, Moses, Joseph, and Joshua lived again in that room. Jesus told stories of these men as if he had known them personally, and had watched their adventures. He told stories about the women heroes, too. Queen Esther, Rebecca, Rachael, and an unnamed Shunamite, they all lived in those children's minds.

Sometimes the little ones would fall asleep in Jesus' lap while he was weaving a world of words. Little eyes grew large with the thump - thump - thump of Goliath's stride before David the little boy sent his own loud thump against the giant's forehead. Even though they knew it was coming, the children still jumped when Jesus yelled the final loud thump as the giant landed in front of little David.

Jesus taught them what these stories meant. He made them real, like any good storyteller would. Soon mothers would come to share to this story time at the end of each day with their children. The carpentry shop was full again, as it had been when Joseph sang.

Legato

Agabus stood at the doorway of the workshop, waiting to be asked in. This was very uncharacteristic of the way he usually acted. It was early morning and Jesus was working alone.

"I w-wa-wanted t-to be here w-where your fa-faaa-fa-father worked. I have such g-good m-memories here."

"Here, sit here in my father's favorite chair, it is where he used to sit peacefully and think about his dreams." Jesus brushed the sawdust off the chair and pushed it toward the nervous man.

"He w-was m-my friend and I m-miss him. I w-wanted y-you t-to know h-how m-m-much he m-meant to m-me. I am so s-sorry f-for y-you and y-your sweet m-mother. They were both always s-so k-kind t-to me."

Jesus put his hands on the stuttering man's shoulders and leaned over to look directly in his eyes. "He loved you, Agabus, he and James often talked about you and how they saw the real person inside you that others missed. He said he forgot your stutter when he listened to you and was able to hear your real voice inside. He wished you could hear that voice and let it out. I do too. I think you have a lot to say having held so much in for so long."

Then something unexpected happened. Silence. Silence that filled Agabus with peace. Jesus could feel the flow as Agabus felt his shoulders relax for the first time in his life. He was letting go of something that had cursed him his entire life. Something that made some people pity him. Something that made other people ridicule him. Something that made him so alone he couldn't even bear the contact of conversation although he wanted it so desperately. His face relaxed, his perpetual wince softened. He smiled. Jesus felt that something that flowed from himself into Agabus, then returned like a harmonic echo. It was love. It was peace.

"Thank you. Thank you for understanding me and sharing our memories of your father. I feel so much better now." Agabus' eyes grew wide. "I didn't stutter. I'm talking. Listen to me. I'm talking – just talking!"

Jesus stared at him and he realized it was true. He was talking without a stutter for the first time in his life. They both laughed and hugged each other.

Joseph would have been proud.

Grace Notes

Jesus was alone on the hillside, harvesting a tree. He felt eyes watching him. Between the loud blows of the axe, he listened for movement. Every time he looked around, he seemed to be alone, but he knew he wasn't. The axe never left his hands, even when he rested.

He could feel the presence of danger behind the ridge just in back of him. He chose to keep his back to it, not face it. He wanted it to show itself, whatever it was. His ears were ringing from the waiting and his beating heart. He decided to cut faster, let the sound of the axe drown out the noise, and give whatever it was a chance to sneak up on him. He wanted it to relax.

He worked until the sweat was pouring off him. Each stroke was followed by the next in a rhythm that flowed into a constant echo from the hills. Everything disappeared into the noise, until he swung around to face what stood a step behind him.

He had turned at the last moment to see the heavy rock raised in both hands above the head of the man who wanted to kill him. It was a familiar face. He had killed his father.

He was naked, as usual. His matted hair was wild as a donkey's mane. His bloodshot eyes glared hatred. Saliva drooled down his beard. He shook with the weight he held, and the rage.

Jesus knew no one was watching. He moved quickly with the axe in his hand to solve the problem. One quick move was all it took. He knocked the stone backwards and it fell behind the madman with a thud harmlessly.

They stood facing each other silently. Jesus had the axe in his hands. The naked man had nothing. Jesus spoke to him gently, as his father had long ago.

"Do you want me to kill you? Do you want to be released from the prison of your mind? You must be suffering terribly in there. Do you want to be free?"

"I want to dance on your body! I want to see your brains spilled on the ground like your father! I want to rape your mother until she likes it! I want you gone forever! There is no dog or father to save you from me now. You're mine at last."

Jesus felt the grain of the wood of the axe-handle in his hands. He remembered his father's body, and his sobbing mother. He remembered the way they struggled to gather all that had spilled to bring home to bury. He remembered the lifeless eyes, the silent lips. The wood in his hand felt good, and terrible. He looked down at his white knuckles, and the straining tendons. His body had taken over and his heart was pumping with rage. He felt the taste of metal in his mouth. He was panting and getting dizzy with not moving.

The naked man lunged at him, tearing at his throat and eyes. Jesus thrust the axe handle forward, held vertically to the ground. It knocked him loose, and sent him spinning to the earth, uninjured, but stunned. He was back on Jesus in a moment, tearing at him with the force of madness. His long nails drew blood from a dozen wounds. His hands were red with Jesus' blood. Again, he was knocked to the ground. He sat there smiling, as he tasted the blood, licking it from his fingers. "I want more."

Jesus felt the blood drip from his face to the dusty ground below. He saw the blood running down his arms. The mad man picked up a sharp stone in each hand and screamed as he lunged at Jesus' face again. The axe pushed him back to the ground, but he was on his feet again immediately. Jesus had to hit him harder. Still he only used the handle, keeping the blade of the axe facing away from the man.

He wouldn't stop. The madness gave him inhuman strength; it was as if he were battling a demon from hell. His eyes stared deeply into Jesus' eyes and there was a shocking recognition. He saw *it*.

The sharp stones found their mark many times, and Jesus was bleeding from deep wounds now. The battle had gone on for almost an hour. A battle he could end at any moment with a single stroke of the axe in his hand. He had the power of life or death over this man who wouldn't stop until he was dead. Jesus was tiring. He knew one of these cuts could slash his neck or arm and then it would be too late to stop him, he would be too weak. He wouldn't be able to defend himself, his mother, or his sisters.

He couldn't escape from him. If he didn't stop him, he would die, and then what would happen to his mother and his family? He had no choice. He turned the axe and swung it hard against the man's head. A sickening hollow sound was followed by his body slumping to the ground. The battle was over.

Jesus looked at the motionless form below him. He remembered what his father had told him the day he saved him from this man at the river. He knew he had done what his father would have done. He had no choice. He had stopped him the only way he could. He sat down, resting the axe across his knees. He wiped the blood out of his eyes and bound his wounds with strips of cloth he tore from his clothing. He stared at the man on the ground. He watched the slow movement of his chest. Then he dragged his unconscious body back to Nazareth, it wasn't safe to leave him here, unprotected from the wolves.

Mary stood speechless as her bloody son struggled with the door. She wasn't happy with what Jesus dragged into her home. James entered the room to see what all the noise was about. Joseph added his stunned silence to the room. Everyone stared at Jesus, waiting for his explanation.

Before he could speak, the madman began to stir. Obscene words erupted. He tried to attack Jesus again, even in his weakened state. Jesus shocked everyone when he stepped heavily on his throat to hold him down.

Jesus called to his brother, "Get some rope and a piece of cloth, quickly, James, before he gets stronger"

Mary watched dumbly as Jesus tied the man's hands behind his back. Then he ran the rope around his feet and drew the rope up, so that his hands and feet were held together and useless. The curses grew louder as he struggled against his bonds. Then Jesus silenced him with a wad of cloth in his mouth held in place by a strip of cloth tied around his head.

There was still no word of explanation, so James finally spoke. "I think a dog would have made a more appropriate pet, Jesus."

Mary was in no mood for humor. "You are cut and bleeding, if you have a plan, I'd like to hear it now. If you don't have a plan then I have one. That monster killed my Joseph."

Jesus explained his plan. It wasn't a great idea, but nobody had a better one. The three oldest boys would arm themselves with clubs and carry him far from town to release him. They didn't know what else to do. They hoped he would realize his attacks were hopeless and leave. They were afraid he wouldn't, though. In fact, they were pretty sure he would not give up so easily. But they didn't know what else to do.

At first light they untied his feet to lead him away, but he struggled with them and kicked so much, they finally tied him to a pole and carried him on their shoulders. It was easier that way. They looked like hunters bringing home a scrawny, naked bear. They gave more laughter to Nazareth as they carried him out of the city.

Two hours later, they released him. They all held clubs to protect themselves. But he didn't run away. He lunged at Jesus and James was foolish enough to pull him off. He turned and went for James' eyes. Joseph pulled him back, but then the three of them were rolling together on the ground like some twisted knot of snakes. Jesus tried to pull him off and only succeeded in getting the full force of his fury directed at his face, opening wounds that had not had time to heal.

James and Joseph held him down and beat him for what he had done to their father and what he had done to them. Jesus yelled at them to stop, but they wouldn't. They were angry, and wanted this madness in their lives over at last. Jesus had to pull them off him to make them stop, but when he did, the madman jumped on them and beat them as they were pulled back. So Jesus had to let them loose.

For ten more minutes this insane battle raged, until James had enough and used his club to knock the man unconscious again. Mad as he was, one more blow to the head couldn't make things much worse.

The three brothers sat panting on the ground. Before he could wake again, they tied him tightly to a tree. In a few minutes he woke and struggled with the ropes. They knew it would hold him briefly, but that he would free himself soon. It gave them time to get away. They hoped he had enough for one day and wouldn't follow then.

They were wrong. Madness doesn't know *enough*. A half-hour later he jumped Jesus from behind, and it all started again. James didn't wait so long to use the club this time.

The village of Nazareth roared when they carried him back home again, all of them bruised and bloodied this time. Mary wasn't happy with her boys. They came up with another plan. They loaded him directly into a donkey cart with some large pieces of wood they selected that were longer than a standing man. They carted him and the wood the rest of the day and overnight to the shore of the Sea of Galilee. They built a raft without a rudder, only a sail so that even if he worked his ropes free he could only travel to the east with the wind. He could not return to them this way. They tied him securely to the raft, removed his gag, and launched the raft into the water. The sailed filled and took it quickly to the east. It was eight miles across the freshwater lake called the Sea of Galilee. If the wind died down he would not die of thirst. But it was much too far to swim.

Jesus watched the raft sail away and said, "I hope someone will find him on the shore and know how to deal with him safely. I hope they see our note explaining what we did and why. May God protect whoever finds him."

The madman's curses could be heard fading as he floated to the east for almost a mile.

It was a long but peaceful journey home; they stopped to sleep along the way. They imagined he was still screaming as he sailed across the lake, frightening birds and turtles along the way. They wondered what sort of person would rescue him and set him free. Careful, they hoped, and strong.

They took turns watching for his return through the night. One son after another sat with a club across his knees. They did the same all through the next night after they were home. When that day had passed, they felt somewhat relieved. When a week passed, they felt safer, then safer still after a month. They hoped he wasn't dead, but decided that might be acceptable, too. When a month had passed, they began to finally relax.

They gathered for the Shabbas meal. Mary added a line to her normal prayer as she lit the candles. "I am so grateful that we sit around our table in peace at last, and that monster is gone from our lives."

" I wonder where he is and what he is doing now?" said James.

" Probably howling at the moon and scratching his fleas.," said Joseph.

Jesus rested his head in his hands and looked down. "I hope he made the journey safely, but that he didn't cause anyone any harm when he was released."

Joseph snorted. "Not very likely, brother. I'm sure wherever he is if he is alive he is causing trouble."

Mary said, "I don't care what he is doing somewhere else, I'm just glad my family is safe at last. He has hurt us all enough. Too much. If it were not for him, my Joseph would be sitting in this empty chair."

"Do you think he has found another target wherever he is now and has forgotten us? Or is the sun bleaching his bones?"

"I don't think he is dead, I would feel it if he were. But I don't think he is a threat to us anymore." Jesus said.

"What do you think happened? Do you think some fishermen found him and set him free?"

"I hope they read our warning first, and took precautions."

"You mean like hitting him with a club and throwing him overboard first? Hitting him in the head always seemed to be our most effective way of reasoning with him."

Jesus sighed, "I hope someone took pity on him, and maybe the time he spent tied up let him think and decide to change his ways. I hope so."

"Yeah, maybe they took him home and cleaned him up and married a difficult daughter off to him to get him in line. At least they could tell from a glance that he was a fellow Jew. His outfit made that easy."

After the laughter, Mary crossed her arms and spoke. "He is some mother's son, and I hope for her sake he will change. I am proud of all my children, I can't imagine how terrible it would be if one of you were like him. There once was a time when he was an innocent child, some mother's son. Being like him is worse than being dead. It would be even worse for his mother. Plenty of people in Nazareth once thought I was mad, probably some still do. Children, even though he killed your father, and then tried to kill the rest of us, let's offer up a prayer for him."

Jesus said, "That is what Abba would do, and what he did when he brought him back to life after he tried to drown me. If we don't forgive and pray for him, we dishonor Abba's memory, and all he taught us. Even when he was trying to kill me and we battled for an hour, I could see that down inside his eyes there was still a fragment of a person who was like us. I could see the real person who had been frightened into hiding deep inside. He was still there; I could see him, feel him. But the madness was too loud, too strong to let him out. But I believe God can heal and redeem even someone like him. There is hope."

Anything is possible, Jesus knew.

Coda

Mary, your son is going to make a wonderful father, just like Joseph." Miriam and Mary relaxed while Jesus entertained the three youngest children. Giggles wove the beautiful melodies that only happy children can create. His stories continued into the afternoon, until one by one, each of the children had fallen asleep, sprawled in the awkward poses that come from dropping in the middle of play into instant sleep. Jesus covered them with blankets and smiled at the tiny mouths wide open, like fish reaching to the surface, swimming in dreams.

In the quiet of the afternoon, older children played in the street singing songs Joseph had written for them or their parents. Songs that were passed down with the names. Simple songs, written for the heart of a child desperately needing a sense of worth. Songs written to the rhythm of the saw cutting to make something valuable.

Daniel's spirit can't be caught
By the heaviness of earth
His mind soars like the eagles
As he peers from his high perch
Where he can see beyond today
To surprises that he sought.

Mary closed her eyes and hugged herself pretending it was Joseph's arms around her once again. She spoke to Jesus from her reverie. "He understood them. His songs changed them. They changed me."

Jesus said, "Me, too. Abba's songs were a part of him and have become a part of me. He taught me everyone needs to be loved. Just to know that someone is listening to what you say and seeing something in you that is worth encouraging makes a great difference."

Another song from outside told the story of what one human soul can do for another in pain. It was about the healing power of love of one child for another.

Suzanna is as beautiful as the flower that is her name,
Her eyes are bright, her spirit sweet
As the fragrance from the field.
She will find a broken heart
That with her love is healed.

New songs they had never heard before came from the children outside. The children of children used what Joseph had taught them to create songs on their own.

The saw set the rhythm.

* * *

The next book to follow in this series is *The Other Mary* about Jesus' ministry from the point of view of Miriam. (The Other Mary) along with Mary his mother and Mary Magdalene.

Another character who continues is Agabus, who is mentioned in the book of Acts as accurately prophesying the future twice. Also returning are Jesus' brothers and sisters as well as Miriam's twins James and Joseph,

Women disciples are only briefly mentioned in the Gospels. *The Other Mary* with her close relationship with Mary and Jesus provides a woman's point of view of what it was like to be a loving disciple.

Those who have known Jesus since he was a child fear what may happen to him as he becomes more visible and controversial. They have seen horrible Roman punishment up close. Wadji also returns to eventually found the Egyptian Coptic Christian Church along with Saint Mark, the writer of the earliest Gospel written in the Bible.

Thanks to my dear friends who made this book possible.

First, my gratitude to three professionals in the publishing world, Phyllis Tickle, Lil Copan, and Toni Lopopolo, for believing in me and guiding me through this publishing maze that is changing daily.

And to writing professionals Annette Haines, Liz Conway, Kevin Duke, Joy Ward, Bernie Mackinnon, and Joe Leibovich for many hours of technical advice or editing suggestions. Especially Annette who volunteered immense work for the tedious final edit.

And to Bill Oates, my dear friend and very talented graphic designer for the cover art that he carefully crafted to accurately reflect the essence of the book. Thanks to his skill, in this case you *can* tell a book by its cover.

My great gratitude to Kathryn Manzo, who set an example with her fine new series of paintings that can open minds to a larger world. But more than that, she has brought me into a larger world to understand love in a new way. Not the simple love of teenagers, but the love of two creative adults sharing a vision to make the world a better place through the individual work of two dedicated to their art and to each other in that very complicated world that artists share. She has helped me understand Mary in a new way with her love for me and her dedication to her child.

And thanks to Jim Dunham, Jr., Janet Haire, Rev. Paulette Wittenbrink, and Jim Watkins, my dear creative friends who talked with me often and listened patiently as I worked out what *Joseph* would be. Each saw the value in this book in his own way. And each found a way into some familiar words and actions in the characters in this book. They taught me something important about their lives and their relationships with their children that I used in Joseph's life.

And thanks to friends who believed in me and saw what Joseph could be and helped in many ways – Daniel Mullins, Jim Williams, Elizabeth Wirls, Lee Silber, Charlee Graham, Maria Bizzel, Beth Hume, Cheryl and Jim Dunham, Sr., Heather Wilson, Hud Andrews, Larry Ohrberg, and Perry Walker. And to Richard Ball who first encouraged me to live a life of creative work four decades ago.

Thanks to Dr. Charlie Kenny for the insights I gained into the psychology of motivation and fear while working as an analyst with *The Right Brain People*™ on forty projects over a decade. He has been a generous mentor into the hidden world of the human mind.

To my mother who read an early draft before she died and didn't hate it. She even surprised me and told me that she liked it a lot. And to my father who never got to see this, but was a model for the patience of Joseph and his love of trees. And to my nephew Al and his wife Mary and their son Peter for sharing their love and family and honoring me with the ultimate honor that made my middle initial important.

And to the last group of true friends who tried to temper my enthusiasm with reality and get me to focus more of my attention on making a living in more sure ways - Kevin Duke and Wilson Justice - who both did much to help me survive in the meantime to get to this point. That bit of sanity is a vital part of getting a book finished. Writing a novel and getting it published is very close to insanity with the characters' voices living in your head as merely the starting point. A touch of reality is needed once you have been intoxicated by the Muse.

Special thanks are in order for Jim Dunham and Jim Watkins for their unwavering belief in me and this book through some of the darkest hours of my life. They believed in me when I couldn't and always encouraged me.

And of course, to Gabrielle Slemons with her love of music that started when she was a baby – she who gave me the seed of an idea with her appearance on St. Joseph's day and gave me a glimpse of Joseph's love.

Cover credits:

Graphic design by Bill Oates, Oates Design

All photography by Peter Ceren

Close-up woodworking hand model on back cover - Sam Tickle, Jr.

14665882R00140

Made in the USA
Lexington, KY
14 April 2012